Lambert made his move

Annja bent her knees slightly, prepared for defense, but cautious.

"I've got my eye on a new treasure," he announced. The epee swept the air in a hiss. "It is another sword. A magical one."

"You believe in magic?" Annja countered.

"I believe what I saw when I watched you in the file room on the security cameras. You wielded a fine sword, Annja Creed. And you produced it from thin air. Where is it? Bring it out of wherever it is you keep it. I want to see it."

She remained silent. Alert. Ready.

"I know something about you," he said in a singsongy tone. "Your Monsieur Roux wasn't quite so careful as he should have been."

Roux had come here? What was the old man up to now? She didn't like what that implied.

"I've done my research on your Roux and Joan," he said. "I know, Annja, I know."

Titles in this series:

ROGUE Angel

Alex Archer

SWORDSMAN'S LEGACY

A GOLD EAGLE BOOK FROM
W❁RLDWIDE®

TORONTO • NEW YORK • LONDON
AMSTERDAM • PARIS • SYDNEY • HAMBURG
STOCKHOLM • ATHENS • TOKYO • MILAN
MADRID • WARSAW • BUDAPEST • AUCKLAND

First edition November 2008

ISBN-13: 978-0-373-62133-0
ISBN-10:   0-373-62133-7

SWORDSMAN'S LEGACY

Special thanks and acknowledgment to
Michele Hauf for her contribution to this work.

The
LEGEND

...THE ENGLISH COMMANDER TOOK
JOAN'S SWORD AND RAISED IT HIGH.

The broadsword, plain and unadorned,
gleamed in the firelight. He put the tip against
the ground and his foot at the center of the blade.
The broadsword shattered, fragments falling
into the mud. The crowd surged forward,
peasant and soldier, and snatched the shards
from the trampled mud. The commander tossed
the hilt deep into the crowd.
Smoke almost obscured Joan, but she continued
praying till the end, until finally the flames climbed
her body and she sagged against the restraints.

Joan of Arc died that fateful day in France,
but her legend and sword are reborn....

PROlogue

Iowa, 1978

Jack and Toby Lambert had been inseparable until the day Toby collapsed after baseball practice. Twelve hours later in the hospital, Jack clung to his seven-year-old twin's hand. Toby's skin was a funny yellow color. He couldn't speak, but his eyelids did flutter when Jack spoke.

Not far from the bed, behind a curtain, Jack heard a doctor announce to his parents that Toby's liver had failed. He called it something like acute. Toby would need a transplant. Jack's parents were instructed not to be too hopeful, for the waiting list was long, and there weren't a lot of donors out there.

Pressing his face against the hard hospital mattress beside his brother's prone body, Jack sobbed quietly. He didn't want his parents to hear. They had enough to worry about.

He and Toby had planned a raid on Nasty Black George's awful gang of four tonight. The entire neighborhood— boasting seven boys under the age of ten—regularly organized pirate raids and booty captures. Jack and Toby wore the monikers "Mad Bloody Jack" and "Evil Gentleman Tobias" proudly. No one stood in their way when they came a-pirating. Their plunder was piled high at the bottom of Evil Gentleman Tobias's closet. Dirty Joe still fumed about his pillaged Atari.

If his parents had money, they could buy a new liver for Toby.

Jack knew that wasn't possible. His mom had been putting on a skirt and jacket every morning before he and Toby left for school. She was looking for work, they both knew, because dad's job was "cutting back the fat." Whatever that meant.

"I'll help you," Jack whispered. His brother had not moved since his collapse. "Mad Bloody Jack will plunder a real treasure so we can buy you a new liver. I promise, Toby."

MAD BLOODY JACK KNEW just the landlubbing wreck of a ship to raid. Hidden in the tower at the center of the playground gym, he and Toby—er, Evil Gentleman Tobias—had kept a keen eye over the goings-on across the street from the city park using their plundered telescope.

The purple house with the gray shutters and wild hedges always kept its curtains pulled shut. The craziest stream of traffic steadily pulled up the driveway, and then away. Some visitors were there less than five minutes. Toby timed them on his Cap'n Crunch watch.

Pirate Silly Ned had once said his mother was always calling the cops on that LSD house. They did nasty things, and shouldn't be in this neighborhood.

LSD was a drug. Jack had looked that up in the encyclopedia on the bottom shelf in his dad's office. It made people see visions and act funny. And people paid a lot of money for it. It was also illegal.

Putting two and two together, Mad Bloody Jack decided where there was LSD, there had to be money.

He eyed the purple house through the telescope. The sun had risen an hour earlier. Jack should be in school. But he knew the purple house would be quiet until at least noon, so he had to act now. Toby's life depended on it.

Skipping across the street, Mad Bloody Jack insinuated himself behind the freestanding purple garage, which was where he'd seen most of the visitors go when they stopped. Tramping a patch of dandelions, he pressed his body flat against the wall. A good pirate should practice stealth—he'd learned that word from last week's spelling test. The window on this side of the garage was blocked with black paper. He checked and saw it was the same on the other side.

A thick steel padlock secured the door, but the wood was old and warped. Mad Bloody Jack was able to slide a finger under the crack at the bottom. And there, under some kind of rug, he felt something cold and metal.

A key.

"I DON'T KNOW where he could have gotten this…." Jack's mother choked on her astonishment and clung even tighter to her husband's arm.

Her son had dumped out a pillowcase on the floor in the bathroom attached to Toby's hospital room. "Plunder," he'd muttered, and then had gaily announced the family now had enough money to buy Toby a new liver. He dashed to his brother's side.

Jack's father toed the pile of rubber-banded bills. Hundred-dollar bills. "There must be tens of thousands here."

"We can't—"

"Of course not. I'll ring the police," he said and instructed his wife to remain in the bathroom and keep an eye on the money.

A PIRATE NEVER GAVE UP the location of his best plunder. Never. But when two police officers escorted Jack's mother from the hospital room where they'd been questioning Jack and his father, Mad Bloody Jack became irate.

"Don't touch my mother!" he shouted.

"They're not going to hurt her, Jack," his father reassured. "Though I don't know where they're taking her. You have to tell us where you got the money. Please, Jack, to keep your mother safe."

In a rush of fear and utter exhaustion, Mad Bloody Jack gave the details of his raid. He didn't take it all. There had been too much to carry. Now would they please let his mother go and get to ordering that new liver for his brother?

Toby died three days later. The police had confiscated the money. Jack had been inconsolable. He'd done it. He had found a means to save his brother's life. And the adults— they'd done nothing! What was wrong with them? Didn't they want to save Toby?

"It was never that simple," his father said. Keith Lambert's face was drawn and his sigh chilled across Jack's shoulders.

1

France, present day

Ascher Vallois unlocked the trunk of his car. The hydraulics squeaked as the trunk yawned open. He was ready for a new car, but given the finances, the ten-year-old Renault Clio would have to serve.

He set a practice épée and mask onto the trunk bed. Tearing the Velcro shoulder seams open on his jacket, he then tugged that off.

Wednesday afternoons demanded he wear the leather-fronted plastron. The teenage students he taught were overly confident about their lunges. Actually, they thought themselves indestructible. They didn't give consideration to their teacher's destructibility. That was why he also wore a full mask. The scar on his jaw had been a lesson to ensure he wore complete protection around kids at all times.

Tomorrow he planned to bring his collection of instructional videos to the studio. The students could learn the importance of a well-designed weapon from watching a master forge a blade. As well, there was much to be gained from watching fencing masters in competition.

Ultimately, he wanted to have a camera set up in the studio so he could record students, and then play back their practice matches for them to study. The best way to learn was by observing your own bad habits and then correcting them.

All things in good time, he told himself. And if his latest expedition proved successful, the aluminum fencing *piste* he'd been dreaming about could become reality. It was wireless, which would be more practical for movement and scorekeeping, considering he hadn't the cash to hire an assistant.

He slammed the trunk shut. It was well past sunset, yet a rosy ambiance painted the horizon, reminding him of a woman's blush. An autumn breeze tickled the perspiration at the back of his neck, drying his sweaty hair.

The noise of traffic from the main shopping stretch had settled. Sens had relaxed and let out its belt. The citizens of the French city were inside restaurants chattering over roasted fowl and a bottle of wine, or at home watching the nightly news or shouting at the quiz shows.

Shoving a hand in his pants pocket, Ascher mined for his keys, but paused. A tilt of his head focused his hearing behind him and to the left.

He was not alone.

Swinging a peripheral scan, he paused only a quarter of the way through his surroundings.

Standing at the front left corner of the Clio, a tall thin man with choppy brown-and-blond hair rapped his knuckles once upon the rusted hood of the vehicle. A silver ring glinted, catching the subtle glow from an ornamental streetlight up the street. Small bold eyes smiled before the man's mouth did.

Ascher felt the salute in that look. A call to duel. The foil had been raised with a mere look. He stood in line of attack.

From where had the man come? This narrow street was normally quiet, save for the business owners who parked in the reserved spaces where Ascher now stood.

Suddenly aware that others had moved in behind him, Ascher stiffened his shoulders but kept his arms loose, ready. He jangled his keys. A tilt of his head, left then right, loosened his tensing muscles.

The air felt menacing, heavy, as if he could take a bite out of it.

The smiling man offered a casual *"Bonsoir."*

Wary, yet not so foolish as to leap into a fight—this may be nothing more than a man asking directions—Ascher offered a lift of his chin in acknowledgment.

"Mr. Vallois, I am a friend," the man offered.

His French accent wasn't native, and he looked more Anglo than European, Ascher thought. A dark gray suit fit impeccably upon a sinewy frame. Probably British, he assumed from the slim silhouette of the man's clothing.

He knew his name? Caution could be a fencer's downfall. Confidence and awareness must remain at the fore.

"I have many friends," Ascher said forcefully, lifting his shoulders. "I know them all upon sight. I do not know you."

Sensing the potential threat level without moving his head to look, Ascher decided there were two men behind him. Bodyguards for the man standing before him?

Ascher eyed the practice épée through the window of the Clio. "Are these gentlemen behind me my friends, as well?"

"You amuse me, Mr. Vallois. And yes, if you wish it, they can be your very best friends. More preferable than enemies, wouldn't you say?"

What the hell was going on? He'd been keeping his nose clean. In fact, the past few years Ascher had gone out of his way to remain inconspicuous. There was nothing like a run-in with the East Indian mafia over rights to claimed treasure to cool a man's jets.

"Jacques Lambert." The man thrust out a thin hand to shake—an advance that put him to lunge distance—but Ascher did not take the bait. This guy was not British. An American using a French name perhaps? "My business card claims me CEO of BHDC, a genetic-research lab in Paris. You have not heard of us."

No need to verify that one. Ascher's interests covered anything athletic, sporting or adventurous. Science? Not his bag. "Genetic research? I don't understand," Ascher said.

"It is a difficult field to get a mental grasp on," Lambert replied. "But the beauty of it is that you don't have to understand. Simple acceptance is required."

"Sorry, I gave at the office."

"I'm not on the shill, Vallois. In fact, I have an interest in financing your current dig."

The dig? But he'd only that morning gathered a small crew of fellow archaeologists online. They weren't set to convene in Chalon-sur-Saône for another two weeks.

Who had brought in this fellow without consulting him?

Ascher trusted the two men he had chosen to assist on the dig. Jay and Peyton Nash had accompanied him before. They were his age, far more knowledgeable in archaeology than him, and also enjoyed a challenging mountain bike course, like the one they'd conquered in Scotland's Tweed Valley.

Although…he'd recruited another. A woman. He did not know her beyond what he'd learned while chatting with her online. And admittedly, knowledge of her character had been not so important as her figure and those bewitching amber-green eyes.

"I'm sorry, Mr. Lambert, if you have been led to believe—"

The sudden heat of breath hissing down the back of his neck did not disturb Ascher so much as piss him off. He stood tall, not about to back down or cringe from the bully behind him.

If the trunk were still open…but it was not. The only weapon he had to hand was his ring of three keys and a rudimentary grasp of martial arts. He slipped the ignition key between his forefinger and middle finger, point out.

"I have been following your research online for months," Lambert said. "Fascinating how you tracked the Fouquet journals in the Bibliothèque Nationale."

Ascher thought about the days spent in the huge Paris library that he had genuinely enjoyed. "I haven't posted that information publicly," he said.

"Yes, I know. You made it very difficult, but once I tracked your conversations with the Nash brothers, I continued to follow them."

So his friends hadn't invited this man. Yet they had inadvertently lured an outsider.

"I've hired all the men required for the dig, I'm afraid."

"You misunderstand, Vallois." Lambert made eye contact with the thugs over Ascher's shoulder. He went for the riposte, slipping something out of his suit coat's inner pocket. It unrolled with a shake. Lambert then slid one hand into the surgical glove. "I—" he gave the glove a crisp snap "—have a keen interest in the sword."

Ascher's intuition screamed this was not the place he should be at this moment. Sometimes it was better to run, and risk injury, than to stick around and risk death. Fencing skills aside, now was the time to employ street smarts.

Ascher jabbed an elbow backward, catching one of the thugs in the ribs.

A meaty arm snaked about Ascher's neck. A vicious squeeze choked off his cry of surprise. Levering his foot against the door of his car, he tried to push off the man, but his attacker leaned into the force, making escape impossible.

"No, no, mustn't struggle," Lambert said calmly, as if directing a child afraid of the dentist's drill. He tugged the fingertip of one glove, snapping it smartly into place. "This is not what you might suspect."

"I suspect everything," Ascher hissed. "I know I do not like you—"

Chokehold released, Ascher's arms were wrenched behind him and upward. His shoulder muscles were forced beyond their limit, and his deltoids stretched painfully. Bent forward, he intended to kick backward, but Lambert's next move stopped him.

Further utilizing the dread calm of a looming dentist, Lambert withdrew a vial from inside his suit coat.

"The musketeer's sword has been tops on my list of plunder for quite some time. I believe you have discovered the only possible resting place for the sword, Mr. Vallois." Lambert tapped the finger-size vial against his wrist. There was something inside, white, stick-like. "Surprising, the conclusions you made about the location, but when I thought about it awhile, very believable. I wish you great success."

"The sword is not for sale," Ascher said.

"When one acquires plunder, sir, one does not pay for it. But I am willing to put forth something for your efforts. You will require cash to finance your dig."

"Already taken care of."

"Your check bounced at the bank. My guess? You should

start seeing the overdrafts immediately. I know you are two months behind on rent for that little fencing salon around the corner. Pity. The children will be deprived of your witty yet charming teaching manner," Lambert said.

Ascher grunted against the increasing force straining his muscles.

"As for that cottage you call a mansion out of town, I've made it my business to know your electricity will be shut off two days from now." He bent close to Ascher's face. "Allow me to ease your financial strain."

"There is no amount you can offer for the sword."

Ascher twisted. Two meaty hands held firmly. It was quite embarrassing how easily he'd been wrangled. As long as his aggressor held his arms back at such a painful angle, he could not escape.

"That sword is something I have searched for for years," Ascher hissed. The gloved hand waggled its fingers before him. A disturbing threat. "I could not possibly put a monetary value to it—"

Suddenly pierced from behind, Ascher's body clenched, his chest lifting and his body arching upward as his shoulders were wrenched further backward. He was impaled. Stuck like a pig. The pain was incredible, so much so that much as he wanted to scream, he could not put out a single breath.

A blade had entered his left kidney. The thug behind him shoved it to the hilt.

Lambert stood right before him now. An intelligent and greedy gaze followed Ascher's gasps of pain. "Of course, it would be difficult to fix a price to so intriguing a find as the sword."

Wincing, Ascher groaned low in his throat. He felt tears roll down his face. It was impossible to make a defensive move or push away his attacker. Barely able to stand, he battled against his fading consciousness by drawing in deep breaths through his nose.

"I wager you'll hand over the sword for a kidney." A snap of the rubber glove released a haze of cornstarch powder.

"I need only one!" Ascher defiantly managed to declare.

"Sure, a man can survive with one, but you won't have that one forever."

The other thug, who had been standing to the side, stepped forward. Ascher cried out as he took a punch to the right kidney. But, held carefully, his torso did not take the blow with another cringe. It seemed they wanted to ensure the knife remained firmly placed.

"Should you refuse to cooperate," Lambert continued, "I shall return for the other. But know, I can give you a replacement in exchange for your cooperation."

Feeling blackness toy with his consciousness, Ascher heard something crackle like plastic.

"Open his mouth."

His mouth was wrenched open from the right by the one who had punched him.

Lambert stabbed something into his mouth and rubbed it inside Ascher's cheek. "DNA evidence. I'll take it back to the lab and immediately begin to grow your new kidney. Therapeutic cloning. Quite the marvel. Think of it as your new life insurance policy."

The thug clapped Ascher's jaw shut, and Ascher briefly saw Lambert deposit a white swab into the glass vial.

"What do you say, Vallois? Do we have a deal?"

"I…" He was losing it. Pain shot up and down his spine and spidered through his entire nervous system. He had never known such agony. He couldn't think, let alone move.

"If you refuse, I'll have Manny tug the knife from your back. Within twenty minutes, you'll bleed out internally. You will be dead, Mr. Vallois."

Death sounded much better than this torture, Ascher thought.

"But, keep the knife in place and accept the escort to casualty that I am willing to provide, and you'll have a pleasant hospital stay, and be back in the field in, oh, ten days? Of course, the left kidney is a loss." The plastic rattled before Ascher's closed eyes. "What do you say?"

The man behind him tapped the blade shoved deep inside his body. Ascher yowled as the vibrations sent out new waves of shocking anguish.

"In or out?" Lambert asked. "The blade, that is."

Feeling his body release the tense cringe and fall forward, Ascher chased the darkness. Passing out would stop the pain. And so would his compliance.

"In," he muttered, and then the world stopped.

2

Court of Loius XIV
Seventeenth century

"History shall revere Charles de Castelmore d'Artagnan."

Queen Anne nodded to Charles, who stood in full regalia—musket and bandolier spread across his black coat trimmed in gold. A red plume dusted the air above his right brow, and his boots were polished to a shine to rival the mirrors in Versailles.

To the queen's right, a liveried foot guard stepped up, proffering a red velvet pillow with a sword laid upon it.

Containing his excitement, Charles drew in a breath and maintained a solemn expression.

The queen took the sword by the gold hilt and held it before her, seeming to look it over, but moreover, displaying it to all who had congregated in the king's private chapel to celebrate one of Louis XIV's musketeers. She handled the weapon with skill, though d'Artagnan doubted she'd had occasion to use the weapon.

"For bravery and valor," Queen Anne recited in a regal yet quiet voice, which was her manner. "For honor among all men. And for all that you have done for your king and queen. You serve our country well, musketeer."

She presented the sword to Charles, blade extended horizontally to the right. The hilt sparkled. A bit of damascening curled up near the *ricasso* of the blade. It was a rapier, and quite ornate. No simple sword for this simple man.

Head still bowed, Charles held open his hands to receive the gift. It wasn't coin—which he could much use over another sword, especially one so decorative. But the gold on the hilt should fetch a year's meals, and perhaps even outfit the ranks with the grenades Grosjean had demonstrated at Lille a fortnight earlier. They exploded on contact with the ground. What Charles wouldn't do to put his hands to those marvelous weapons.

The rapier landed on his palms. It was well weighted; he could determine that merely by holding it. It was likely fashioned by Hugues de Roche, the king's sword maker, and a most sought after craftsman.

This honor meant the world to Charles. To be publicly awarded this gift made him stand a full boot heel taller, and he felt his shoulders should never again slouch.

Perhaps he'd keep this prize to hand. Though a gold hilt was never practical in active combat. The enemy would see it as plunder, instantly transforming Charles to a keen target among the ranks.

Charlotte would insist he keep it. Yes, perhaps his sons should have this. It was rare he got a chance to visit the boys. It had been over a year since he'd last seen them.

Now the queen bent slightly and leaned forward, which startled Charles. And it wasn't because her heavily gilded dress creaked and the pearls roped about her neck and across her bosom clacked. The queen had reduced their proximity to close confidence. She had never done such around so many.

"There is more to the eye than what glitters without," she whispered.

Straightening, she then stepped back and placed her hand in that of her son King Louis XIV.

Remaining bowed before his majesties, Charles knew the king would send him off with a few words. But even as Louis spoke, he could not concentrate, for the wonders Queen Anne had stirred with her cryptic statement.

Present day

CHALON-SUR-SAÔNE WAS a thriving city nestled on the shore of a river that saw barges and tourist cruise boats heading northwest to Paris. The Saône was one of Europe's largest commercial waterways.

After her flight from England, Annja Creed had rented a car in Paris. She'd come from Stonehenge, after filming a segment for *Chasing History's Monsters.* Since the builder's settlement had been discovered not far from the stone monument, the archaeological world had been astir. Annja hadn't been able to resist the assignment, but it was not finished, nor did she believe it could ever be truly completed. Stonehenge would offer marvels and mysteries for centuries to come.

Upon arriving in Chalon, a quaint half-timber-and-brick restaurant lured her to park. Now she sat before a table on the restaurant patio beneath a maple dropping its leaves. Pea soup and a side order of potatoes and sausage made her forget that fast food ever existed. She was in pure, fattening, butter-laden heaven. She'd work it off later with a few hours of practice lunges.

The restaurant was on the ground floor of an eighteenth-century building, just across from the river. Since Annja was half an hour early, she had taken advantage of the opportunity to eat. Her first rule of thumb when on the road was to eat when the opportunity presented itself.

Finishing her cup of coffee, she dug out some bills and coins and left them on the café table in payment.

Last night she'd received a hasty instant message from Ascher Vallois—a man whom, until today, she had only referred to as AnjouIII while communicating with him. He'd asked her to meet him as quickly as possible. Ascher knew from a previous online conversation that she had been wrapping things up at Stonehenge. His message had been littered with exclamation points.

Ascher's excitement had injected Annja with renewed exhilaration over a side project she'd been working on for years. It was one of her favorite geeky obsessions. And Ascher believed he had found it.

She made him promise not to look at the find until she arrived.

The *find* was the infamous sword alluded to in notes found in the nineteenth-century research journal of adventure writer Alexandre Dumas. The sword was gifted to Charles de Batz-Castelmore d'Artagnan by Queen Anne, the Austrian import, while her son Louis XIV reigned over France in the seventeenth century. Research notes written in the margins of Dumas's notebooks—but not necessarily in his handwriting —had postulated that the sword had been a gift for a job well done serving as lieutenant of the king's First Company of Musketeers.

"D'Artagnan's sword," Annja murmured, a smile irresistible. "Finally."

Standing outside the white picket fence that corralled the café's customers, she looked across the street and stretched her gaze beyond the parking lot before the river.

"If Ascher is right, this day will so rock."

Though her specialty was the medieval and renaissance time periods, Annja had started following the life of the real-life musketeer—upon whom Dumas based his infamous hero—after reading a tattered copy of *The Three Musketeers* during her first year at college. If her fellow archaeologists discovered she spent her rare free time poring over copies of Dumas's journals for the sword, they'd laugh.

And a laughing archaeologist was a rare thing.

Annja considered what she knew about the real musketeer. When Charles Castelmore, one of eight children born to minor nobility, signed on to the musketeers—some thirty years *after* Dumas had chosen to place him into his fictional version of history—the adventurous young Gascon used his mother's maiden name of d'Artagnan. At the time, it carried more cachet than the Castelmore surname. His mother had been a Montesquieu, and the d'Artagnan name hailed from ancient nobility. His grandfather had been well-known to Henri IV, a valuable alliance to the Castelmore family.

Castelmore lived an illustrious career serving the king's First Company of Musketeers. Dumas had included many of the man's actual adventures in his stories, including the capture and imprisonment of Nicolas Fouquet, the notorious superintendent of finances who had been arrested for embezzling royal funds.

Not many people were aware that the swashbuckling hero from one of their favorite classic reads had been a real person; even fewer were aware of the sword. An allusion to the sword's existence was marked by a notation in Dumas's notes. Most literary researchers put it off as an abandoned plot line.

Annja, on the other hand, had found that notation and had run with it.

There were too many correlating facts for her to ignore. But she'd turned up nothing but a few enthusiastic historians and the occasional document signed by d'Artagnan for her sleuthing efforts. Once she realized that the real man had signed his name "d'Artaignan" she had also uncovered a few more items of interest, such as a copy of his marriage certificate—signed by Louis XIV—as well as the document of divorce.

She had explored the few sites d'Artagnan was known to have occupied or lived at, and had even been involved on a dig in Lille where d'Artagnan had served as governor of the city for a few miserable months. That dig had turned up nothing more than a few Spanish coins circa the sixteenth century and a dented copper pot.

She'd thought of Gens, the region close to Lupiac in southwest France, where he was born, but that had turned up little more than the usual facts about the musketeer's military accomplishments. Though there was a nice museum dedicated to the musketeer in Lupiac.

Of course, Charles Castelmore's last residence was not Lille, but in Paris on the rue du Bac. The site where his apartment once stood bore a small plaque commemorating the musketeer, but the building had long been torn down and replaced with a more modern design.

Annja had known Ascher Vallois for over a year, having met him online at alt.archaeology.esoterica, her frequent hangout when stuck in an airplane flying over any number of oceans. Ascher began instant messaging her after she'd filled in some information for him on Henri III, his favorite historical figure.

An unabashed flirt—yes, even though only in e-mail—the man had managed to wheedle some of Annja's personal information from her, such as favorite color, favorite country to visit, and favorite geeky obsession—d'Artagnan.

That information had started an amusing and often informative cyber friendship. Ascher had been on the sword's trail for years himself. Thanks to some extra research efforts the past two months, Ascher now believed the sword could be found in Chalon, the final resting place of Charlotte-Anne de Chanlecy—d'Artagnan's ex-wife.

It was a solid theory, one that had caused Annja no amount of chagrin to realize someone had beaten her to the punch.

But though he'd called the moment something had been unearthed at the dig site—it appeared to be the end of a wooden sword box—she knew it could be any number of things.

If the sword had been found, then this detour before heading home to Brooklyn could prove most exciting.

Annja knew exactly what she was getting herself into by meeting Ascher Vallois. She'd already done a background check on him. Her good friend Bart McGilly, NYPD homicide detective, usually ran names through the law-enforcement system for her, but for overseas contacts Annja was left to her own devices.

It had been easy enough to find information on Ascher. He had his own Web site, which focused on fencing and *parkour*. While Ascher styled himself a part-time archaeologist who enjoyed extreme sports and who also taught at a children's fencing school in Sens, Annja had decided he was really a glorified treasure hunter.

To be called a treasure hunter by a fellow archaeologist was a real insult. Duel worthy. Ascher had laughed her off when she teased him. Or rather, he LOLed her.

At least he wasn't a pothunter. Their sort were unauthorized amateurs who scavenged marked-off sites, digging up fragments and then selling them on the black market.

Annja favored the social aspects of archaeology. She loved

learning about the people behind the treasures. A treasure hunter was all about the find, the bling, the prestige over nabbing a valuable artifact and then selling it.

Not that she didn't get excited over a find, but she was very rational and followed the law when it came time to turn treasures over to the proper authorities.

She had made Ascher swear that, if he located d'Artagnan's sword, selling it was not his intention. He had promised it would go to the Lupiac museum.

"Chalon," she murmured, smiling to herself. "I should have thought of Chalon."

Exhaling, Annja then drew in a deep breath. The river, about a hundred yards off, sweetened the air with a marshy tang. She strode across the street, heading for her rental car to wait for Ascher.

Since inheriting Joan of Arc's sword, Annja's life had been completely turned on its head. It wasn't a bad thing, but neither always good. Her job description had become more than a simple archaeologist turning up finds at a dig. She was so much more than a field reporter on a cable television program.

Around every corner she turned, it seemed she encountered danger. She had escaped from bullet fire, swum away from harpoons, battled demons and had come close to death too many times since she'd discovered Joan's sword—her sword.

Almost daily, the world proved to Annja it was far more wicked than she could have ever fathomed. When Joan's sword came to her from the otherwhere and fitted itself ready in her hand, it was because it was needed to stop evil or counter adversity.

And of late, Annja had been wielding it a lot.

Today felt like a vacation. An escape from the day job. For once the world did not sit heavily upon her shoulders. This trip to Chalon was a free moment away from Annja Creed, sword-wielding defender of innocence. It was a chance to breathe and to indulge herself.

"I need this," she said aloud.

Leaning inside her car, she deposited her backpack on the front passenger's seat, then closed the door and went around to sit on the hood. From here she could see the two steeples of Saint-Pierre, the city's largest cathedral. She loved touring European cathedrals. And there were so many of them to see, she felt sure to never run out in her lifetime.

The parking lot bordered the shore of the river Saône. The scent of fresh water and grass overwhelmed even the leaky-oil smell coming from the rental car. Blond brickwork danced along the verdant shore, and the paved walkway was shaded by huge chestnut trees.

A white swan called out as Annja scanned the pedestrians, mostly tourists carrying shopping bags and maps. A newly remodeled strip of shops and cafés lined the street behind her. This part of the city catered to tourists, and offered hourly boat tours along the river.

"Tous pour un."

At the deep male voice Annja turned and offered an enthusiastic reply to his "all for one," with *"Un pour tous."*

"Annja!" A six-foot-plus man with a smile as broad as his sunburned shoulders and curly, dark hair strode up and embraced her. He gave her a kiss on the left cheek, and then the right.

It happened so quickly, Annja just went with it. Normally she did not allow a stranger such ease with her. She enjoyed the social aspects of her trade but she protected her personal space keenly.

But Ascher wasn't really a stranger. She'd been communicating with him for a year. And beyond the knowledge gained about him online, she couldn't deny he smelled great.

"Ascher Vallois," she said. "It is you?"

"*Oui,* I am not to accost the beautiful star of *Chasing History's Monsters.* Mademoiselle Creed, you are more gorgeous in person."

"And you are…" *Handsome* popped to her mind.

His body moved sinuously, and the sleeveless shirt he wore revealed a defined muscle tone that could only come from intense workouts. The man was an extreme sports enthusiast, so the muscles were no surprise, but his attractiveness startled her. Of course, she had expected a rogue. His e-mails had not hidden the arrogant pride and underlying flirtatious manner.

Ascher was, she realized with a start, the epitome of what she imagined d'Artagnan must have looked like. He was a boundless adventurer with a devil-may-care attitude and a charming glint to his pale blue eyes. A mere wink from him could be capable of dropping women in his wake.

"I am what, Annja? You think I am as you expected?" Ascher asked with a grin.

He moved to shake her hand, which relaxed her, and she shook off the weird schoolgirl reaction that had risen. She was no swooner.

"You are exactly as expected, Ascher. Friendly, athletic and handsome," she said, smiling.

"Ah, the American television star, she calls me handsome? What my buddies at the dig will think of that!"

"How many are there?" Annja asked, suddenly anxious.

"Two others I have worked with previously. You know I trust them. Oh." He dug something out of his pocket and handed it to her.

Annja accepted the item, loosely wrapped in a white hand-kerchief. Her enthusiasm ratcheted up the scale. "Is it—?"

"Just look," he urged. Crossing his arms high on his chest,

he watched her, the gleam in his eyes rivaling any glittering treasure he had ever claimed, Annja felt sure.

She unwrapped a piece of wood about six by four inches. She ran her fingers over a design impressed into the end. Sniffing it, Annja scented the dirt and clay, or maybe limestone. Limestone was excellent for preserving artifacts.

Turning the wood, she decided the impression must be a coat of arms. It was divided into four quarters, and in the first and fourth quadrant were double towers. A bowing eagle was impressed in the second and third quarters.

"It is the end of the sword box that I removed accidentally." Literally bouncing on his feet, he gestured enthusiastically to the object in her hand. "It is real, Annja. The sword has been found."

"I'll believe it when I see it," Annja said, forcing herself to remain calm.

"Very well." He hooked an arm in hers and tugged her around the car. "Come, we must be off to the dig site before the sun sets. We will take your car. You rented?"

"Yes, in Paris."

"City of love!" He dashed ahead to open the driver's side door for her, and closed it behind her after she'd slid inside. "To a dashing good adventure," he said as he climbed in the passenger's side.

And Annja dialed into his enthusiasm. "To adventure!"

FIELDS OF GRAPEVINES LINED the narrow country road they traveled. A symphony of crickets demanded Annja switch off the radio—tuned to a news-and-weather channel—and take in the natural performance.

"Just ahead." Ascher gave directions to the dig site that once harbored an Augustine convent before it had been demolished by fire in 1690.

Charlotte-Anne de Chanlecy had initially moved into the convent following her husband's death, but quickly retired to a quiet family estate just off the convent grounds. Chalon was her hometown.

There was not a lot of documentation on d'Artagnan's wife, she being a minor historical figure, but Annja guessed the convent might have been a bit too stifling for a woman who had once been married to an adventurous musketeer.

Window rolled down, the September air brushed a warm breeze across Annja's face and arm. It was a far cry from the ocean-kissed air that had buffeted Stonehenge, but not unpleasant. The countryside smelled like centuries of history, hobbled and roped and beaten into the ground by defiant hooves. *Liberté, Égalité, Fraternité.* She did love a French motto.

"I have to wonder why, when I studied documents and files and researched dusty old archives for years," Annja said, "I was never led to Chalon-sur-Saône."

"Because it makes little sense." Ascher hooked a palm over the outside mirror. A bend of his fingers flexed his muscular forearm. "To find the sword in possession of the wife?"

"And the *ex*-wife, at that," Annja returned.

"Such a cad! D'Artagnan had no true affection to any particular woman," Ascher said.

"Exactly," she agreed. "Dumas certainly got that part right. The musketeer basically married for money, got the wife pregnant and then went off to play shoot-'em-up with his military buddies. Though, part of me likes to believe he did love Charlotte. Initially."

"There is no doubt that he did. A Frenchman does not take love lightly," Ascher said. He spoke English, and it rang with a delightful accent. "But a soldier—especially a Gascon—was more devoted to military service than family."

"Yes, the Gascons. Born and bred to the fight. They served in great numbers in the French army. You mentioned you are originally from Gascony?"

"*Oui!* But I would not be so foolish had I a lovely wife at home," he said.

Without turning her attention from the road, Annja could feel Ascher's glance heat the side of her face. The man was a charmer.

Nothing wrong with that, she thought.

"'A plague upon the Gascons!'" she said, quoting Rochefort's vehement frustration from the text of the Dumas story.

"'Monsieur, I love men of your kidney,'" Ascher quoted back. "'And I foresee plainly that if we do not kill each other, I shall hereafter find much pleasure in your conversation.'"

"Athos to d'Artagnan," Annja said. "But I see you more as the young Gascon."

"I am flattered. Then you shall be my Constance Bonacieux."

"I hope not. She was strangled by Milady de Winter while awaiting d'Artagnan's straying affections," Annja exclaimed.

"True, true. Very well, I will hold reservation on your fictional counterpart, Annja. For now."

She smiled and stepped on the brake lightly as they made a sharp curve that took them onto a narrow gravel road that edged a thick forest of colorful maple and leaf-stripped birch. If anyone approached from ahead, she'd have to pull into the shallow grassy ditch to pass.

"Back to the mystery of the sword." Annja flipped the inner vents closed to keep most of the gravel dust out of the car. "It's surprising to think our musketeer would gift a woman, who likely did not love him because of his obsessive call to duty, with a valuable sword."

"Maybe it was given to her with the intention his children would reap any reward found? He had two sons," Ascher said.

"Yes, Louis and Louis," Annja agreed.

"Both claim Louis XIII and Louis XIV as godfathers. Now, that is a family who loved their king."

"Charlotte-Anne must have been quite the woman," Annja said

"Yes, she divorced her husband in a time when divorce was not considered. But they remained friends. I believe it was not just for their children, but that d'Artagnan was genuinely in love with his wife."

"He was more in love with adventure," Annja said.

She knew the feeling. Relationships took a back seat to her wanderlust. And defending the world from evil tended to put a damper on romantic notions.

She noted that Ascher had not relaxed in the seat since getting in the car. He leaned forward, his eyes to the road and, often, on her.

"I think the seat is adjustable, if you're not comfortable?" she said.

"Ah, no worries." He smoothed a palm along his left side. "An injury that is yet stiff, you see."

"How'd it happen? Base jumping? Extreme running—what did you call it?"

"*Parkour.* Running all over building tops and jumping at high speeds. You use the architectural landscape as your obstacle course. Very exciting. Good for the quads, glutes and delts. You should give it a try."

"I just may."

He tossed her an approving nod.

"But that was not how I came to this injury. It is of no importance. Up there, just around the corner, we'll find the dig site. Why are you stopping, Annja?"

In the rearview mirror, the sight of the big black SUV that

had barreled up on them put Annja to caution. The pistol jutting out the passenger's side could not be ignored.

She couldn't outrun the monster truck in her little beater. While her gut prayed it was merely mistaken identity, her intuition screamed that this vacation had suddenly taken a new yet familiar twist.

3

Annja stopped the car on the country road. The sun had set, but the sky still glowed yellow. The SUV's headlights dimmed in the rearview mirror.

"For reasons that elude me, we've been followed," Annja said.

Tilting a glance across to her passenger, she was taken aback to spy him nervously swipe a palm down his face.

What had she stepped into?

Certainly she had jumped into the adventure with little more than anticipation for a fun excursion. No parachute, that was for sure—parachutes were for wimps. Yet now that she had jumped, it had become apparent she should employ caution at all turns.

"Ascher, do you know the hulking, black-suited men who are currently getting out of an imposing SUV, tucking pistols into their inner pockets and marching toward us?"

The man's sudden lack of conversation struck her to the core. Annja sucked in a heavy breath.

"Ascher, my background check on you didn't turn up any jail time or criminal leanings."

"You checked me out?" he asked, sounding offended.

"Obviously not well enough. What have you involved me in? Have you enemies who feel the need to keep tabs on your every move?"

"Every man gains an enemy or two in his lifetime, no?"

"No—"

A thud against the window alerted them both. Annja twisted in the driver's seat to spy two palms pressed flat to her window. Ten fingers disappeared, and were replaced with the barrel of what looked like one of her favorite pistols, a 9 mm Glock. It wasn't her favorite at the moment.

From outside the car, a staunch French voice commanded they exit with their hands up.

"Be cool," Annja said. "And get out slowly."

"I am cool. You be cool, Annja."

"I'm cooler than—oh, for cripes sakes, what are we doing? Now is no time to act irrationally. Let's do this slowly and carefully and together."

"Exactly. We cannot allow them to divide and conquer us."

Holding back the retort, "Whatever you say, Napoleon" seemed wise.

Each slowly opened a car door, and before Annja could get her hands up, the gun barrel pressed into her rib cage. She wore a white, sleeveless T-shirt and khaki hiking shorts, and she was sweating.

A tall, brutish man dressed in nondescript dark pants and a short gray coat wielded the gun. A thick gold chain snaked about his tree-trunk neck. High-top sneakers rounded off the attire that was strange for only a drive in the countryside. He looked ready for a hike through an urban nightclub.

Pressing the backs of her thighs to the car door, Annja surreptitiously glanced over the roof of the rental. Ascher stood with hands raised, and a gun about a foot from his nose.

"You had no intention to invite us to the dig?" the gunman beside Ascher asked in French.

She heard Ascher fumble for a reply. "And have you get your hands dirty? Of course not."

"Who is she?"

The gunman eyeing Annja lifted a blocky chin and eyed her down his nose. One crushing palm to the tip of that nose and he'd be snorting blood. But though she knew Ascher was athletic, she couldn't be sure he'd know to react defensively when she did. Just because he was an enthusiast for sports didn't make him a self-defense expert.

"A girlfriend," Ascher volunteered. "No one you know, or need to know. She can stay in the car while we go on to the dig."

She felt to her bones that Ascher knew these men, or at least wasn't as surprised to see them as she was. And while his efforts to protect her fell flat in the chivalry department, she wasn't about to stay behind when the situation could turn dangerous.

And did you just hear your own thoughts, Annja? You know it's going to be dangerous, so you intend to march right into the fray. You really buy into all this protect-the-innocent stuff the sword has brought into your life.

If she couldn't avoid danger, she figured might as well join it. That would grant her more control than if she simply surrendered. Besides, she was armed, but the sword wasn't exactly a weapon to win against bullets.

"She comes along." The gunman gripped her upper arm, hard, and poked the Glock into Annja's back. She hated unnecessary aggression focused through the barrel of a gun. "Vallois, you will take us to the sword," he ordered.

They knew about the sword? And they knew Ascher's name.

Good job on checking the online contact's history, Annja, she chided herself.

Once around the hood of the car and shoved to Ascher's side, Annja saw he had a pistol barrel stuck against his temple.

"Does she know where the sword is?" the thug with the gun stuck into her side asked.

"I—I'm not—" the safety on the pistol aimed at Ascher's skull clicked off, which made the truth flow easily from him. "No, but I have told her about it. The dig site is through the forest."

"Then lead us." Both of them were given a shove.

Annja stumbled in the growing darkness as they descended into the shallow roadside ditch, but kept her balance. Her hiking boots squished over soggy grass, but didn't sink in far. An owl questioned them from somewhere in the distant forest. A cloud of gnats pinged against her shoulders and neck. She didn't shoo them away. Any sudden moves could result in a bullet wound, which was less desirable than a few insect bites.

As she trudged up the incline and through the long grass, she felt fingers touch her hand. Ascher tugged her up the opposite side of the ditch and they continued onward, close, hands clasped.

"Trust me," he whispered.

"So not going to," Annja replied. Keeping her voice to a whisper, she asked, "Are there others at the site?"

"Two. They camp overnight."

Not good. Annja didn't want to endanger anyone else, and it wasn't as if she expected a rescue team to be waiting for their arrival. Archaeologists did not the cavalry make.

At the moment, no other option presented itself. She'd play this one with a feint, holding back the riposte for the right moment. Now was no time to bring out the sword. Not until she determined if their guides were eager to use their weapons, or if they were more for show. She wouldn't kill unless her life was threatened or the lives of others were. But a few slices to injure were warranted.

Ascher stumbled and she instinctively reached to catch him. A shout from behind, "Don't touch him!" parted them quickly.

Ascher and Annja entered a copse of maples capping the tip of the forest. Surrounded by trees, twisting branches and leaf canopy obliterated any light lingering in the sky. Verdant moss and autumn-dried leaves thickened the air with must. They slowly navigated the uneven ground, snapping twigs and dodging low branches. Boots crunched branches; leaves brushed her skin. Briefly, she hoped there was no poison ivy.

"It is growing difficult to see without a flashlight," Ascher hollered over his shoulder. Rather loudly, Annja noted. The dig site must be close. Ascher might be trying to warn whoever was camped there.

A fine red beam zigged across the ground between the two of them. It came from the rifle scope one of the men had pulled out of his coat. It was bright, but only beamed a narrow line across the forest floor. It illuminated nothing.

It occurred to Annja to be worried about wild animals as they tromped over an obvious trail worn into crisp fallen leaves between birch trees. Wolves were rampant in France, though Annja knew they were most prevalent in the southern Alps.

Right now, taking her chances with one of them almost sounded favorable. At least with a wolf she stood a chance of escape, or if she was attacked, knew it wasn't personal.

Was this personal for Ascher?

Knowing little about this situation notched up her apprehension. Annja flexed the fingers of her right hand, itching to hold her sword. Was Ascher an ally or foe?

"Just ahead!" Ascher suddenly shouted.

The small golden glow of a camp light beamed across the front of a large pitched tent. Inside the tent, another muted glow lit up the two visible sides of the structure.

She hoped no one would rush to greet them and thus freak out the gunmen and result in someone getting shot.

The tent was pitched outside what Annja determined to be a shallow dig site. Pitons and rope marked off a territory about thirty feet square—a guess, for darkness cloaked most of the area. A small leather case, likely for tools, sat open next to the roped-off area alongside two buckets and a short-handled shovel.

Pale light illuminated the interior of the tent, and as the foursome approached, a man in slouchy blue jeans and crisp yellow button-up shirt emerged, saw the situation and immediately put up his hands.

"Vallois," the surprised man said in English. "Didn't know you were bringing more than the girl. Guns. Christ, two guns. Evening, gentlemen. What's up?"

"You have the sword?" the thug who held the gun on Annja demanded.

"Ah." The man considered that request for a moment. He eyed Ascher, who remained stoic, the gun at his temple. "The sword."

British, Annja decided of the man. Probably midthirties, and slender, with long graceful fingers. He had expected Ascher to bring her along with him, but the gunmen were a surprise.

Of course, when were gunmen *not* a surprise?

"Are there others in the tent?" Annja asked, and then mentally kicked herself, because if there were others they might have been planning an ambush. Until she had opened her big mouth.

"Just the one," the Brit offered. "Jay is sleeping."

"With the sword?" Her henchman was persistent.

"Er…most likely. Yes, the…sword." Again the Brit looked to Ascher, who offered nothing by means of physical comprehension.

"We all go inside," the gunman said.

Shoved roughly, Annja tripped forward, past Ascher, until she stood before the confused Brit. They exchanged furious gazes, but no matter how hard she tried, Annja couldn't decide whether to compel anxiety or reassurance. She knew nothing, beyond that she wanted to stay alive—and figure out why everyone was being so evasive. To do so required following orders. For now.

"Go in! Go in!" the gunman shouted.

Annja shuffled in behind the nameless British man, with Ascher on her heels. As the pair of gun-toting thugs tromped into the tent, another man, looking like a teenager and lying upon a makeshift camping cot, woke and pulled a pillow from his face. "What the bloody hell?"

"Ascher has brought along some friends," the other explained, with a flair for understatement.

"The woman from the television—" Jay suddenly noticed the guns, and chirped off his sentence.

"Hands up!" Annja's gunman shouted, and the recently risen boy dropped his pillow to the tent floor and complied.

"What do they want?" he asked, standing and shuffling over to the older Brit's side. He wore long flannel sleeping pants and a clean white T-shirt. His feet were bare.

"The sword," Ascher said. "The one you found last night. You know?"

Last night? But he had only just called her this morning to announce they had yet to completely unearth the sword.

Annja couldn't read Ascher's expression in the dull light, but beyond him, she noticed a folding table laid out with a few pieces of crockery—obviously dig finds—and another item covered over by a white cloth. The sword? It couldn't be. Well, it could be. But that would mean Ascher had lied to her when he'd promised he'd wait to unearth it.

"Where is it?" the gunman asked.

"On the table," the younger man answered, bowing his sleep-tousled head and toeing the ground. "Under the cloth."

"D'Artagnan's sword?" the other gunman finally spoke, and his deep, throaty tones startled Annja. It sounded like a ten-pack-a-day rumble.

"I guess so," the teenager said. With an elbow nudge from his cohort, he continued. "It is. We uncovered it last night. Bloody hell, you're not going to take it, are you? That's a valuable—"

The gun that had been focused on Annja found a new target on the nervous teen. He immediately shut up, offering a pantomime of zipping his fingers across his lips.

"It hasn't been authenticated," the other Brit spoke up. "There's no proof it is real. I'm not an expert in weaponry—"

"You are trying to trick me," the gunman said. He motioned at Annja with his gun. "You. Get it for me. Keep your hands up where I can see them."

"Don't mind if I do," she muttered under her breath.

Annja walked carefully toward the table, hands up near her ears.

For years she had researched, tracked and searched for this very sword, and now, before she could barely glance at it, it would be taken from her hands?

But I will have seen it. Touched it. All that matters is that it exists.

"Careful," Ascher directed over his shoulder.

Careful? No freakin' kidding, she thought.

The dry, chalky scent of limestone-infused earth wafted up from the table. A dusting brush sat upon a piece of terra-cotta pottery. Not worth salvage, the shard, but no find is ever overlooked on a dig. All bits and pieces of size are cataloged in field notebooks. Nearby one lay open upon the table.

And there, beneath a wrinkled white cloth, that she now saw to be a pillowcase, sat the shape of a sword.

Peeling back the cloth, Annja slid her fingers over the dull metal blade, crusted with dirt and probably rusted or eroded for its rough texture. The camp light did not illuminate the table well with her body blocking the light source. The hilt, perhaps blued steel, did not shine. Common for a sixteenth-century weapon—but for all the dirt she could not be positive.

D'Artagnan's sword should be seventeenth century.

"Bring it here, quickly!" the gunman said.

Tucking the pillowcase about the hilt, Annja then took it in a firm grip. She stood there, waiting to feel the infusion of power, that triumphant surge of knowing that always came with claiming the talisman, medallion or sacred cup the hero quested for. It had to be there. It wasn't right without it.

It didn't happen. In fact...

"This is—" she started.

"A fine specimen," Ascher broke in. "Handle it carefully, Annja."

The hilt was not gold, Annja realized.

Right. A fine specimen, indeed.

Walking forward, the sword held out before her, Annja reached Ascher's side and glanced to him. Perspiration sparkled on the bridge of his nose. And yet, she didn't feel the nervousness he displayed.

The sword was torn from her grip.

"Careful with it!" the teenager said, which ended with an abrupt tone. One of the gunmen kept the foursome under watch.

Annja felt her body relax, her shoulders falling until one nestled against Ascher's shoulder. He didn't flinch at the contact. Despite appearances, his posture and breathing seemed equally relaxed as hers. Almost...content. To be watching the grail be stolen away?

The gunman near her tucked away his Glock. He then grabbed the sword, rather roughly for an artifact, and gestured with it toward the back of the tent. "Back by the table. All of you!"

The foursome, Annja, Ascher, Jay and the man who had not been allowed an introduction, shuffled backward, hands up. The other gunman returned with a red gas can and began to soak the edges of the tent.

Annja shook out her hands, her fingers aching to grip a weapon, a sure defense against all that was wrong.

She did not want to reveal her secret to the three witnesses. Ascher, she wasn't even sure whose side he was on. The risk wasn't worth the payoff—yet.

The tent lighted to a blaze and the gunmen took off.

"*Allez!*" Ascher shouted. "Let's get out of here!"

"If we flatten the tent we can smother the flames," Jay said.

"Get out, Annja!" Ascher shoved her, and she stumbled toward the tent opening.

She did not stick around and wait for a second warning. Though intuition whispered that the sword wasn't *the* sword, she wasn't about to let it get away until she knew the truth.

Dashing over the two-foot-high border of flame eating the canvas tent, and into the clean night air, Annja did a scan of the surroundings. The night had quickly grown dark; there wasn't a moon in sight. A Jeep was parked on the other side of the marked dig. Had they driven across the field and around the forest?

The thugs would return the same direction they had come. Their only escape was the waiting SUV.

Taking off at a sprint, Annja vacated the blazing campsite and entered the dark confines of the trees. It wasn't exactly a forest, more a strip of birch and maple, probably edging an arable block that was once an old medieval plot.

Her suspicions about the sword the thugs had taken off with felt right. And Ascher's silent but effective eye signals had further confirmed her doubt about its authenticity.

But that didn't mean the bad guys were going to get off scot-free.

Generally thugs were just that—big loping oafs with muscle. They usually answered to someone. And Annja wanted that someone's name.

Branches snapped under her rushing steps, but she didn't worry for stealth. Already she could hear her prey ahead, plodding through the undergrowth and cursing the darkness. The forest opened onto the field. A hundred yards ahead, the SUV's parking lights beamed over Annja's rental car.

Annja reached out to her right, exhaled a cleansing breath, and focused her will to that untouchable otherwhere that served her wishes. With her inhale, she felt the weight of Joan's sword fit to her grip.

This sword belonged to her. She had claimed it when she'd fit the final missing piece to the other pieces her mentor Roux had collected, quite literally, over the centuries. It answered no one's bidding but her own. And it had become her life.

She curled her fingers around the familiar hilt. Wielding the well-balanced weapon expertly, Annja swept it through the air before her in a half circle and then to *en garde* position.

One of the thugs sat on the ground, huffing, both palms to the grass. Obviously he'd tripped.

"Get up! The entire forest will soon be ablaze!" The other man beat the air in frustration with the stolen sword.

"Now boys, that's no way to handle a valued artifact," she announced.

Both looked to the woman who stood at the edge of the forest, medieval sword wielded boldly and determination glinting in her eyes.

4

Knowing both thugs carried guns, Annja dashed across the grassy meadow, cutting their distance, and the range for an easy shot, to a minimum.

The one standing reacted by defensively stabbing the stolen sword at her.

Annja took the bait. But she didn't connect her blade to the ancient blade. Instead, she delivered a thrust to the air just over the opponent's shoulder and slapped her elbow against the very tip of his blade, which bounced it out of threatening position.

The man on the ground thrust out his right arm. Annja knew a gun would be in his hand. She swept her blade across his forearm, slicing through his leather jacket. The gun dropped. Blood spattered her wrist as she did a one-foot reel, swinging forward to grab the gun and spinning up into a twirl to land on the other side of the grounded thug.

A cold jab poked her neck. The man with the sword smiled, and charged again. He'd actually poked her with the thing! Yet a slap to her neck did not find blood, only a sore spot.

"You're going to destroy what you believe to be a valuable artifact?" she challenged, and bent to avoid another inexpert swing of the rusted weapon. "You must have come after it for a reason. Why risk damaging it now?"

That question appeared to give the idiot some thought. Tossing the sword to his left hand, his right then went for his gun, tucked in the front of his waistband.

Aware that the man on the ground groped for her ankle, Annja kicked, landing her heel aside his head. He fell unconscious.

Instinctively diving to the ground, Annja's palm hit the grass as a bullet skimmed her shoulder. It burned, but didn't go deep. Rolling to her side, she pushed upright. Her weapon was not designed for choreographed fencing moves. Nor was she. Annja jammed her sword into the thigh of the gunman. The thug took the hit with surprising sanguinity. He grunted, but appeared to swallow back a curse. The Glock found aim with her head.

A dry branch cracked under her boot as she stepped to the side and bent, charging forward. The pistol retort echoed in the sky.

Crown of her head barreling into the gunman's gut, Annja put her weight into the move, and kicked from the ground. They both went down. Thinking she'd land with her palms, Annja willed away the sword. Her fingers slid across dried leaves and grass.

She spied the gun but it was a grasp away. Cocking out an elbow, she jammed it into whatever she could, landing on the tender curves of an ear. It was a choice shot. The gunman growled and dropped his head, rolling toward her.

Again willing the sword into her grip, Annja swung out and with the heavy hilt, clocked the man at the back of his head above his ear. He dropped, out for the count.

Scrambling forward, she grabbed the second gun. Another Glock—the clip was full. Stuffing the first at the back of her waistband, she then stood and held the second on both downed thugs.

"Annja!" Ascher appeared, scrambling out from the trees. "What the hell?"

"I'm fine." She walked toward Ascher, who clutched his left side.

As for her sword, she always seemed to release it without thought. It was safe, wherever it was that it went when she did not need it. That made it very handy when the need to be discreet presented itself. There'd be no long black Highlander coats for this chick.

"How did you do this?" He looked over her carnage. "They both had guns."

"I charmed them," she offered, and then smiled because if he knew the truth, he'd never believe it. "You got some rope back at camp?"

"Yes, but—they're getting back up."

Annja spun, but instead of leaping forward to swing her sword after the thugs, she couldn't move. Ascher gripped her by the shoulders, and she could do nothing but watch as the lead thug grabbed the stolen sword from the ground.

"Let them go," Ascher said. "You have the sword!" he yelled to the thugs. "Now leave us be."

"I am not going to let this happen." Annja twisted from Ascher's grip.

In less than a breath he'd positioned his body before her, his chest up against hers. A bulldog guarding its territory.

"It's not *the* sword," he hissed. "Let them go."

"They were going to kill us. Or at least try. Are the others all right?"

"They are fine."

She took a step to the left. Ascher matched her. Taller than her, and bulked with muscle, his physique didn't give her concern. The idea of simply allowing those men to walk off with the sword—any sword—felt like defeat.

"Come back to camp," he said, his shoulders dropping and his tone settling to a softer plea.

The SUV revved and pealed across the gravel, heading back the way it had come from.

"There's more to this than a simple treasure hunt, isn't there?" she asked.

Ascher rolled his head and shrugged his shoulders in an aggressive move. Then he sighed and walked toward the forest. He left her to follow.

Annja sucked in the corner of her bottom lip. She could walk across the field, hop in her car and be done with this treasure hunt masquerade.

Or she could turn around and hound the deceitful Gascon for the truth.

Seventeenth century

NICOLAS FOUQUET LOOKED UP from the list of expenditures Cardinal Mazarin had handed him.

"Where is it?"

The king marched into his office, red heels clicking and garish blue silk rosettes bouncing at shoulders, hips and toes.

"Your Highness." Mazarin turned on the chair where he sat before Nicolas's desk. He didn't offer a bow. Instead he held out his hand, for the king to kiss his ring. Louis did. "What troubles you this day?"

"Where are the jewels?" Louis rubbed his fist against his stomach, which was a common habit of anxiety. "My mother's private stash. Some are missing. Have they been stolen?"

"And how are you aware of these so-called missing jewels?" Nicolas asked, but immediately cursed himself for being so bold. Mazarin may have had the king's respect, but he yet strived for that elusive confidence.

"Surely—" Mazarin sent a cruel glance toward Nicolas to reprimand "—she must have handed them to the royal jeweler for cleaning?"

"No." Louis paced between the bookshelf where Nicolas kept his legal volumes and the window that overlooked the Tuileries. "I check our coffers every Sunday. Today there are many pieces missing. She is not wearing them. There are some items she has never worn. I cannot understand that."

The king looked imploringly at his financier and the cardinal. So young yet, and with an entire nation depending on his guidance.

Nicolas cleared his throat. But when Louis beseeched him silently, he looked down and merely shook his head. He couldn't reveal that he had seen the map. He valued Queen Anne's trust immensely.

"They were given to her by a lover," Louis suddenly said in a very quiet voice. "Or so I suspect as much."

The cardinal chuckled. "You cannot spite your mother a lover."

Mazarin rose, but instead of going to the king's side, he walked in the opposite direction, toward the wall of legal books. Tracing a finger along their leather spines, the cardinal said nothing more.

Nicolas knew why the silence. Queen Anne and Mazarin were very close. And her son, the king, could never imagine such an alliance right beneath his very nose. Which was why Nicolas valued Anne's trust more than the king's. For the time.

"She has a lover?" Louis prompted.

Mazarin answered with a guilty silence and splay of his liver-spotted hands.

When the king looked to Nicolas, the financier swallowed back the urge to confess the intrigues he knew, in hopes of gaining the king's confidence, and merely shrugged. "Possible," he said.

"If she has a lover—" Louis paced as he spoke, head down in thought "—those jewels may have been gifts."

"Should not the queen be allowed to accept gifts?" Mazarin posed. "Surely they were mere trinkets?"

Much more than trinkets, Nicolas knew. For he kept detailed records of the royal assets. Though Anne had shown him the jewels, she had insisted he not tally their value.

"It matters not the size of the bauble, or the conditions in which the trinkets were received." Louis fisted his hips, a petulant child. "All monies within the royal palace are the king's property. The queen cannot give away an asset without giving away mine. I will have them back."

Louis marched to the door, but swung back to admonish them with a pointing finger. "I will discover the truth of this matter, *messieurs*. With or without your assistance."

The king did not close the door. For long minutes his heels echoed out jaunty clicks as he strode the marble hallway toward the west wing.

Finally, Mazarin heaved out a sigh. He rapped Nicolas's desk with his beringed knuckles. "Quite the intrigue, eh?"

Nicolas could not be sure if the cardinal could know the complete details behind the missing jewels—that the queen had hidden them, and had plans to then give them away.

To hide her indiscretions.

And so he but nodded, and watched as the cardinal sauntered out of his office.

It was interesting to Nicolas, now that he considered the recipient of the treasure cache of jewels. A musketeer. And what was that silly little phrase the musketeers spoke as a literal statement of faith?

All for the king.

Yes. Interesting, then, that a very particular musketeer should be taking from the mouth of the very man he had pledged to serve faithfully.

Actually, it was rather amusing.

5

It neared midnight, and exhilaration overwhelmed Annja's exhaustion. The tent lay flattened, its perimeter burned and the canvas smoking. The center remained intact thanks to Jay's fast actions to snuff the flames.

A flashlight had been retrieved from the Jeep's glove box, and Annja could now make out faces. The teenager's face was blackened with ash, and his short blond hair stuck out in tufts. His slouchy jeans and fancy sneakers led Annja to believe he was a charmer. Or maybe it was the wink he tossed her way.

"Now what?" Jay asked Ascher, but he danced his look up and down Annja.

Boys and their blatant hormones. Annja looked away to conceal her smile.

"Formal introductions," Ascher said as he slung an arm across Annja's shoulder. "Jay and Peyton Nash, I introduce you to the one and only Annja Creed."

"Chasing History's Monsters," Jay said in weird fan-boy

wonder. "I never miss an episode. Your stories are fascinating, Miss Creed."

"Thank you, Jay. Glad to know you appreciate the history and research."

"Oh, yeah, the research," he muttered, but it wasn't very convincing.

"A pleasure." Peyton Nash leaned forward and offered a hand, which Annja took as opportunity to slip from Ascher's too comfortable embrace. She returned the proffered shake. Good, firm clasp. And a keen sense of decorum. She liked the man. "Jay's my little brother. We've had the ill luck of digging out holes with Vallois on more than a few occasions. I suppose that is our fault. He calls, we come running."

"I guess that makes you a winner," Jay said to Ascher.

Ascher shook his head subtly, but from the corner of her eye Annja caught the move. "A winner? What does that mean?" she asked.

"I do not know what he is talking about," Ascher pleaded with a shrug.

Peyton, the elder brother, shook his head, but could not hide a grin in the glare of the flashlight.

"Did you make a bet that you could get me here?" she tried. It wasn't a stretch to imagine after his attempts at online flirtation. "Was that the only reason you invited me to the dig?"

Jay answered, "Yes."

Ascher spit out a resounding "No."

"I may have put forth a friendly wager," Ascher then offered quickly, "but only *after* inviting you here."

"Because you were guaranteed you would win," she said.

"No, because I wanted you to see the sword."

"You didn't have the sword when you called me last night. Or that's what you said. You had *some* sword. The one the thugs got away with looked sixteenth century from what I saw," she said.

"Found it after but three dips of the shovel into the ground," Peyton explained. "Nice find, but quite damaged by the elements."

No surprise. France was covered with lost weapons and armor and spoils of war. Most of it was found by farmers, who took the rusted artifacts home and hung them over their fireplaces or tossed them in the truck beds filled with an assortment of odd finds including stripped tires, chipped pots and the occasional silver coin.

"Do you even have the real one?" Annja prompted. "If this was a ruse to get me here—"

"Annja, settle. You saw the coat of arms on the piece I showed you in Chalon. Do you doubt your own knowledge?" Ascher asked.

She'd left the wood piece in the rental car. It had been the Batz-Castelmore coat of arms. Of course, anyone could have easily forged it. Especially someone with ulterior motives to trick her here.

"Who were those thugs?" she asked Ascher. "You weren't surprised we were followed."

Peyton took this moment to conveniently slip back and stroll around to join his brother at the edge of the dig site, leaving Annja facing Ascher in a tense stare-down.

It may be three men to one woman, but Annja's testosterone raged enough for all of them.

"I can honestly say I have never seen them before," Ascher said.

"They acted as though you had intended to give them the sword all along," she said.

Ascher shrugged. "You know how the cyber community

can be. If you are an expert hacker, you can find out any number of things."

"Your lack of concern disturbs me."

Annja tugged out the pistol still tucked at the back of her waistband. With no intention to use it for anything more than a sly threat, she didn't thread her finger through the trigger, but did snap up her arm against her shoulder—barrel pointing to the sky—and made it clear she wasn't about to back down.

"Trust me, Annja." Ascher splayed his hands before him. "I have no intent to deceive you, now or when I called you this morning. I want to share this discovery of d'Artagnan's sword with you. It is as much yours as it is mine."

"If it does exist, it belongs to neither of us," she stated.

"I understand that. All historical artifacts belong to France. But I mean the find, the joy of discovery. It is ours to share."

"I don't like the sound of sharing any joy with you." She dropped the gun to point downward. The man wasn't a threat. She wasn't sure if he was an opportunist or just arrogant. Probably both.

"You've got two minutes to prove to me I haven't wasted my time today, Vallois. I don't have an expense account, and the flight to Paris was not cheap."

"The proof awaits!" Ascher gestured that the Nash brothers join his side. Each of the three men nodded, knowing. The air hummed with an unspoken excitement.

"What?" Annja eagerly followed as Ascher urged her toward the dig site. "Have you found another sword? *The* sword?"

"It's still half-buried," Jay said excitedly.

"But we'll have it out in a jiff," Peyton agreed. "We've been waiting for Ascher to bring you here before digging it out completely. He made us promise we would not peek. Well, I was waiting, Jay was—"

"Just resting my eyes. I was not sleeping. You've got a gun," he said to Annja.

Annja dropped the Glock to her side. "Spoils of war. So show me the prize."

Both men jumped down into the pit, about three feet deep and seven or eight feet wide. Ascher started tossing them tools, trowels and the small shovel. Grinning at Annja, he then jumped into the pit and began to direct them.

So he hadn't lied about promising to make them wait. But Annja sensed he still lied about something.

"Light, please, Miss Creed," Peyton said.

Annja flashed the light over the pit. She saw that indeed something was embedded in the dirt. It looked like a corner of a box. An old wooden box that had once held—and maybe still did hold—a valued sword?

"It's a sword box," Ascher explained as he carefully brushed away dirt. "Jay opened the end. That is when I contacted you. And you did ask me to wait."

Trowels clicked against wood and the men worked furiously to uncover the entire box.

Annja didn't even mind the chill that had settled with nightfall. Brushing her fingers over her bare shoulder, she felt an abrasion. The thug's bullet had barely damaged the skin. No blood. Though her flesh did feel warm. Excitement fueled her temperature up a few notches, she felt sure.

"There is a sword inside!" Jay announced grandly. He had a hand poked in the exposed end of the box where the coat of arms had been removed. "I can feel the curve of the pommel through the cloth. It must be wrapped in a sword bag. And it will be d'Artagnan's sword!"

Annja smirked. "I'll believe it when I see it."

AN HOUR LATER, Annja believed.

The box was open, she squatted next to it, holding the sword that Ascher had carefully laid upon her palms. Jay held the camp light above their heads as they all preened over the weapon.

It was a rapier, apparent by its short and narrow blade. The hilt was ornamental. Not a fighting sword, but one worn by a gentleman as an enhancement to his wardrobe, a decorative accessory.

Surprising. Yet Annja assumed if the queen had commissioned it, she may not have thought to gift her favorite with a fighting weapon.

The light Jay held flickered. "We're losing juice," he said.

"We'll take it to my home for a better look." Ascher reached for the sword, but paused. "You hold it, Annja. Let's pull out the box and then leave."

CLUTCHING THE SWORD BAG to her left shoulder, the base of it stretched onto the small floor space in the rental, Annja nodded off as Ascher drove. She didn't feel the need to chat, so long as she held the sword.

She'd left the pilfered Glock with the Nash brothers, with an encouragement to decamp and leave quickly. There was no telling how quickly the thugs would discover the sword dupe and return for the real thing.

Two hours later they arrived at Ascher's home just south of Sens. The town was once the capital of the Gallo-Roman province. Abelard's doctrines were condemned here, and Annja recalled, Thomas Becket once lived in Sens during exile from England. Perhaps she'd find a few hours later to explore the city, after the sword had been examined.

The sun had yet to rise. Annja guessed it was 3:00 a.m. but

she couldn't get a view of the digital clock on the driver's side of the dashboard.

Ascher lived in an estate that resembled a castle with tiled pepper-pot turrets to each of the four corners. It was probably officially considered a château, she thought. It even had a dry moat. The brickwork was streaked with black, and more than a few tiles were missing from the roof and turrets. It needed a bit of tender loving care, Annja figured. As the car's head-lights flashed over the exterior, she saw climbing vines painted the limestone block and seamlessly blended the house's corners into the large rectangular yew shrubs that hugged it.

A house in the country replete with a sexy Frenchman?

Hell, she really did need to sleep. After the encounter with the thugs, she felt quite certain she could spit farther than her trust extended toward Ascher Vallois.

He offered to carry the sword inside. Determined not to let it out of her sight, Annja walked past him. For some reason she felt an attachment to the thing, though it hadn't even been her dig.

Because you've wondered and obsessed over it for years— that is why, she told herself.

And what would she do if it was authentic? It wasn't her find. Nor Ascher's. According to French find laws, all artifacts belonged either to the living relatives—if the artifact could be verified as to owner—or then to the city of provenance, and finally to France itself.

Standing in the dark foyer, Annja clung to the weapon as she looked about. A low ceiling lamp switched on, illuminating the immediate area, but fading out into a dark hallway. Dark stained oak coated the foyer from floor to ceiling and gave off a musty odor Annja associated with the stacks of old libraries.

There were a few swords displayed point down from ornate

hangers on the wall opposite the door. Nothing Annja immediately recognized to century or country of origin.

What caught her eye were the acoustic guitars of every design hung high on the walls. Art deco glass lamps focused spotlights on an ivory-inlaid fret board or the shiny gold tuning pegs on a small instrument that resembled a ukulele more than guitar.

"Do you play?" she asked.

"No, but I appreciate." Ascher strummed his thumb across the strings of one specimen. "Mid-nineteenth century. A real Spanish guitar once played by Paco de Lucena, famed flamenco artist from Granada, and not to be confused with the contemporary Paco de Lucia. You like music, Annja?"

"Of course. I never travel without my iPod." She dangled her backpack from three fingers. "Usually use it as background when I'm researching. I've some Sabicas on my playlists."

"Ah, an aficionado. Sabicas is real flamenco *puro*."

"I'm not even close to being an expert. I just like guitar music," she said.

Her eyes trailed lazily away from the guitars and across the tiled floor, which resembled the rusted color of dried clay from Spain. In her backpack were her laptop, iPod, digital camera, her ever present notebook and a clean pair of shorts and T-shirt, not to mention bra and underwear. A change of clothing felt necessary, but trying. She found it impossible to stop a yawn.

"You can stay the night," Ascher offered as he led her left into a small room. "Or what remains of it."

A fieldstone hearth and shelves of books lined the walls of the small yet cozy den. Brown leather furniture sat as if it had been built with the house, so regal, yet aged and in need of repair. A ragged-edged map hung over the hearth. France, post-

Revolution, for the names of the monuments were all changed, such as the Temple of Reason instead of Notre-Dame.

All the room needed was a lazy mastiff lounging on the bearskin rug before a crackling fire to complete the look.

"I'm tired," she said. "But I don't feel like sleep."

"You stole a nap in the car."

So he'd noticed.

"Much needed, I'm sure, after your certain brilliant actions against those men with guns," Ascher said.

"Certain brilliant actions?"

He shrugged. "Treville told d'Artagnan such actions were a requirement—"

"To become a musketeer."

And despite her exhaustion, Annja smiled. Now she remembered what had attracted her to Ascher in the first place, and why she had enjoyed his cyber company so much. They shared common interests, such as sporting and adventure, and archaeology. And a love for Dumas's famous story.

Resisting full collapse, Annja sat on the edge of a comfy leather ottoman. Carefully laying the sword across her lap, she then burrowed into her backpack for the cool rectangle of her digital camera. "Let's take a closer look at the sword, okay?"

Pushing aside some books and magazines, Ascher cleared a marble table against the wall opposite the hearth. "I will lay out some clean paper and find us some gloves."

He produced a large sheet of butcher's paper from a drawer under the table, which he laid over the white marble. A box of disposable latex gloves was produced from a cabinet on the connecting wall. Annja realized that an archaeologist, even if only part-time, would have all the essentials.

"So why only part-time?" she asked, still clinging to the ancient, dirty velvet bag as Ascher smoothed out the crisp paper.

"What? You mean the digging? It is no more than a hobby."

"Treasure hunter," she teased.

"Call me what you will. But you knew before coming here my experience and education."

"Yes, too bad you left out the part about consorting with thugs."

"Annja." He dug out a few surgical gloves and leaned against the table. "My real passion is teaching."

"Fencing." He had a little shop in Sens, but lately, struggled to make the rent. How then, could he afford this mansion? Perhaps more than the exterior was crumbling, she thought.

"Fencing is a romantic sport, *oui?*"

"Yes, but it also emulates armed manslaughter."

"Touché! Ah, but the children. They are so agile and quick to learn. It is a delight to watch them develop their skills."

She was surprised to hear the enthusiasm in the man's voice. It was something he'd never mentioned during their online chats. "You teach full-time?"

"I'm down to three days a week. The rent—ah, it is of no import. I have to be free, you know?" He gestured with excited fingers as he smoothed out the paper, yet took moments to punctuate his speech like an air typist. With a wince, he clutched his side, but recovered as quickly. "I live to experience adventure. Jump off of buildings. Trek across mountains. Swim in the Amazon."

Annja lifted a brow. "I've had a few adventures myself."

"I like that about you, Annja. That time on *Chasing History's Monsters* that you pursued the blue flash down the hillside?"

"Not planned, I assure you." She recalled an episode on the blue flames, which, according to Bram Stoker's *Dracula,* were places where buried treasure could be found, but only on Saint George's Eve. Legend called them flames from all the dragons Saint George sent to Hell. Annja had decided it was the oxidation of hydrogen phosphide and methane gas, though she hadn't ventured anywhere near a swamp where that should normally occur. "But it did make for good viewing. My producer held the clip for ratings week."

"You were on Letterman that week, as well. You should flirt more with the man."

Annja bowed her head and tried to force up another yawn. Why couldn't she summon one when it was needed?

"You are a very sexy woman, Annja," Ascher said.

"Yes, well." The compliment felt great. She didn't hear things like that often enough. "Right now I'm feeling far from it. Tired, dirty and close to falling asleep on my feet."

"So! You want to let go of that, or must I pry it from your iron grip?"

"Hmm? Oh. Sure." She set the sword bag on the paper with a crisp crinkle, and rubbed her hands together. "Hand me some gloves. And focus that light, will you?"

"Your wish is my command, *mon amour.*"

"Watch it, Gascon. Just stick to the business at hand. All right?"

"Of course. Gloves. And light."

Snapping the latex gloves onto her hands released the smell of powder. She then drew out the sword from the bag to place it on the white butcher's paper. Bits of dirt and particles of the desiccated velvet that had lined the box fell onto the crinkled surface. In their excitement at the dig site, she had already handled the sword without gloves. Hopefully, it had no incurred damage.

Annja let out a huge breath and pressed a hand to her chest. Yes, her heartbeats really could pound that quickly. Here beneath her fingertips, sat a remarkable history.

She concentrated on the weapon, leaning in to study the length of the hilt, from the flat, slightly curved pommel to the *quillon,* curved back to protect the hand, yet abbreviated as it swept into the decorative hilt. The blade was about three and a half feet in length, and the hilt designed for a large hand to fit comfortably about the grip.

A gorgeous sword for any cavalier to wear at his hip when out on the town and looking to show his worth or to attract a lady's eye.

She clicked the camera on and snapped a few pictures.

"Damascened blade," she said, drawing a gloved finger over the slightly rusted blade. The arabesques were worn to mere suggestions, but still there was no denying the quality of work. She leaned in and adjusted the camera for a close-up shot. "Blackened steel. Folded…I'm not sure."

"Twelve or thirteen times," Ascher tossed in. "Most seventeenth-century swords crafted for the French court were designed by Hugues de Roche. Especially the more decorative rapiers. He folded his steel a dozen times and signed them with a mark on the *ricasso* of the blade, just near the hilt."

"What was the mark?"

"A simple *R* in a circle," Ascher said.

Annja tilted the sword to catch the light at the base of the blade. Smoothing a finger through dust and dirt, she located a small marking. "It's here. It's real," she gasped, not wanting to succumb to the tremendous feelings that threatened to make her squeal like a silly schoolgirl. Not yet. Look it over completely first. And take more pictures, she ordered herself.

"Swept hilt," Ascher noted. "Gold."

"Yes," Annja agreed. "The hilt is three strands of gold, which sweep to form the suggestion of a basket. The grip is wrapped in silver, maybe, and it looks like a black cording twists around it, almost as if it was meant to fit within the channels of silver."

"The inventory documents of Castelmore's belongings detailed two swords," Ascher said.

"One of black steel," Annja confirmed, "the other gold. But they were believed sold to pay off his debts."

"How do you suppose Charlotte-Anne got her hands on this sword?"

"Well, that's assuming this was one of the swords remaining in Castelmore's home after his death. Neither one was indicated as a rapier. He could have received this from the queen, then immediately handed it to his wife for safekeeping. This rapier could be entirely different from the two documented swords."

"True. But I don't think so," Ascher said.

"You just don't want to believe so."

There was only one sure way to determine if this was the actual rapier once wielded by Charles de Castelmore d'Artagnan, gifted to him by Queen Anne as thanks for many dangerous missions, all for the king.

All for one, and one for all.

Such a noble phrase. And yet "all for one" could bear a much greater meaning.

Annja surreptitiously slid a latexed finger along the hilt, tracing the smooth gold. Now she met Ascher's eyes. The two of them challenged without words. A lift of her brow was matched by Ascher's grin.

"Shall we check if rumors hold truth?" he asked.

6

"When did you have the time to research this legend, Ascher? In between jumping out of buildings and swimming the Amazon?"

"Exactly. I like the quiet of the *bibliothèque* stacks. So still and haunted by the ghosts of centuries past. It offers a balance to my busy lifestyle."

Annja felt the same whenever in a library. Rarely did she find the time lately. Her own loft back in Brooklyn had become a minilibrary. And if she waded beyond the piles of books, field notebooks and research documents, there were artifacts stacked without order. The loft wasn't a complete disaster; she liked to consider it comfortable disarray.

Balance, yeah, that was something she should never allow to tilt too far out of whack. A good meditation session wouldn't hurt after her long day.

"Besides Dumas's journals, which you have read," Ascher said, "I've had opportunity to pore over some of Nicolas Fouquet's voluminous writings."

"The royal financier who was imprisoned for embezzlement," Annja said.

"Yes, unfortunately he is known for that small mistake."

"And for being a pornographer, thanks to Louis XIV."

"Falsified evidence. He merely copublished a racy little tome with Madame de Maintenon. She did the majority of writing—he edited. He really was so much more."

Annja smirked. "And here I thought your favorite Frenchman was King Henri III."

"The most reviled of the Valois kings—because of his homosexual tendencies—but I'm interested in them all. Do you know Fouquet also had a huge lending library that was the greatest collection of research books in all of Europe? It attracted political advocates and patronages. Fouquet intended to use it to rise in position in the government. But the king wasn't having it. I'm not sure why Louis XIV was angry with Fouquet. This all happened *before* the infamous arrest after the lavish party at Vaux le Vicomte."

Annja hadn't known about the library. "What happened to the library after his death?" she asked.

"It was divided up and sold. Madame Fouquet managed to save his personal journals. I'm surprised I found the little I did at the Bibliothèque Nationale. The man made copies of virtually every important document he created for the royals, be it for purchases of land or certificates of patents to the nobility or coded secret missives. He was a secretive Saint-Simon, if you will."

The duc de Saint-Simon had been an infamous chronicler of the seventeenth century, his diaries amounting to thirty published journals. Much like a modern-day entertainment program, Saint-Simon had reported all the salacious and juicy details of court life.

Annja had always wanted to get her hands on Nicolas Fouquet's private journals, for he had been close to Charles Castelmore during his imprisonment for embezzlement. Castelmore had been forced to stay with and tend him while imprisoned as Fouquet waited the king to either call him back from exile or begin proceedings for his trial. It took well over three years, during which the musketeer had not the opportunity to command his troops or engage in martial combat. It must have been hell for d'Artagnan, she thought.

"I believe Dumas had access to the Fouquet papers, as well," Ascher said.

"To look at you, no one would mistake you for the scholarly type," she commented, turning her attention back to the rapier.

"Please don't let the word get out."

She gave a little laugh. "And here I thought you were nothing more than a treasure hunter."

"You say the title as if it is so offensive."

"Treasure hunters have no reverence for history, the condition of a dig site or the people who left behind the objects. Archaeology is all about learning the why, what and where. Treasure hunters could care less. They storm in, kick aside the dirt and haul away the booty."

"I'm very meticulous before I haul away the booty." He delivered her a charming wink. "I know how to backfill a site, returning it close to its former state."

"Even when you've got gunmen breathing down your neck?" she asked.

"I am very busy man, Annja. I have…had alliances."

That statement struck Annja oddly. But she knew now she should not be surprised at anything Ascher said or did.

"Those men who tried to steal the sword," she said. "You knew them."

"As I've said, I have never seen them in my life."

"That may be, but you were not surprised by their arrival," she pointed out.

He drew himself up straight, but with a sudden wince, he clutched his side.

"Did you get hurt tonight, Ascher?"

"It is nothing. An old injury, as I said earlier. Just surprises me now and then. I'm usually quite fit, and can perform remarkable feats with my body. As a *traceur,* one uses his whole body to perform. An injury keeps me from participating."

"The *parkour?*"

"Yes. A *traceur* is one who practices *parkour.* I do not like it when I am injured."

"It's been a trying day. Maybe a heating pad?"

"Perhaps."

Ascher pressed his palms to the white paper and leaned in, his shoulder brushing her arm. Annja could hear his breath catch—he was in pain.

Compassion didn't come easily for her. She wasn't a hugger, nor did she often feel inclined to ask anyone "How are you?"

She'd give him some space. He'd take a moment if he needed it.

Tension strummed through her, but it was divided between excitement and the nervousness of being close to a man she had thought to know better than she apparently did. A man she had initially thought to trust.

"Enough small talk," Ascher said in a whispery tone. "I am well. Are you going to check to see if it is in there?"

"You're giving me the honor?" she asked, surprised.

"But of course."

Tilting her head, she peered into Ascher's eyes. When

fencing, it was critical to maintain eye contact with the opponent. The enemy's next move always first showed in his eyes. But she saw nothing to clue her to defense. And when had she started calling him an enemy?

His mouth slightly parted, Ascher waited expectantly. A shadow of a soul patch dabbed his chin, and lower, a pale white scar curled out of view under his jaw. The adventures that drew him appealed to Annja perhaps more than he did.

Annja let out a breath and placed both palms to the paper, before the rapier. "Can I trust you, Monsieur Vallois?"

He propped an elbow on the marble table. Mischief now danced in his pale blue eyes. A dangerous mischief. While it threatened, it also intrigued. Adventure or not, Annja wasn't completely oblivious to the opposite sex.

"How can we know when to trust anyone?" he asked.

"That's not the answer I was hoping for."

"I can ask the same of you, Annja Creed. Can I trust you?"

"You invited me here. I'm just along for the ride. Amusement-park ride, as it may be. Just tell me before we do this— who wants the sword?"

Huffing out a sigh, he pressed his chin into his palm and eyed her straight on. He was hiding something, and Annja could sense his need to blurt it out. Men always kept their feelings bottled up. Yet their secrets often simmered just beneath the surface, easily excavated with adept care.

Kind of like you, eh, Annja?

"Annja, believe me when I say I have always intended to hand the sword over to France if and when it was found."

"But now…?"

"I have been forced to look differently upon this discovery. The people who want the rapier," he stated slowly, his vision now directed at the tabletop, "have ensured, by use of devious means, that I will hand it over. But it is merely the sword they want, not anything that we may find inside it."

"You intend to hand this valuable artifact over to a collector?" Annja asked.

"Collector or weapons enthusiast? I don't know what he is, or why he wants it. All I know is I've but one kidney remaining, and haven't the desire to lose the other."

Annja straightened. He'd lost a kidney? What was he talking about?

Ascher drew up the back of his shirt to reveal muscular and tanned flesh. A long red scar, where his left kidney should be, looked angry and new.

"Sounds crazy, doesn't it?" He tugged down the shirt. "But it is not a lie, Annja. I did not want to deceive you, but the truth is so humiliating."

Not sure what to say to his confession, she made the conclusion that whoever Ascher was dealing with was not the friendly sort. And this so-called treasure hunt just took a dangerous curve downhill.

"Someone injured you so grievously that you lost a kidney. For a sword?"

He nodded. "It was insurance that I would comply. I value the one I have remaining."

"But—" Incredible, yet the scar did appear new. He could have injured himself doing any number of things, mountain climbing, bike racing or whitewater rapids. But Annja sensed he spoke the truth.

Even so, she thought. "I can't allow you to hand d'Artagnan's rapier over to a private collector," she said.

"Then we will come to arms over that." He tapped the table. The butcher paper crackled. "It is my favor to you, Annja, to warn you in advance of my intentions."

"Fair enough." So what would she do? Grab the sword and run?

Not without first looking for the real treasure.

"Let's do this, then," she said.

Placing the gloved fingers of her left hand about the hilt, a test wiggle concluded the pommel was firmly attached. Wincing and closing her eyes as she torqued her grip, she tried the pommel again. Fine particles of dirt sifted to the paper. The dry aroma of limestone lifted in tendrils.

"Is it moving?" Ascher wondered enthusiastically.

"I don't know. I think I'm just twisting off the debris. But…maybe. It's giving."

"Really? Don't break it," he said.

"Break it? What do you care? You've probably already alerted Monsieur Kidney Stealer to come pick up his prize. Have you?"

Ascher shrugged. "I don't contact them—they contact me."

"I think…yes, it is moving."

"Let me see." Ascher leaned in as Annja twisted the pommel loose and carefully removed it from the hilt.

Holding the round piece upon her palm, Annja flicked away particles of dirt. Interesting how the sword, though encased in a wooden box and velvet bag, had become encrusted with so much soil. Of course, the box had been split down the center. Centuries of dirt had sifted through.

The pommel was the size of a silver-dollar piece in circumference. It was convex, and heavy to counterbalance the weight of the blade. Both sides of the piece were impressed with a design.

"The coat of arms," she blurted out, recognizing the design on the pommel.

"The Batz-Castelmore coat of arms?"

"Yes," she said, elation lightening her tone. "Two castles and the eagle. The queen went to great lengths in having this gift handcrafted and personalized specifically for d'Artagnan."

"Do you think they were lovers?" he asked.

"What?" Drawn back to reality by that conversational detour, Annja eyed Ascher's enthusiastic smirk. "Lovers?"

A waggle of his brows preceded a shrug. "Anything is possible."

True. There was no documentation that would lead anyone to believe the real Charles Castelmore had an affair with the queen of France, yet novelists and filmmakers had alluded to it over the years. And Annja couldn't deny it a salacious fantasy that she could consider placing to her favorite musketeer.

Only problem was, Dumas had placed d'Artagnan in the story earlier than actual history, which had made him closer to the queen's age. In reality, Annja wasn't sure of the age difference, but a guess had to place the musketeer and the queen at least thirty years apart, the queen being older.

She set down the pommel on the white butcher paper. A few digital pictures were needed.

Ascher tilted the end of the hilt toward her, revealing the open inner chamber. The inside was no wider than a man's thumb. She took a few more pictures.

"Annja, you must do the honor," he said.

This was it. As usual when on the verge of what she felt to be a fortuitous historical discovery, Annja grew intensely calm and almost zen. Now was no time for frantic excitement. The joy came in careful exploration of what was once only a mystery or legend.

She bent to look down. There *was* something inside the hollow hilt of the seventeenth-century rapier.

"Careful," Ascher coached.

"It's a rolled paper. Do you have a—?" Bent-tip tweezers

slapped onto her palm before she could finish the request. "Thanks."

She knew the slightest jolt could damage the centuries-old paper. If she tugged too hard or clasped the tweezers too tightly, she risked tearing the parchment.

Annja drew in a breath through her nose, and went for it. A roll, about four inches long and tightly coiled, slid out easily.

Ascher redirected an overhead lamp to focus on the roll that she set before the rapier blade. The roll wobbled, then stopped. The twosome exhaled in unison.

"Do you think it is?" she whispered.

"The map!" Ascher said. "To the real treasure."

"Yes," she answered, surprise softening to agreement. A relieved exhale unraveled the tightness in her core she hadn't been aware of until now.

"Rumor tells the map will lead to a treasure," Ascher whispered. "A treasure the queen wanted d'Artagnan to have in thanks for all he had done to serve France and its king."

"Right. But it wasn't for chasing after missing diamonds for her collar, as Dumas wrote," Annja said. "Though there may have been a morsel of truth to that."

"That was pure fiction! There is no historical record of the diamond studs," Ascher said.

"Yes, but never say never, eh? It is alluded that the treasure might have been a collection of jewels the queen had received over the years from her lovers," Annja replied.

"Evidence she wished to be rid of, for some might have placed her to having an affair with Mazarin."

"And what better way to do that than give them away. This sword was a gift for heroic deeds such as defeating the Spanish at Lille while the king marched his troops to help, or heading the vanguard at La Rochelle, while the king dallied at Fontenay."

"Yes!" Ascher's excitement vibrated between them, bouncing against Annja's chest and throat. "Let's have a look."

"We can't yet," she said, poking the map with the tip of the tweezers. It was rolled so tightly, that she could not think to unroll it and risk it crumbling to flakes. "We'll need…"

"Humidity. We can relax the parchment by steaming it. I'll boil some water."

"We should wait," Annja said.

A panicky look deflated Ascher's joy. "Why?"

"We need a good six to eight hours for the humidification process."

"I know—I've done it before. Ah, you are tired? You can rest while I begin."

She ran a hand over her scalp, wishing for a good solid eight hours of sleep. Heck, she'd take four. The sun had yet to rise. She should be sleeping. Normal people were sleeping right now. Couldn't she manage one day as one of them?

But to be truthful, normal wasn't interesting to Annja.

Ascher possessed unbounded energy. But she did not trust him with the process on his own. There were many things that could go wrong if he did not have the proper equipment. One could not simply boil water and steam the roll open. A humidity chamber had to be created and the parchment had to be protected from droplets with a sheet of Gore-Tex.

"Maybe if I had some coffee," she muttered.

"I can do that. Be right back."

THE PHONE RANG in the kitchen and Ascher picked it up on the first tone. He barely said, "Hello," when the voice on the other end began to berate.

"You know the new kidney is not completely developed. You risk your very life by refusing to hand over the sword today."

"You got the sword, I just—"

"I know my swords, Vallois. This is sixteenth century," Lambert said.

"Perhaps the queen gifted her musketeer with a family heirloom?"

"It does not ingratiate you to me to lie. You have the real thing?"

"Yes," Ascher gasped, hating himself, but seeing no other option.

"I'll send a man round to retrieve it. Again. Will you cooperate and hand it over?"

"Of course." Now that they'd discovered the map within, he had no need for d'Artagnan's rapier. Annja would be disappointed but he had no choice. "Give me an hour to get rid of the woman."

"Who is she?"

Ascher tightened his jaw. He hadn't intended to get Annja involved like this. He'd merely wanted a worm to dangle before her to get her to come to him. Things going as they were, he highly doubted he'd have the time to romance her as originally planned.

"Just a friend. A fellow archaeologist. She doesn't know what's going on. And I'll be sure she is gone."

"You had better, Vallois. That map is too valuable to risk losing."

The phone clicked off and Ascher stood there clinging to the receiver. The constant ache high on the left side of his torso would not allow him to forget he was playing with his very life.

And yet, what Lambert had said: *That map is too valuable….*

This was the first time he'd heard anything about the map from Lambert. Ascher had always assumed he knew only about the sword and was perhaps a zealous collector.

But if he expected to find a map, that meant Lambert was on a much bigger treasure hunt.

"Time for a change of plan," Ascher muttered.

7

Seventeenth century

"He refuses to talk about this, and I find that most disagreeable. It is as if he hides something."

King Louis XIV paced the drawing room before the damask chaise that had just arrived from Venice. The wooden crates used to pack it sat in shambles on the floor. Discarded in billowing piles, soft Venetian cloth once wrapped about the chaise dotted the floor in turquoise blobs.

Cardinal Mazarin found the chaise most comfortable, though Louis complained it was overstuffed. If any were overstuffed, Mazarin thought, it was the French. Italian craftsmanship was exquisite.

"I insist we have Fouquet investigated," Louis declared. "Why do you shake your head, Eminence?"

"Forgive me, Your Highness. Any valued asset gone missing is a grievous thing. I do not wish to discount the gravity of this dilemma. But these were the queen's jewels.

Perhaps she has a perfectly rational reason for moving them from the usual storage place."

"You think she still has them? She had better."

"Have you spoken to her? Asked her? Expressed your concerns?"

Louis shrugged, reverting to a childish wallow. "Might you speak to her in my stead?"

Mazarin nodded, finding the room was only getter warmer. Why the king persisted upon this small detail astounded him. The king had his own cache of jewels. Was not his mother allowed the same? Some privacy to her belongings?

Well, the cardinal knew the answer to that one. All correspondence with Anne was written in code for the very reason that nothing in this court was ever secret. Nothing.

Though he had managed to hide their affair for the short time it had occurred. Cheers to Anne for finding a sensible means to be rid of the jewels. They could be traced back to an Italian jeweler. He'd not been thinking properly at the time. His heart had been in the fore.

"I will, Your Highness," the cardinal said.

Present day

LEAVING THE TIGHTLY ROLLED parchment on the table and placing the pommel to one side so it wouldn't accidentally roll to the floor, Annja then slipped off the latex gloves with a snap and wandered out to find the kitchen.

Exhaustion clung to her shoulders and pressed upon her temples. She needed more than a short nap in a car. But elation could carry her a bit longer. More than a few times in her life she'd uncovered artifacts or legends that had been thought only myth. She'd never lose the giddy feeling each time that happened.

It really existed. A piece of fiction come to life.

The citrus scent of Earl Grey tea seasoned the air as she found her way into the dimly lit kitchen designed with masculine black marble countertops and stainless-steel appliances.

"I didn't know Frenchmen drank tea," she commented as she slid onto a chrome stool and propped her elbows on the counter.

Ascher shot upright from his bent position over an open drawer. "I didn't hear you come in."

"Sorry, didn't mean to surprise you. Did someone call? I thought I heard a phone ring."

"Wrong number."

"Ah. Pretty early for a crank call. What time is it?"

"Three a.m."

She started to calculate how long she had been awake, almost twenty-four hours, then stopped.

"So." Ascher set out a teacup. The delicate white porcelain looked frail against the masculine black countertop. "D'Artagnan's sword, or rather, rapier. We've done it."

"You've done it. I was the one skeptical about the Chalon site," Annja said.

"Yes. You are right. It was all my doing." Pleased with his triumph, Ascher's shoulders straightened and his cocky smile reappeared.

Annja could claim nothing more than observing the entire operation, though she had chased after the bad guys—and let them get away with an artifact.

"You encounter men with guns a lot on your digs? You seem pretty blasé about the fact any one of us could have been killed," she said.

Only then did she remember the abrasion on her shoulder. She fingered the rough skin absently.

"No, it is not often men with guns try to take away my dig finds. Maybe someone saw my post online?"

"You didn't post about the Chalon site publicly. So how did the men who took your kidney find you?"

"Listen, Annja, I don't know them. They were likely pot-hunters. You know they are rampant, stalking dig sites and stealing the artifacts for their own gain. I once worked a site in Ireland where two of the hired hands were just that. They played along like students until we uncovered a cache of silver beads and plating. They slipped out at night with the booty."

"Speaking of booty. What about the treasure?" she prompted. "If we find that?"

"I've a small fencing *salle* in dire need of fixing up. You are hurt?" he prompted at sight of her touching her shoulder.

"Just a burn. A bullet skimmed my flesh. Didn't even bleed." She brushed over her shoulder. A red abrasion marked it. Such luck.

"A fencing studio?" she wondered. "You intend to keep the rewards for yourself? What about the found-treasure laws? And if there's family?"

"There are no descendants to Charles Castelmore's line," he said.

"How do you know there are no relatives? His brother's children?" Annja asked.

"You claim to be an authority on the musketeer's history, and yet, you are not aware of the family tree?"

"There was a family tree published in a book mid-twentieth century—"

"Yes, and why do you not believe it, eh?" Holding up one finger in a sign to remain patient, Ascher then left Annja in the kitchen. She heard him walk down the hallway, and contemplated following him, but the sight of the teapot redirected her intentions.

Pouring a cup, she sipped as Ascher reappeared with a small, dusty gray book, sans cover jacket.

"I have that volume," she said as she tilted her head to read the spine. *"D'Artagnan: The Ultimate Musketeer,* by Hall and Sanders. Published in the sixties."

"Have you read it?" he asked.

"Of course. It's the one with the family tree on the end papers. You collect books printed in English?"

"If it's about d'Artagnan I do." Ascher laid the book on the counter before her. He opened the front cover. The olive-green end papers featured a family tree of the Batz-Castelmore line.

Annja nodded. "I've seen it. It is incomplete."

With a heavy sigh, Ascher then paged through the book until he came to what he was looking for. He pointed out a specific paragraph, said, "Have you a disagreement with this?"

Annja read the paragraph. It stated Charles de Batz-Castelmore's bloodline had indeed been extinguished when both his male grandchildren died, without progeny.

"Just because it's written doesn't make it historically accurate. Scholars have disproven historical texts throughout the centuries. And d'Artagnan did have a sister who survived his death, as well as Paul, his brother, who lived to the amazing age of ninety-four. No matter, we still can't keep found treasure," she said, finishing on a yawn.

"You should lie down, Annja. I will get a blanket for you to rest. I've a private guest room upstairs. The sun will rise in a few hours, and then we will attempt to unroll the map, *oui?*"

Ascher left her again and called back he was getting a blanket.

"Sure," she said, but absently, she wasn't even aware of her mouth moving. The bergamot steam from the fragrant tea should waken her senses but she wasn't feeling it.

She shrugged a palm up her arm, feeling fatigue plunge upon her like a mallet. It had been a long day, but well worth it.

The sudden loss of light startled her to alertness.

The piercing scream of an alarm bit into the back of Annja's neck.

An alarm? Had someone broken into the house? But who—?

Instantly, she knew. The gunmen. They must have followed them from the dig site.

The sword dupe must have been discovered. And if someone had been cruel enough to rip out Ascher's kidney in warning, then they likely wouldn't stop until they held the real prize in their hands.

The rapier was in danger.

The kitchen was small and in the center of the house. Darkness unhampered by windows disoriented Annja. The hallway was about ten paces to the left, she knew.

Stepping around the last bar stool, she slunk forward. Sliding her palms across the chair rail that dashed waist level along the wall, she found the main hallway that led to the front door. The den had been to the left of the entrance. Narrow decorative windows hugged the front doors, but no light shone through for it was still dark outside.

The alarm chirped loudly. Annja wondered if it was connected to a security office somewhere in Sens. Would the police soon arrive? That could either be a good thing or not so good. You see, Officers, we have this map—which we were going to follow to a treasure without reporting it to the state of France…

That was Ascher's plan. But not hers.

Annja arrived at an open doorway. The den. The pervading scent of earth lured her to the cool marble table. Paper crinkled at her touch. The rapier blade was cool beneath her palm. She grabbed it—no time for gloves—then carefully felt around for the pommel and the map. She didn't feel anything. A cursory check of the sword proved the pommel had been screwed back on. She was sure she'd left it off, setting it against the map to protect it from rolling to the floor.

A twist easily removed the pommel. Blindly poking about inside the grip, she did not feel anything.

Rushing toward the doorway in the foyer, Annja saw a shadow move outside.

"You think so, huh? Not on my watch," she muttered.

She pulled open the front door. There were no yard lights. But there, to her right, footsteps crunched across the pebbled gravel driveway.

Transferring d'Artagnan's rapier to her left hand, she then willed Joan's sword into her right. Annja got a strange thrill to note she held swords that had once belonged to two remarkable historical figures. Who would have thought the two would ever combine forces?

With a sure grip about the hilts, she rushed out and ran after the dark figure.

The night had cooled considerably. Stars sprinkled the sky, yet the moonless dark made everything appear as gray shadows and unedged ghosts.

She got close enough to the intruder to hear breathing and called out, "Stop!"

The shuffling of gravel ceased. Annja could make out the silhouette of a person standing about twenty paces from her. Dressed all in black, he was probably wearing a mask for the lack of definition to the face. To her left stood a building, which might have been a sort of barn.

A brief glint rising before the intruder's shoulder set off Annja's instincts.

Lunging, she slashed low, aiming for wrist or hip, but the powerful sword merely cut air. The thief had dodged into black on black. Footsteps were no longer audible. There must be a stretch of grass along the gravel. Yet Annja knew he—or she?—had not left the area.

The sound of steel hissing through the night alerted her two seconds before the cool kiss of a blade struck the outside of her elbow. Not a cutting blow, but it did electrify her funny bone.

The thief had come armed with his own sword? Or had he stolen one from Ascher's collection?

Bending forward and low to avoid the next sweep of blade, Annja, balancing awkwardly with d'Artagnan's rapier thrust out behind her, moved in to strike the black silhouette, yet missed again.

A great sweep of her opponent's blade whooshed past her face, but it was too far away to do any harm. Did the night steal the thief's prowess, or did they not intend to harm? Anyone could have made that strike, even in the dark.

"The property you stole belongs to France," Annja tried. She lunged and her blade connected.

Her opponent grunted, but in a manner that clued her he'd not taken grievous harm.

A tremendous creaking alerted Annja to something outside the immediate duel range. A *whoosh* and the feeling of impending danger made her dodge to the left. Something struck her cheek with quick, lashing strokes.

Annja staggered. She brushed the back of a fisted hand across her stinging cheek. The crash of a wooden pallet landed but a foot from where she stood. Startled off balance, Annja went to her knees. Dry hay shards rained about her. She spit out a stray bit of straw.

The nondescript building she hadn't been able to physically see must be a barn. A pallet of hay had been dangling overhead from the pulley system, in wait of storage in the loft. The thief had cut the rope.

Annja spit more hay from her mouth. She snapped out her right hand in frustration, literally throwing Joan's sword back into the otherwhere.

"Luck is not with me this evening."

The map was gone. Along with a bit of her pride at such an easy defeat.

Annja slashed through the air with d'Artagnan's rapier. The musketeer's presence hadn't helped the medieval warrior to succeed. He and Joan would have never made a good pair, anyway.

She wasn't sure what to believe anymore. Was this a futile quest for a mere artifact? She could only make conjectures to what the map was worth. Anyone who knew about it would take a chance to get their hands on it. But very few did know about it. Or so she suspected.

Unless a certain treasure hunter had been babbling about his find online. Or if he was working with someone who had a bead on his only remaining kidney.

Said treasure hunter was strangely missing at the moment. Where is Vallois? she wondered.

Shaking her shoulders and brushing them with her free hand to remove the loose hay, Annja then transferred the rapier to her right hand and stalked back into the house.

There was more to this. Annja felt it in her very bones.

And now the most valuable piece of evidence had been stolen.

HIS MEN WORKED all hours of the clock. They had no concept of night and day and when a man should be sleeping or even eating, for that matter. They were machines. They slept when there was opportunity, and if there was not, they did not.

Jacques Lambert now paced before the two men he had sent to retrieve the sword from Ascher Vallois.

"Such a simple task," he hissed. His alligator loafers clicked crisply across the marble floor. "And you actually admit you allowed a woman to get the upper hand over the two of you? Three-hundred-pound behemoths with guns?"

He eyed both men, but they remained silent. As they should.

Jacques walked to the wall and stopped, eye level with the exquisite sword he'd obtained two years ago off the Spanish coast. An eighteenth-century saber of blued steel inlaid with gold. A real pirate's booty. "Which of the two of you is responsible?"

Silence.

And then.

"He is, Monsieur Lambert." Thornton had spoken. From the corner of his eye, Lambert could see he hung his head so eye contact was impossible.

Gripping the hilt of the Spanish sword with his left hand, Jacques tore it from the rack. Turning in a swift spin, he thrust the blade through the center of Thornton's heart. He pushed the blade steadily, stepping forward as it glided through flesh, thick muscle and cartilage as if through an aged soft cheese.

Thornton's mouth gaped. His eyes went wide, unseeing. Blood drooled from his mouth. But he still stood. Jacques did not have to support his weight. Yet.

"See how the blood runs down the center of the blade?" Jacques said. "That divot in the blade is called a blood groove. There is a misconception that it is there to allow the blood to flow down the blade. But in fact, it is there to prevent suction when removing the blade."

The other man had nothing to say. Until— "But…he was right. It was my fault."

"Magnanimous of you to confess, Manny." Jacques slowly withdrew the blade from Thornton's chest. "There. You see? A flat blade would have given a struggle to remove." Blood spattered his wrist and the front of his white Armani shirt. Such a bother.

"Why didn't I kill you instead, you wonder?"

The man nodded, a cross between a yes and a no.

"I'm not much for tattlers, truth be told. There now, catch him as he falls. And do carry him out before he bleeds on the floor. Italian marble is so difficult to clean."

The man caught Thornton as, indeed, his body teetered forward. It was an obvious struggle to contain the behemoth, but Manny managed to hook him under the arms and drag him from the room.

"No mistakes next time," Jacques called as the door closed.

He drew up the sword before him and observed as the blood pooled at the base of the blood grove and drooled over the swept hilt. "I'd preserve this DNA evidence if the idiot weren't such a loathsome individual."

Drawing the blade across the sleeve of his opposite arm, he cleaned away the blood then returned the sword to its position on the wall. A closet with a dozen clean white shirts waited in the adjoining room. He walked inside and sorted through the shirts, all identical, and each bearing a simple white embroidery of the pirate's skull and crossbones just over the left breast.

"A woman, eh?"

Manny had described her as young, athletic and gorgeous. Also, she had been fearless.

"This adds a new twist to the adventure."

8

Rapier clutched firmly in hand—no way was she letting it out of sight now—Annja stalked into the foyer of Ascher's home.

The lights were on.

From around the corner, and inside the den, Ascher dashed out. "Are you safe? I took chase after the thief…"

"So did I." She crossed an arm over her chest, but held firmly to the sword in her other hand. While not exactly angry with Ascher, she was troubled. "Where were you? I didn't see you outside."

"You have the rapier!"

Annja wasn't feeling the Frenchman's elation. Nor did she trust him at this moment. "Where were you?"

"I took after a man out the back door. It was wide open. The thief must have entered that way."

"But *I* chased someone through the front yard and over in front of the barn. Do you think there were two of them?"

"Annja, your cheek. Are you hurt?" He reached for her face, but she flinched.

"Rope burn. You're so cavalier about this, Ascher. Your house has been broken into. You've been robbed. How are the lights on?"

"It was the circuit breaker. Someone must have thrown the switch."

While Ascher had gone to get the blanket for her? And then to get to the sword so quickly and not run into Ascher, who should know his own home in the dark? There must have been two of them.

The same two she'd battled outside the forest? Annja hadn't given either any capacity in the brains department— at least not to plan so successful a heist.

"The map is gone," she said.

"It is?" He stepped back into the den, and Annja heard a growl, and what sounded like a fist punching into the butcher's paper. "I thought they wanted— Bastards!"

"It's probably crumbled to flakes by now," she muttered. "There is no way a thief could have had the forethought to know what the map would be like and what precautions would be required to keep it in one piece."

"Annja…" Ascher rubbed a hand over his tousled hair. Sweat glossed his forehead.

"Did you see me fighting the thief out by the barn?" she asked.

"No. It was too dark, but I heard struggling. Is that how you were hurt? I'm so sorry."

"I'll live. So you heard commotion?"

"*Oui.* I thought I heard someone run by me, so I took chase. I gave up at the edge of the property. The neighbors grow wheat. There's a freshly plowed field that edges my property. Impossible to run through the clods of dirt with any speed. I figured I must have been chasing a ghost."

"I didn't hear a vehicle. Whoever it was had to have parked far away. Your driveway is very long."

"Yes, but the main road is half a mile to the east, across the wheat field. If the thief had a flashlight, he could have made a quick escape."

"We should go investigate. Grab a flashlight," she said.

"It'll be daylight in less than an hour."

"By then the thief will be long gone."

"He's already gone, Annja!"

"Have you no yard lights or a searchlight? I can't believe the lack of—"

Annja stopped herself and pushed out a breath through her nose. It wouldn't help to argue. Nor would traipsing across a field of plowed-up dirt get them any answers. She had to accept that the map was no longer in hand.

Deciding that if she remained, this night could only get worse, Annja stepped back outside through the open doorway. There were too many questions and she hadn't a notion which one to ask first.

Rose-and-violet strands of light dashed across the sky, promising a gorgeous autumn day. Ascher joined her on the front stoop. He touched her shoulder. Annja shrugged him off violently. No Frenchman's charm was going to soften her suspicions.

"I'm sorry, Annja. I know the map was the real treasure," he said.

"No, this was the treasure. Knowing that there really is a sword. Proof." She pressed the hilt of the rapier to her cheek. The cool steel burned against the spot where the rope had whisked her. The weapon had been handled so inelegantly since its unearthing, she was ashamed to think about it. "The map would have merely been an added bonus."

"Surely many millions of added bonuses," he said.

She wasn't in the mood for a snarky Frenchman right now. "Not like we expected it to really lead to something, right?"

"We'll never know without opportunity to look at it."

"I'm going back to Paris. There's nothing more I can do here." Paris was an hour northwest. A motel bed sounded like heaven. "Will you bring me the velvet bag for the rapier?" she asked.

She reasoned Ascher couldn't have anticipated this would happen. But the man rubbed her the wrong way right now. Something about this didn't feel right. She needed clarity and peace. To be alone to sort through the little facts she had. To think.

He returned from the foyer and placed the bag over her arm. Annja took care to pull it over the weapon. "You have the keys for my rental?"

He stroked a hand over her hair, and this time she didn't flinch away. "I'm sorry. My security system was working, but who can know what it will be like to catch a thief in the dark. There must have been two. They gave us the slip. I will call the police. You should leave the rapier here as evidence," he said.

Annja clutched bagged sword to her chest. Evidence. Yes, but she had only just obtained this treasure, and it seemed there were people who had an interest in taking it away from her.

It's not yours.

She knew it wasn't. But neither did it belong in the hands of a thief or a treasure hunter.

If she kept it, it would be safer. Unless Ascher ratted her out to his conspirators.

Or had the thief gotten what he wanted? How many people in this world could be aware of the infamous sword? Only scholars and historical researchers. Maybe a few zealous

Alexandre Dumas fans—such as herself. But then to have further knowledge of the hidden map? Not any more than a handful, she figured.

That left her and Ascher.

"Did you post about the map online, Ascher?"

"You have read all that I've posted about the sword, and you know I was very cautious to simply conjecture, never admit that I thought I was close. Annja, do you not trust me?"

"Take a look at the evidence from my point of view. There's a lot to be said for your guilt. What about this guy who took your kidney?" That incident still blew her mind. "How did he find you?"

Ascher shrugged. "He followed my personal posts to the Nash gentlemen. I don't know how he did it, but you know there are hackers who can do that kind of thing."

Yes, there were. Which was why Annja used a false name when online and half a dozen different addresses for her e-mails. Impossible to trace.

"I need some sleep. And I'm taking the rapier with me," she said.

"You dare to show up and take off with the sword? My find?" he asked

He was right. She had waltzed in and claimed it, which made her as much a pothunter as the thief. But Ascher had proved himself incapable of keeping valued archaeological evidence safe.

She had an idea.

"I want to have it looked at. Authenticated. The map is gone, so until we find that, we're both out of luck, eh?"

Ascher shrugged a hand through his thick hair, his gaze fixed to the velvet bag in her hand.

"I'll bring it back," she reassured. "I promise."

VACILLATING BETWEEN following Annja and remaining at home, Ascher reasoned that to follow her now would get him nowhere. But to remain at home could prove even more dangerous. Lambert was sending his men even as he stood in the entryway watching Annja drive away in the rental car.

Acting upon impulse, Ascher sprinted through his house, gathering up supplies. A change of clothes, a backpack that he kept stocked with a cell phone, passport and a flash disk of all his important financial and personal files.

He stopped by the circuit breaker in the cellar and switched everything off. Just in case.

From the safe behind the bar he retrieved a stack of euros totaling a couple hundred. Normally, he kept a thousand in cash on hand. He'd forgotten to restock the last time he'd had to make a quick departure.

He had this escape scenario down pat.

Swinging into the den, he retrieved one vital essential, and then ran outside to his car.

ROUX LIVED in a gorgeous estate south of Paris. When Annja arrived it was around 7:00 a.m. The guard at the perimeter gate admitted her with a nod and a smile.

Henshaw, fit out in smart butler's livery, greeted Annja, and informed her Roux was out for the evening. Meaning, he hadn't returned home since last night.

The man kept the same hours as her, though Annja figured he'd probably had a much better time at it than she had last night.

Initially she was hesitant to accept the guest room Henshaw offered for her to rest, as Annja knew Roux wasn't always happy to see her. Finally, lack of sleep trumped her reluctance. After a long, luxurious shower, she snuggled into what were probably Egyptian cotton sheets of extremely high thread count. Nothing but the finest for Roux.

Within minutes, Annja fell asleep.

9

It was such a delight to see his protégée wander into the study around two in the afternoon. In Roux's mind she was a protégée; in Annja's, she was probably more of a partner, or more likely, a woman of her own means.

Possessed of a gorgeous athletic figure, she wore khaki cargo shorts and rolled-down socks and hiking boots with style. The T-shirt stretched across her ample bosom was wrinkled, perhaps from being tucked inside a duffle bag. She had an awful tendency to pack her essentials as if a nomad.

Roux set aside the day's copy of *Le Monde* and, seated in his leather chair behind the desk, nodded at Annja's entrance. Her chestnut hair drifted across a shoulder and her bright tiger eyes, as always, held a smile much longer than her mouth ever did.

"I thought you were across the channel?" he offered. "To what pleasure do I owe your company, Annja?"

She ran a hand through her long, unbound hair. Crossing the marble floor in, admittedly, the largest room in the estate and stuffed to the rafters with antiques, artifacts and assorted ephemera collected through the ages, she stopped at the desk and set a velvet sword bag before him.

"Joan's sword?" he asked, but knew it could not be.

Oh, it could be, but, no, she would not give up the job just like that. Nor could he reason that the sword would allow itself to remain fully formed *out* of Annja's grasp. She had developed *sentiment du fer* for the sword, a feel for the blade. And it, in turn, answered dutifully to her commands. It was an extraordinary duo of deadly blade and feminine prowess.

He had oft wondered if Annja would ever grow wary of the great responsibility put upon her by carrying the sword, but had faith that she would meet most challenges, and those she could not, would at the very least stand before and show her teeth with a defiant snarl.

"It's good to see you, Roux," she said. "I had hoped to get a chance to stop by. I've been filming a segment for the show at Stonehenge, but I've become sidetracked."

"Another calling?"

"Not exactly. Maybe. I'm not sure." Her lack of confidence granted a tender blemish to her tough facade. "Actually, I had hoped it would be a sort of vacation. A self-serving venture."

"A most delicious undertaking, those tasks that serve ourselves. It is a fine man who can feed his soul so that others will reap the benefits. But it's not so much the vacation you had hoped for, I can judge from your grim expression. Show me your prize, then. Let's get this figured out."

She withdrew a rapier from the velvet bag and presented it to Roux.

"Yet another sword?" he asked.

"A girl can never have too many swords."

He stood and accepted it with a finger at midblade where

the foible began, and two fingers to the gold hilt. "Ah, this looks familiar."

"It does?"

"Oh, indeed."

Poker face dropped, Annja's excitement gave Roux a bit of a chuckle. Interesting, some of the things that lit this woman's fire.

He looked over the rapier, carefully handling it by the blade.

"I guess I expected something more ornate," she offered, "coming from the queen of France, and especially during the baroque period."

"That's the beauty of the sword—any sword. It is not the exterior, but the talents within, if you will. What the sword master folds into the steel is the true estimate of its value. This particular rapier, though, has more than a fine blade to its merits, if rumor holds truth."

Annja crossed her arms over her chest and leveled a smirk on him. "Tell me what you know."

He did admire her challenging nature. Not about to rush out with details until she first heard his side of the story. Just so.

Turning the rapier about and tracing the gold hilt, Roux's thoughts journeyed back three centuries to a sweet time that hadn't seen him in the ranks, but rather socializing with the soldiers in the king's army and the many women who followed them about. Fan girls, they would call the sort nowadays. Lusty wenches was what he'd called them back then.

Room and a fine meal had set him back no more than a few thin coins. The wenches had been free. He'd marveled at the excess the French royalty enjoyed, while the subjects—well, it would be another hundred years or more before the Revolution.

"The Croix-de-Lorraine tavern, every Tuesday night. A musketeer favorite," Roux said. "Louis XIV was struggling to get Mazarin in hand, while the cardinal much preferred the aging Queen Anne's company. Er, I do believe Mazarin died not too soon after. The musketeers had been disbanded—no, they *would* face disbandment—but not for another decade. And then they would be resurrected, and yet disbanded again. When was that? I believe the year 1650…or, something—oh, the year is not important."

"You served in Louis XIV's army?" She pressed both palms to the desk. Eagerness flashed in her amber-green eyes. Roux did love those eyes. Bewitching. So much there that he could never know, but worth the exploration of soul required to learn what he could.

And he would. All in good time.

"I did not serve the Sun King, finding my tastes at the time led me to debauchery and drink."

"What's changed?"

"Ah, you think to cut me, but you merely make me smile, Annja."

"It wasn't a cut," she said with a teasing smirk. "You know who this rapier belonged to?" she prompted, fishing for his truths before she would offer hers.

"Whose weapon is this? That Gascon fellow. What was his name?" He feigned consideration, though only to see the fire in her eyes spit off a few sparks. "A musketeer, I believe. He garnered a certain bit of postmortem fame after that adventure novel was published. Ah, yes, Charles de Castelmore. A fine fellow with adventure flooding his veins."

"D'Artagnan," she said with gasp of glee.

Roux understood her enthusiasm, yet at the same time, felt pity toward anyone who could only imagine the past. He had lived it. And holding a piece of it in his hands brought it all back as if it were only yesterday.

"Why, Annja, you've given me a tickle. You said this was a self-serving quest. You have a passion for the musketeer?"

"A certain geeky fascination, yes. Fiction glorified d'Artagnan, but in real life, he wasn't quite so famous. Certainly, he had been the king's right-hand man for a time. But history wagered that Paul, his older brother, may have actually received more military glory than Charles."

Roux nodded, considerably impressed. "Yet Charles was the one who received this gift."

"From the queen. I doubt Louis XIV would have shown the same generosity. He kept a tight hold on items of value," she said.

"I thought your expertise was much earlier than the seventeenth century?"

"It is, but this particular historical figure is irresistible. It's an obsession. Life can't be all about danger and demons, can it?"

"I should hope not. Er, meet any demons lately?" he asked.

"None I've wished to converse with." She traced the rapier blade, still held in Roux's hands. "You knew him well?"

"Charles? Drinking buddies, actually. I did once play against him in a match of tennis. Boisterous idiot. He was awful. I won, as usual."

He tilted the sword, noting the pommel. A coat of arms. Likely Castelmore's, but he was not up on the history of heraldry. Hell, keeping his own family crest to mind was oftentimes a challenge.

"Castelmore was gifted this rapier by the queen for his service to the crown. I recall him mentioning the ceremony was held in the king's chapel. A small to-do. Only musketeers and family invited. Of course, I wasn't there." He twisted the pommel and noted the tiny thread, or rather… "Is this a hair?" he asked.

He carefully unwrapped the thin strand from around the base of the pommel.

"One of d'Artagnan's hairs, do you think?" Annja leaned in, observing as he unwound the six-inch specimen. "Or it could be mine."

"It isn't dark, as yours. It was so tightly wrapped about the grip, I had to break it to get it off. None other than your illustrious musketeer, I'm sure."

"Is there an intact root?"

"A—what?" He studied her face from over the blade.

"If there's an intact root you can do DNA testing on it. That would be cool."

"Annja, dear." Roux set the sword down and carefully placed the hair to the side. No root on that little bit of history. "I've never before seen you so excited about a dusty old piece of history."

"Old stuff always gets me excited. You should spend more time with me."

"Perhaps so." He marveled at the exquisite spirit of her. "Musketeers and DNA?"

"I'm no expert on the DNA bit. In fact, the little I know was gleaned from *Scientific American,* a magazine. Though I do have experience in ethnography—genealogical research—I don't often utilize what I've learned out in the field. What I do know is, genetic archaeologists are using DNA testing more frequently these days to date artifacts and determine lineage. The DNA would not tell us who the hair belonged to unless there was a living maternal relative to compare to."

"Really? That's quite interesting. So if you've DNA evidence of a historical figure, you could match their genetic, er, *code* to a modern-day relation?"

She shrugged. "I'm going to have to bow out of this conversation. Dead civilizations are my thing. Not genes and

DNA and all that current science stuff. Though, either way, this sample has been contaminated, so it's probably useless."

Roux nodded, and again lifted the rapier. He recalled what he knew.

The tavern had been ablaze with candlelight that evening. One of d'Artagnan's cohorts had just announced his engagement to a Russian princess, and had bought ale and candles for the entire room. Poor fellow. He could have had no clue about the Russian winters.

It was that evening that Roux and d'Artagnan had leaned over the table to inspect his newest prize. They hadn't wanted anyone else to witness their curious inspection. Captain Treville had arrived but moments after their secretive endeavor, and d'Artagnan had put away the rapier. Roux had never seen it again. Nor had he spoken to d'Artagnan about the map.

He forgotten about the secret of the sword until now.

Curious, Roux twisted off the pommel from the hilt and handed it to Annja, who traced a finger around the circumference.

He peered inside the hollowed column of the hilt. "Gone, eh?"

"You know about the map?" she asked.

"Looked it over with Castelmore one drunken evening while we wagered on the value of the treasure. So it's riches you're after? Annja, are you in need of funds?"

She laughed and shook her head. "No, but thanks for the concern. The treasure was merely a bonus above and beyond the actual existence of the rapier."

"But of course it exists. You had merely to ask."

"Yes, well, good to know for future reference. And believe me if I had thought you might have known the man I would have sought to pick your brain a year ago."

"Pick away, my dear. I welcome the conversation we could have."

"Have you ever thought about writing a book?" she asked.

"Wouldn't have the patience. Perhaps you could ghost-write my history?"

"We'd have to publish it as one of those fictional memoirs. Anyway, I'll have to take a rain check on that. I think I've stepped into something a little more self-serving than a simple quest for treasure. The map did exist. I held it in my hands. Half an hour later, it was stolen."

"That's curious." Roux set the blade on the desk and crossed his arms over his chest. "A stolen treasure map. Seems a very obvious outcome. Treasure tends to involve conspiracy, adventure and pirates. Right up your alley, Annja dear. So who took it?"

"I don't know. Ascher's home was invaded—"

"But you're not giving me all the details. Ascher?"

"The man who invited me to the dig. Ascher Vallois. I've known him for some time online."

"Ah, an online tryst." He couldn't resist a suggestive lift of brow.

"Keep your insinuations to yourself, old man. He's a fellow archaeologist. Treasure hunter. I may have been a little uncertain on his actual profession. We share a fascination for the musketeer. We were followed to the dig site last night, and though I was able to fend off the thugs, later, back at Ascher's home, they returned to steal the map."

"But not the rapier."

"The rapier is not the treasure. And we hadn't expected the map to still be intact, let alone inside the sword."

She crossed her arms over her chest and tilted out one hip. Roux noted her eyes fell upon the collection of Egyptian scarabs he'd only recently received from Cairo. An exquisite find. But if she thought to question him on its provenance, his lips were sealed.

"Tell me this," she said. "You spoke to d'Artagnan. You looked over the actual map. Did Castelmore have no desire to claim the prize? Do you think it still exists?"

Roux shrugged.

"He died in debt. So I have to believe he didn't claim it," Annja said. "Yet, why not? Or did he gift it to his wife?"

His acquaintance with the musketeer had been brief. Roux had known the musketeer's exterior, but not his heart. Castelmore had spoken fondly of a nameless *amour*. Conjecture as to whether that woman was the one he married—or perhaps one of nobility—remained conjecture. Yet, try as he might, the life of a soldier did not allow for an easy, close relationship to any woman—Roux could vouch for that. It was the very reason he hadn't been in the ranks at the time. Things such as e-mail and video conferencing did not exist centuries ago, which might make things easier for today's soldiers, but never painless. The ache of separation dug like a bleeding wound.

"I might suppose he left the rapier for his family," Roux offered. "But it is only an assumption. I had no opportunity to learn if Castelmore had discovered the treasure before my path led me toward the Irish Sea."

"That was Ascher's and my guess, as well. We found the sword at the site of a former Augustine convent in Chalon-sur-Saône. The very convent where Charlotte-Anne de Chanlecy was reported to live before moving to a private family estate in her final days."

"So one may assume Charles Castelmore gave the valued sword to his wife as a means to compensate for a love he could not manage," Roux said.

"He was all about the adventure," Annja offered.

"Indeed. Devotion to one's king is a demanding position. It is the musketeer's faith—all for the king." Amused, Roux tilted his head. "Now what are your plans? Pursue the map. Find the treasure. Have a jolly time with the plunder?"

"I've no clue where to begin to find the treasure. Dumas's references to it were vague. I'm surprised there was anyone else out there actively searching for it. For a while I had to believe Dumas might have claimed it. And yet the sword was found buried exactly where d'Artagnan's wife may have left it. Two hundred years *before* Dumas was even born."

"The Dumas thing doesn't make sense," Roux stated.

"But it can. Dumas uncovered information about the sword during his research for *The Three Musketeers*."

"Didn't the man work with various collaborators? Research assistants?"

"Yes, many. In fact, Dumas was criticized by his peers for operating a 'ghosting factory' of nameless writers who handed him stories, to which he then merely signed his name to the cover page. Auguste Maquet being his most lucrative and famous collaboration.

"And there were notations in Dumas's journals that did not appear to be in his own handwriting." Such as the notation that had led Annja on the quest for the sword. "Well, no matter. The treasure map was mentioned, but nothing beyond that."

"Sounds like you've been relying exclusively on Dumas to find your way. Not that he doesn't have a lot to offer, but he did turn our hero into a bumbling, sex-crazed fool," Roux said.

Yes, while touted as a romantic, adventurous hero by those who read the modern-day, abridged version of the classic, the truth was, Dumas's d'Artagnan jumped from milady's bed to her maid Kitty's bed, and then went gallivanting off to

England to assist Queen Anne while his supposed true love, Constance Bonacieux, withered away in a convent, only to be murdered just when d'Artagnan remembered he had a girlfriend. Not the epitome of a romantic hero, in Annja's book.

So many alliances, yet dedication only to the king. Had Ascher Vallois as many assorted alliances?

"Ascher has provided corroborating evidence found in Nicolas Fouquet's journals," Annja explained. "It's not just Dumas I'm following. Do you remember anything about the map from looking it over with d'Artagnan?"

"If I recall, we had decided it was a map of the aqueducts beneath the Louvre, or perhaps the catacombs beneath Les Innocents. Well, I'm not positive. It's been three centuries since the evening d'Artagnan and I looked over the map, and we were very well soused, I'm sure. Sorry."

"Tell me again why I spend all my time sitting in libraries, surfing the Internet on quests for historical facts and details, when I've got you, a virtual living history book?" Annja asked.

He shrugged. "Some women never realize a man's value. But I'm willing to forgive if you'll have dinner with me."

"I am starving. Can we eat soon?"

"I love a woman with a healthy appetite. Henshaw has prepared the patio for an afternoon repast. Let's step outside, shall we?"

10

Seventeenth century

Three years of incarceration at Pignerol, and he hadn't gotten any closer to learning where that damned sword was.

Any treasure found as a result of the map was owed to him. He'd been framed. Mon Dieu, that they'd made him to be a pornographer! Forced into prison by Colbert and Mazarin— yes, even Mazarin was instigating control over him from his very grave.

So he had diverted some funds from the royal coffers. Not nearly so much as Colbert had led the king to believe. And now to make him sit in this miserable estate that was nothing more than a prison waiting a trial. It had been three years! Would he never be given his due? The king merely shuffled him about the French countryside, from one prison to the other. First it was Angers, followed by Vincennes and then a brief stint in the Bastille, and now the dismal Pignerol.

And always at his side, his indomitable guard, faithful to king and country, Charles de Castelmore d'Artagnan.

Nicolas called him d'Artagnan, as most others in the musketeer's company did. The man was a lieutenant of the king's First Company of Musketeers, but he'd not served in any official capacity over his regiment since the day he'd taken Nicolas under arrest and began his duties.

It bothered d'Artagnan greatly that he could not be out and at the vanguard, active, defending his king. Instead he was forced to play nursemaid and sit about while the king ignored his former financier.

They had become quite amiable toward one another. Nicolas even went so far as to believe d'Artagnan considered him a friend. But he would make no doubts that the king was who d'Artagnan served, and if the king said to bring in Nicolas Fouquet to be hung, then d'Artagnan would do just that.

Easing his fingers about his neck, Nicolas tried for the hundredth time not to consider the pinch of the rope about his neck. But how could a condemned man *not* regard such things?

"You are thinking on it again," d'Artagnan said from across the large cell that Nicolas had recently been moved into on the Pignerol estate. "How many times must I tell you it does no good to live in an uncertain future."

"You appease me with your optimism, my friend." Yes, he always used "my friend." D'Artagnan would correct him if he believed differently. A small reassurance that was most needed. "Were you able to arrange a duel with the bailiff?"

D'Artagnan sighed. "You know how I ache to be active. No, Balmaroille would not agree to the match. He is rather staunch. I am not convinced of his effectiveness in running a prison. Though you must admit your quarters are rather luxurious." He swept a hand to encompass the room.

Damask bedclothes hung from the corners of the four posts and encased pillows and mattress. A fine damask chaise, to match the fabric on the bed, held d'Artagnan's relaxed frame. A marble washbasin matched the marble writing desk, which was outfitted with paper and ink thanks to d'Artagnan's rallying for supplies to keep his prisoner from going completely lunatic.

"And the view." The musketeer pointed out the barred window, which framed an idyllic verdant forest that hugged a narrow stream.

"Trees and grass. But never without the bars. A man's soul requires fresh air and exercise. What of your soul?" Nicolas asked. "How fares it during my incarceration?"

"I am ever faithful to the king—you know that."

"And the queen?"

"Anne appreciates my loyalty to her son."

Yes. Anne the Austrian. D'Artagnan spoke of her in the familiar. As had Nicolas once. The queen had once trusted him with all her correspondence, and he'd learned early on to make copies of it all. For evidence. For blackmail. For his own safety.

Perhaps, for his future security. Pity, he could not access his files now. His wife, pray she kept them safe.

"That was a particular fine sword the queen gave you a few years ago," Nicolas tried.

"You bring that sword up so frequently, I wonder if you pine for it yourself," d'Artagnan replied.

"Who would not? I hope you've tucked it safely away while far from your home?"

"Planchet watches my home in Paris. I've no worry to be robbed. There's not much I own in this world of great value beyond the intangibles, such as honor and respect."

"And a fine gold sword."

D'Artagnan sighed and delivered that tired smile he so

often did. He would not reveal where he kept it. But how to discover if he'd yet found the map in the hilt that Nicolas knew should be there?

But even more important, the *key* to the map.

That exclusion gave Nicolas no amount of wonder. Anne had been particularly elusive after he'd tried to tease it out of her. She did enjoy a good puzzle. Certainly, here in this prison, Nicolas did have the time for it.

Present day

ROUX'S SHOCK of bold white hair and white goatee did not lend to age, but rather life. A life well lived. He brandished a few wrinkles at the corners of his blue eyes and some age spots on his strong, wide hands, but other than that, Annja would place him as perhaps midsixties. He was handsome, and a rogue of the finest water.

She did admire the old man. "Old" being a relative term, for he was well over five hundred years old, and still going strong. Though there was some question as to whether or not he was truly immortal. Since joining together the lost pieces of Joan of Arc's sword—and that sword finding its way to Annja's hands—it wasn't clear if Roux, and his nemesis Garin Braden, possessed the immortality the curse of the sword seemed to have put on them. The mystery did not appear to bother Roux, though Annja knew Garin was desperate for the answer.

The salmon was grilled to perfection and laid upon a creamy lemon sauce speckled with white pepper that Annja promptly put down her gullet. Aware of Roux's peculiar grin as he watched her eat, she finished the salad and the proffered crème brûlée before sitting back and closing her eyes to the high, warm sun that kissed the clear Parisian sky.

"Are you getting along well with the sword?" he asked. "Your sword, not the musketeer's."

"Best as can be expected." Wincing against the sunlight, she blocked it with a hand over her brow and peered through half-closed eyes at him. "There's an incredible emotional price that accompanies the wielding of it, I'm sure you know."

"If there were not, then you would become sick with the power. There must be a balance. You do meditate?" he asked.

"Wouldn't think of not meditating. It is what keeps me grounded," she said.

"Those who live by the sword…"

"Die by it?"

"Is that how it goes?" He downed the remainder of his wine. "I've spoken to Garin recently. He won't let it go. He will pursue the sword until his end days."

Garin Braden had once been Roux's protégé in the fifteenth century. A slave to a kind master who had taught him skills of stealth, defense and the martial arts, until the boy had betrayed his teacher. The twosome had engaged in a reluctant alliance over the centuries, bonded together by a common quest, but each having his own direction.

Now, since the sword had been re-formed, Garin had been at odds with both Annja and Roux. He wanted the sword back, and though he'd yet to prove successful in nabbing it from her, Annja could always be assured of his shadow lurking not far from her travels. He showed up in the most unlikely places, and possessed rather interesting contacts and knowledge of esoteric artifacts even Annja could not begin to grasp.

And he'd once almost been staked as a vampire. To summon that image gave Annja a certain amount of glee.

"Garin will have to take it from me himself," she said. "If

a man wants something, he can't depend on others to snag it for him."

And he had tried that method, more than a few times. To no great success. Was it because Garin feared going head to head with her?

No. While he paid others to do his dirty work, when it came down to it, Annja knew Garin would stand before her, determined and ready to take her on. For now, they had only engaged in a teasing play of sorts.

She tilted her head, eyes closed. A man obsessed with something he held of great value would take it for himself, wouldn't he?

Another obsessed man, Ascher, had been very concerned she was walking away from him, sword in hand. Yet, he hadn't been at all upset over the stolen map—arguably the greater treasure.

Annja rubbed a palm along her opposite arm, chilled even with the bright sunlight.

Had he?

The robbery at Ascher's country estate still didn't feel right. For a masked man to have sneaked in and taken so delicate an object? If she had only navigated the dark by feeling her way, how could the thief have proved any more capable? Unless he'd had a flashlight, which she would have noticed.

When she'd gone back into Ascher's house, he'd come out of the den to see where she had been. And yet, now that she thought on it, he'd been surprised when she told him the map was missing.

If he had been in the den, shouldn't he have known that it was gone?

Had there really been two thieves? And then, to battle her in the courtyard, while also holding that very delicate map? It didn't fit.

Because it hadn't been stolen?

"Oh, crap." She sat upright. Roux winced against the bright sunlight, having gone quiet during her retrospective mood. "It was too easy." She pounded the glass-topped patio table with a fist. "And when we returned to the house, the lights were on again. They'd gone out, and then—he has it. That bastard has the sword."

"Your online lover?"

She scoffed at the old man's salacious suggestion. "I don't know who the figure in black was that I fought with, but he was a distraction. Had to be. Someone else had the map. And they couldn't have taken it far, or in a great hurry. Which only means…"

Standing, Annja walked to the edge of the stone patio where a honeysuckle vine shaded the side of her face. She dug her cell phone out from her pocket. She hadn't exchanged numbers with Ascher, but—yes. When scrolling to the last number received, an unidentified number showed up. She dialed it, and he answered on the first ring.

"You have the map," she insisted. "You have it, I know. There was no one else in your house this morning, except perhaps the decoy you hired to take me on a wild-goose chase away from the map."

"There are wild geese in the area? Annja, I did not know—"

"Nice try, Frenchman. Sit tight. I'll be there in an hour."

"I'll save you the trip," he said. "I am in the car right now, on the way to Paris."

"You'll hand over the map?" she asked.

"If you bring the musketeer's rapier."

So he did have it. "What value is the rapier to you?" She glanced to Roux, who, though he appeared to be intent on his crème brûlée, followed her conversation carefully.

"A personal quest completed," he replied. "I want to ensure the rapier gets placed in the proper hands."

"Those hands have blood on them? Your blood?"

"No, there is a museum dedicated to d'Artagnan in Lupiac. We discussed this online, Annja."

She did not for a moment believe he would hand the rapier over. Not without recompense. But the map would provide that. If it were genuine, and if there was even a treasure to be found.

He had warned her they may come to arms over the ownership of the sword.

"Tell me what you know," she said. "Who were those thugs?"

"Annja—"

"No details, no sword, treasure hunter."

"Very well. They may have been with the investor who gave me no choice but to ally myself with him. But I got the map out for us, Annja. I didn't want to lose that. All he wanted was the rapier."

"Who is this investor?"

"He gave me the name of his company. Uh…BHDC."

"What do they do?"

"I don't know."

"Don't believe you."

"Well, perhaps I know they are into making new organs for transplants."

"What?"

"You know…what is it you call it? To make a new organ from nothing. Cloning. Yes, that is it. So if a man loses a kidney, they can make a new one, *oui?*"

What he was telling her sounded not at all related to a stolen map. But he was either rather clever to summon such a story on the run, as it were, or else telling the truth. And he *had* lost a kidney recently. Unless that was another lie.

"That's the truth?" she asked.

"On my honor and cross my heart. Annja, please, I need to hand over the rapier to this man or…"

"Or what?"

"He'll take my other kidney from me. He's already stolen the one. I can't afford another. So will you bring me the prize?"

She recalled his flinching in the car, and his explanation that it was a recent injury. Someone had attacked Ascher, destroyed his kidney, all for a sword? Without the treasure map?

What had she walked into? And how, in the greater scheme of her life, did this relate to what Joan's sword called her to do?

As an archaeologist, she had learned to search for the why of things, not just the what. A couple of treasure hunters squabbling over a sword? Didn't make sense. But the mystery of it intrigued. And if not for the mystery, she did have to see Ascher once again to give him what for on tricking her.

"I'll meet you in the courtyard before Notre-Dame in an hour," she said, and hung up. "I have to go into the city," she said to Roux. "Can I leave the rapier with you?"

"Of course you can, my dear."

She paused in the doorway to the patio, pressing her palms to the frame. A place to rest and a nice lunch was one thing. But she still had not drawn a definite bead on her relationship to Roux. The man could be concerned when it served him, but she wouldn't fool herself by extending blind trust.

"Can I trust you with it?" she asked.

Roux set down his wine goblet and wiped his lips. "Whatever might I do with it? It's not got a treasure map in it, so I might only spend the time looking upon its ancient beauty and being reminded about the certain lovely who shared my bed that night after I had first looked it over with Castelmore."

Rolling her eyes, Annja headed back through the house, but called back, "Keep it safe, Roux. I'll be back!"

11

Annja arrived before the Notre-Dame cathedral a half-hour early and lucked out finding a parking spot right across from the parvis that fronted the tourist attraction.

Two parking slots down from her bumper, a red-and-white-striped hawker's cart sold hot crepes to a stream of eager tourists. The scent of burned bananas permeated the car windows Annja had rolled down an inch. The giggles of children chasing the ever present flocks of pigeons in the courtyard tickled the air.

She remembered the first time she'd visited the cathedral a few years ago. She'd walked right up to the Arago disk set into the ground fifty yards before the cathedral and taken a picture of her feet standing on the timeworn piece of history. The disk marked point zero, the starting point from where all distance in France was measured. There were 135 disks all over the city, and some day she planned to hike about and see them all. Just for kicks.

Laptop set on the passenger's seat of the rental, Annja twisted and tucked an ankle up under her other leg. She leaned across the shift console and opened her browser. After checking all the possible URL combinations and coming up with nothing, she Googled "BHDC," the initials Ascher had mentioned.

There were numerous corporations and businesses with the initials, scattered all across the world. None seemed like what she was looking for. But after the sixth Google page, she hit paydirt.

"BioHistorical Design Corporation," she read. There was no company Web site, merely a small notation in a science journal. The article, dated 2002, conjectured the few European genetics labs that may have successfully accomplished therapeutic cloning.

Ascher had mentioned something about a cloned kidney, so this may be the right lead.

Annja searched "therapeutic cloning" for a definition. Such a form of cloning involved extracting human DNA from a sample, growing an embryo to about fourteen days, then extracting stem cells to then grow human tissue or even complete human organs capable of transplant. The first successful therapeutic cloning had been done in 2001, and the article, written but a year later, supposed BHDC had accomplished therapeutic cloning the year of the article.

"Huh." Annja sat back in the driver's seat.

From her position, she would notice if Ascher arrived in front of the cathedral. The day was overcast, and a few rain sprinkles spotted the hood, but it wasn't heavy enough to dissuade the pigeons or the children.

"Cloning and d'Artagnan," she muttered, not connecting the two. "But only human organs, not complete humans, which is what I thought cloning was all about."

More surfing found that therapeutic cloning had been legal

in Britain since 2001. It was not currently legal in France, though there were a few exceptions, like if the stem cell was drawn from a frozen embryo.

In America they were trying to pass a law where couples who had stored embryos for infertility therapy could donate the unused embryos for stem-cell research. It was a very touchy subject, both morally and politically.

Overall, the law defining therapeutic cloning was different in various European countries and the United States, though Britain was far ahead and open to the technology.

Across the board, human cloning was illegal.

Interesting, that only this morning Annja had watched Roux pull a hair from d'Artagnan's sword. She had then explained to him that DNA could sometimes be used to identify maternal genetic matches. With a hair sample, an intact root was needed to create a DNA sequence. The actual process was beyond her knowledge, but it was interesting enough that she wanted to learn more.

"But why *BioHistorical?*" she mused. "Does it have something to do with historical figures? Why would BHDC want Ascher to hand over d'Artagnan's rapier? Do they believe there might be DNA evidence on the artifact? Which would provide them…what?"

If there had been usable DNA evidence on the rapier, what would BHDC have done with it? Create an organ? But that would only serve the one whose DNA had been used to create the organ. Charles Castelmore was no longer around. The musketeer was definitely not in need of a transplant.

Ascher was one kidney short, but he could never use a kidney cloned with someone else's DNA. It wasn't possible unless the match was a relative, and even then, it was never a guarantee.

Was Ascher related to d'Artagnan?

"No. He would have mentioned that. Over and over."

If anything, the enigmatic treasure hunter might get a thrill to trace his genetic heritage to Henri III, his favorite Valois king. But he'd already checked that out. No match.

She glanced at her watch. Ascher was five minutes late.

She tapped the keyboard. "I'm missing something."

The more she searched the Internet for information on cloning, the more her head spun. It was not her area of expertise, though certainly there were archaeologists who specialized in genetics. When digging up bones and pieces of history, she was more concerned with who the person had been, not *who they could become?*

Cloning a historical figure? It all sounded too like a science-fiction movie to her.

Though, certainly, the DNA for historical figures was out there and was being put to use. DNA testing was used all the time to date archaeological finds. Heck, there was that whole debacle over slices of Einstein's brain.

Why hadn't anyone tried to clone Einstein?

The topic boggled, so she switched gears to focus on the sword and treasure.

Annja searched the law of finds in France. She wanted to be clear on whom, exactly, the found rapier belonged to, and ultimately, the treasure.

Trying a few simple searches, there were no clear details that she could find. What she needed was access to a law library. But she was able to piece together that treasure belonged to the country it was found in.

"Obviously," she muttered, having already known that. "Though there must be a finder's fee."

Not that she cared to claim any remuneration, but she did

want to be clear on what rights Ascher had should the map actually turn up something.

Closing the laptop, she opened the car door and twisted to stretch out her legs. Only yesterday she'd been smiling ear to ear because this venture had been a means to escape her calling to fight injustice.

There was nothing whatsoever world-threatening about this situation. Not that she was ever rescuing the entire world—just small portions of it, most often. And yet, Annja couldn't help wonder what she did not yet know, and if that would push the stakes higher.

Ascher had lost a kidney because BHDC wanted a sword that once belonged to a famous musketeer. Those same *investors* didn't seem to be aware of the greater prize, the treasure map inside the sword.

Or did they? Certainly anyone would be interested if they knew there was treasure.

Tugging out her cell phone, she dialed Roux's number. Henshaw hooked her up within thirty seconds.

"Miss me so quickly, then, my dear?" Roux asked.

"You still have that hair strand you pulled from the sword?"

"I haven't returned to it since you left. I'm sure it's still there. Do you need it?"

"I don't know. I've discovered a new player in this game. They're called BHDC, which stands for BioHistorical Design Corporation."

"Means nothing to me."

"They do therapeutic cloning. With DNA samples—like a hair strand—they can then create new organs for transplant. Although it's clear that it is not legal in France. Thought I'd run it by you."

"DNA from a hair strand? Still sounds incredible to me,

though I will not deny having heard it on the news stations from time to time. I'm sorry, Annja, what do you want me to do?"

"I don't know."

Yes, what could a five-hundred-year-old soldier provide in way of a complicated topic as cloning?

D'Artagnan and I looked over the map.

Incredible.

"Keep your ears open for me?" she asked.

"Will do."

"Annja!"

A thump on the roof of her car startled Annja. She hadn't seen him coming from the right and behind. "Thanks, Roux, gotta go."

She snapped the phone shut and rose out from the car.

Ascher was looking his usual suave, handsome self. Blue jeans and a gray T-shirt emphasized his athletic build. Sneakers for running. The physicality of him made it impossible to look away. He was all muscles and cocky smile. Standing still was out of the question; he either shuffled his weight from foot to foot or paced a few steps before her. Always ready. A bit like an eager puppy.

But trust had been lost.

Ascher grinned his roguish smirk and came around the hood with arms spread as if to hug her. She sidestepped him. His smile fell.

"You bring the rapier?" he asked.

"You bring the map?"

Daring a move, Annja lunged around and grabbed the coiled roll sticking out from his back pocket.

He protested, but Annja did not listen. The feel of the slick plastic in her hands started Annja's heartbeats to a race. He did not!

"Oh, my God, you…laminated it?"

Uncoiling the roll revealed a small map—about six inches square, with a corner missing—completely laminated within a glossy plastic sheet.

"This thing was priceless, Ascher. It's…" What to say when all she felt was utter disbelief? "I can't believe you did this!"

"Would you prefer we walk about in the dark tunnels losing flake after flake like the gingerbread kids until we know not where to go?"

"Dark tunnels?"

This was the first time she'd had the opportunity to look at the map. At first glance it was merely a twist of lines. It was impossible to determine what the lines represented for there were no street names or landmarks indicated.

Sickened at the incredible damage done to this priceless artifact, Annja swallowed back a huge sigh.

"What kind of archaeologist are you to not know the value of such a thing?"

"Part-time, Annja. Archaeology is not my principal interest."

He had that right. Theft and destruction of property topped his treasure hunter's list. "You bloody treasure hunter!"

"I wear the epitaph with pride." He gave a cocky rub of his knuckles against his chest. "Without treasure hunters millions would still be sitting on the seafloor. But look closely, my frantic American friend. It is a copy. I promise you I am not so ignorant to have damaged the original in such a manner."

"Copy?" Annja breathed as she really looked at the paper. It was bright white. Not aged and yellowing. A gray streak ran along one edge where the toner had dusted the copy. "Mother Mary, you scared me, Ascher."

"Just a bit of humor. I had no idea you'd believe it even for a moment. Now, do you want to help, or will you hinder?"

"Help?" Annja crossed her arms. How could the man be

so cavalier after such a stupid joke? "I don't trust you Frenchman."

"Ah, so we are the snippy American this afternoon?" he said

"Don't even go there or you'll force me to—"

"To what? Lay me out like you did those thugs in the forest. Very impressive. I'm still wondering about that one Come, Annja, let me see your fire."

That was exactly what he was trying to do, wasn't it? See the snippy American blow a cog and lose it. Well, she wouldn't give him the pleasure.

Zen, Annja, calm yourself. Move beyond frustration, she told herself.

"Look, I am sorry, Annja. After I—"

"Stole it?"

"It's not theft when one keeps it in the same place it wa discovered, is it?"

She huffed. So her conjecture had been right. He'd had th map the whole time. "Who helped you? I followed a man int the yard. Dueled with him."

"You are very skilled with a sword. Which one did you gra from my collection? I didn't have time to look."

"That was *you* I dueled with in the dark?" At the time sh had thought her opponent was missing some very easy strike. He hadn't wanted to hurt her. What a guy.

"Plans have changed, Annja. I was desperate and had t keep the map myself to ensure its safety."

"Where is it now?" she asked.

"In a security safe. No one can lay hands to it but m. Anyway, after you left with the rapier, I created a humidit tank and it unrolled nicely. It wasn't too fragile, as expected but the idea to copy came to mind. Lamination seemed the be way to preserve the paper copy, especially for the task we are about to undertake."

"What plans have changed? The one where you dupe me out of the rapier and the map? I don't understand why you invited me here if—" She caught his lifted brow. A rogue's smirk of interest. "Oh, don't tell me you just invited me here to— That stupid wager with the Nash brothers?"

"To get to know you better, Annja. But also to share the discovery of d'Artagnan's rapier. It is as much yours as mine. Don't you feel our connection?"

"Please." She'd been lured here so the man could flirt with her? He did enough of that online. So why hadn't she at least suspected that after his initial phone call?

Because, Annja, you are easier to charm than you are to take out with bullet or blade.

It was painful to admit, but true. She was not a shrinking violet, but neither would she ever claim to know a man's mind. Or her own, for that matter.

"Why didn't you tell me you wanted to go after the treasure?" she asked. "Maybe I would have invited you along. Did you ever consider that? Why the sneakiness?"

"You invite me along? Ha! La Directrice! You see? You have already taken over this operation. I knew that would happen. Whenever a woman gets her hands into the mixture—"

"You—" Ah, hell, he was right to make the accusation, she realized. She did have a tendency to step up and want to lead. And why not?

"You've suspected since we met online that tracking the map was my ultimate goal," Ascher said.

"Yes, but for your own gain, or someone else? BHDC doesn't care about the rapier any more than you do, right?

That's why you had to steal the map. Are you going to hand it over to them, or keep it for yourself?"

The man slapped his arms across his chest. An evasive glance made Annja uncomfortable.

"You are very much like me, you know that, Annja Creed?" he said.

"I'm not a sneak, or a thief," she retorted.

"Touché. But you do like a good adventure. And a challenge." He walked around to stop her from completely turning away from him. A flock of foraging pigeons scattered behind him. "I know if I ask you to trust me you will balk. It is your right. There is nothing I can do to restore your confidence in me, so allow me to earn it."

"By telling me everything?" she asked.

"By showing you I can be honorable. I admit stealing the map was sneaky. I had intended to hand the rapier over to BHDC and wipe my hands of them, but someone decided to take it with her when she left me this morning."

"You could have said, 'Hey, Annja, I need that. My kidney is at stake.' Hell, what am I saying? Will they come after your last kidney if you don't hand over the rapier?"

"Monsieur Lambert had followed my posts online—in which, as you know, I was very careful not to mention the map—and discussed only the sword."

"A sword that contains a treasure map. Imbecile."

"Your harsh words have no effect on this adventurer's heart."

Talk about a Gascon set on serving one goal and ignoring the needs of others to the detriment of personal honor. He was going for the gusto, nothing less than valor. This man was exactly like d'Artagnan, she thought.

It was impossible to believe BHDC would merely seek a sword, when the treasure map was the more valuable. The cor poration must know about the rumored map. On the other hand, if BHDC sought historical DNA, then perhaps the rapier could be deemed a prize.

Ascher gazed across the river to the opposite bank where seagulls dived for scraps left behind by tourists.

"They do know about the map," Annja decided. "And that still makes us a target."

"I will protect you, Annja. No one will hurt you if I am able to stand before you."

"If you are able, Mr. Missing Kidney Guy. I think I'll take my chances on my own. Professional fencing is a world apart from down-and-dirty sword fighting."

"You don't think I have what it takes to protect you?"

She could sense his guard go up. The indomitable male pride that most wore silently, until they were challenged, or forced to defend it. She'd grant him that. Admittedly, he wore it well, bold eyes and muscles flexing as they itched to display their strength. She frowned.

"So, let's take a look, *oui?*"

Annja tugged the map from the man.

Tilting her head to the left and then the right stretched out the tension riding her neck. All right, anger dropped. Back to business.

Ascher pointed to the torn edges at the lower left corner of the map that appeared as a fine gray line on the copy. "Someone ripped off the most important part. The key or scale. There is no way to navigate without it because I cannot determine which is north, south or west."

"It wasn't you?"

"No, Annja, that piece was missing when I unrolled it."

"You sure it hadn't disintegrated decades earlier?" she asked.

"If I had the rapier, I could inspect the interior of the hilt for paper fragments, but…"

"I wish I had the original map to verify what you say is true." She examined the map closely. The edges of the missing corner were serrated and thin, showing more discoloration in shades of gray toner, similar to the three intact edges of the map. It was also more intentional than a tear, perhaps cut at a jagged edge. But why?

Ascher turned the map upon her palms, showing that no part of it was marked by a directional compass. It was impossible to tell which side was up and which was down.

"If we can determine the directions," he said, "then we can decide where the starting point must be."

"There is no mark to beginning," Annja said.

"No, but I think this here might be the *X* that marks the spot. Look closely," he said.

At the center of a tangle of lines was a small device, about half the size of Annja's smallest fingernail, but unmistakable in design.

"A fleur-de-lis?" she said.

"Exactly. The symbol of Paris and the royal insignia. That is where we will discover the treasure," he declared.

Annja turned the map to the right, but it didn't make any more sense. "And what, exactly, is this a map of? The streets of Paris? The turns and lengths are too short and curve too much. I know Paris's streets can be short but—"

"I believe this thick line is the Seine, but cannot be positive. It was faintly red on the original. That would make this portion the right bank if you follow the curve of the river. I'm guessing this map is the labyrinthine aqueducts beneath the city," Ascher said.

The aqueducts. Or perhaps the catacombs. A series of

tunnels would match the curving lines much more than an aboveground street did.

"There are tunnels beneath the Louvre—it was the royal palace at the time this map was produced," Ascher said. "I'd guess if a queen were going to hide a treasure, she wouldn't venture too far from her comfort zone."

"Unless she sent a lackey to do the job," Annja said.

"Trust a lackey with a treasure?"

"I cannot picture Anne of Austria traipsing about some dank, dark tunnel. Why ever hide the treasure? Why not simply present it to d'Artagnan?" she asked.

"Perhaps it is because the treasure was baubles from lovers she wished to dispose of privately. No royal ceremony to hand over illicit love gifts."

They had conjectured during their online chats that the queen had indulged a few lovers in her lifetime. Ascher had suspected d'Artagnan had gifted her the jewels, which made little sense if the man had never had money to hand. Although, the queen could have known of his financial situation and sought to return the man's gifts, purchased in a foolish moment of devotion.

Annja couldn't help but wonder if Cardinal Mazarin—or even Richelieu, his predecessor—had held Anne's heart. They were the most common assumptions by historians, as well.

"Okay," Annja said. "We're hunting for gifts from indiscreet lovers. So where do you think the royal palace should be on this map if this wide line is the river? Doesn't it appear as though the fleur-de-lis sits right on that line?"

"Perhaps, but I pray the queen did not expect d'Artagnan to dive for the treasure. Certainly the key to the map was placed in the southwest corner as is common with most maps?"

"Not always. It could be the northeast corner. See?" She handed him the laminated copy.

Looking over the tangle of twisting lines, none marked, but merely creeping like snails' trails across the paper, Annja tried to orient it to a specific direction. The thick line that dissected it did so very evenly. The river should curve rather sharply at the west end. And even though the left bank was less dense and smaller in area than the right, it was impossible to determine which was which for the way the lines had been drawn. And there was no island marked on the thick line, which would indicate the Île-de-la-Cité.

They would definitely need a key. The missing corner of the map.

"This map didn't appear to have been removed for centuries," Annja said. "I wonder if d'Artagnan removed the key? But before or after he'd found the treasure?"

"He did not find the treasure," Ascher said with assurance. "We know that, Annja."

"Maybe. The documents of his holdings after his death detailed very little in personal or property, but…no, you're right. He couldn't have found it. D'Artagnan strikes me as the sort who would have reveled in a fortune and perhaps have given at least part to his family. So, what's the plan?" She couldn't help but be intrigued.

"We could mark out the map aboveground," Ascher suggested. "Walk along the river to see if this wider line coincides."

"Aren't there like five hundred miles of tunnels beneath the city of Paris? This will be like looking for a needle in the proverbial haystack," Annja said.

"Indeed, what else have we but to try?"

She did like his optimism.

"Besides," he added, "there were probably only a quarter so many tunnels two hundred years ago."

"Which will only make navigating three times more difficult. The lines won't match the current system of tunnels," Annja pointed out.

"Just like an American to always see the negative."

"I think I resent that," she said.

"By the way, where is the rapier?" Ascher's voice sounded right near her ear. She twisted and found herself face-to-face with him. His bold blue eyes swept across her face. "In the car?" he asked, looking around.

"I don't have it with me."

"You promised we would trade," he said.

"Not until I know you can be trusted."

"I've told you everything. What more do you want? Blood? I've already sacrificed a kidney! I must have that rapier."

"Not until we've found the treasure and you've given me reason to return it to you."

She tugged the map from his grip and crossed the bridge to the north side of the Seine. She would head toward the Louvre down the quai de Gesvres, figuring that if a queen were to hide a treasure, most likely she would place it close to where she resided.

"ANNJA IS RETURNING for the sword," Roux instructed Henshaw as he strode into the guest room she had slept in that morning.

"I'll tend the room, sir," Henshaw said.

"Right. I want to check she didn't leave anything behind."

Their conversation about DNA and genetic testing had got Roux to thinking. Why hadn't he considered such a thing before? It could answer the one question that occurred to him relentlessly since meeting Annja Creed and watching her take command of Joan's sword.

"There must be something in here," he muttered.

The bed sheets were rumpled and pushed back. Bright sunlight beamed upon the pillow. The impression of her head still dented it. Roux leaned over the bed to inspect. He was looking for something most particular—there!

From beneath the pillow he tugged a long single strand of chestnut-colored hair. Holding it high before his face, he inspected both ends in the sunlight, and found the small root still attached to the end.

"DNA evidence?" he murmured. "Interesting. Very interesting."

12

They left their cars outside Notre-Dame and decided the best course would be to walk up to the Louvre and then try to figure from there if the map matched any landmarks. Not that landmarks would help if the entire map were of the underground tunnels.

It was nearing 6:00 p.m. and the streets were clear before the dinner rush that would see the rue de Rivoli tight with traffic and the riverside packed with the workforce eager to get home.

The shops were still open, hawking musty books and frayed treasures from the past. Annja found herself straying toward one particular stall with huge green bins of books displayed.

Ascher tugged her back on target.

They passed three main intersections where the bridges connected to the island. The Louvre in sight, their pace had decidedly picked up. Ascher grabbed her again.

"What's the problem?" Without waiting for Ascher's answer, Annja tracked their circumference with a twist of her waist and to each side.

Three young men following them, apparent because they were the only ones beating a determined trail in their wake. Not dressed in thug suits, but instead, running shoes and camouflage trousers and loose sweatshirts.

"They look like street punks," Annja commented. "The kind you see skateboarding in herds before the city hall."

"Do you see skateboards?" Ascher slipped a hand into hers. Their pace sped to a slow jog. "They've been following us since Notre-Dame," he said.

"BHDC?"

"Who can know?"

"Well, if you're not sure, that means you've got more enemies than you're letting on to, Frenchman."

"No time to argue." He gave a tug to Annja's hand, and then released it as he took off. "Run!"

While she had never been one to question intuition, the idea of running away from mere— Annja flashed a look over her shoulder. The punks had begun to run.

"Right, then. Run it is."

She took off after Ascher, noting he wasn't in mind to run around the iron fence before him. Instead, he leaped onto the short stone wall the fence poles were anchored into. Climbing the iron hand over hand, his sneaker toes gouging into the iron poles, he pinnacled and levered himself over the top.

"Show-off." Annja went for the same move.

She landed the other side with bent knees and arms out to balance. Instantly, she realized they'd entered the yard behind the Louvre. No doubt, security cameras had spied their illegal entrance. But she didn't give it another thought as their pursuers charged to the fence and began the same climb.

"Time to lose the apprehension," she muttered, taking off at a dash. It was onward and straight forward from here.

"You coming?" Ascher called as he sped across the grassy lawn outside the medieval structure that had been modified for centuries and was now the preeminent museum of the world.

He darted for a low brick barrier, made the top and then leaped, disappearing in a flying, arms-out balletic move.

"Right behind you," she said.

The man was a *traceur*, a practitioner of *parkour*. Annja was now getting a hands-on session with a master. She'd never done it herself, but it was all about running the landscape—including buildings—taking the shortest route, as fast and safely as possible. Physical agility and quick thinking were required. It was about escape or chase, whichever side you put yourself on.

In this instance, she had no qualms with escape.

French cries for her to stop barreled out from the three punks. Far more preferable than a policeman wielding a club. She wasn't keen on spending time in jail.

But how would her time be spent if the punks caught up to her?

Annja raced across the grass. Her hiking boots were not made for high-speed chases, but they were worn enough to allow her ankles flexibility.

The courtyard of the Louvre appeared to her right. The glass pyramid where visitors entered the museum was lit, and the surrounding pond glimmered gold in the twilight.

Ascher avoided the line that queued from the pyramid and darted across the street to enter the Tuileries. Catherine de Medici, mother of Ascher's favorite king, had commissioned the royal garden in the sixteenth century.

Not at all winded, but wondering how far her boots would take her, Annja gained Ascher's side.

He signaled they should run the tree-lined avenue down the

center of the garden. In two great strides he jumped to a concrete bench, sprang high and cleared a low yew hedge.

"Land on your toes!" he hollered back to Annja.

Taking the jump, she did land on her toes, but briefly, as she rolled her body forward, curling across her right shoulder into a ball and pushing upward into a run. The impact had been remarkably light. But then the distance of the leap had been less than ten feet.

Crushed gravel spit at her ankles as her pursuers began to land. They were too close.

Annja sped across the manicured lawn that none in the gardens walked on. She didn't see any Keep Off The Grass signs. Just ahead, Ascher sprinted down the center of the wide gravel-paved main alley.

The garden was alive with children riding the merry-go-round while mothers chatted. It was probably an evening pre-dinner stop for families coming home with schoolkids in tow. A slow-moving donkey cart ferried squealing toddlers beneath the trimmed lime trees that dropped yellow leaves in slow dollops.

Breathing from her chest, Annja focused on keeping the pace. She'd gained some distance from her pursuers. Drawing up her diaphragm and pumping her arms at her sides opened her airway and allowed increased speed.

Ahead, Ascher ran right for the donkey cart. He leaped, toeing a concrete column, and cleared the entire cart with one flying soar through the air. Annja thought it was remarkable that the man virtually flew.

Annja marked her paces, suspecting she couldn't make the same ground-to-air leap. Instead, she was able to step onto the sidebar of the cart, push off and perform a high leap, topped by a snap into a midair roll. She landed on the ground in another roll, and was off with the elation of the chase.

Make that escape.

Was it wrong to be feeling rather proud of her first go at *parkour?* She really should only be concerned with the situation.

"But I so rock." And she sped onward.

Carnival music jittered out from the huge neon-lit ferris wheel to her right. Ahead, the octagonal pond loomed. Ascher dodged to the left, slowing a bit, as Annja caught up to him.

"Take the Concorde," he said in short huffs. "Detour to the Seine. We might lose them there."

He made a jump and landed on the corner of one of the horseshoe ramps that slanted upward to form the end of the gardens. Looking over the highest peak, Annja spied the Eiffel Tower about a mile off in the distance. She followed the leader's example.

The concrete border edging the slanted ground was about eight inches wide with grass topping the ramp. It was easier to balance the faster she ran. Two of the punks followed, while one ran parallel along the ground, though he had to detour around a statue and a flock of ducks waddling toward the pool.

The end of the gardens landed them at the place de la Concorde, where once revolutionaries decapitated cartloads of royals for the macabre pleasure of the citizens. Sunlight glinted on the gold-capped pink granite obelisk. It stood in the courtyard to their right where a crew of cars honked in echo of the gruesome cheers from centuries past.

To her left, Ascher dashed to the edge of the bridge and leaped to the top of the guard rail. Balance exact, he leaped forward in the direction his body wanted to sway. Airborne two seconds, he then landed on the top of a moored house-boat. A bounce set him into the air like an acrobat, and he landed on the sidewalk with an easy spring.

Annja followed in kind, dropping to the cobblestone

sidewalk that hugged the Seine. Houseboats were moored up to the edge, lined all the way to the next bridge.

A water bus motored slowly by, transporting tourists on a lazy river tour of the city. A loudspeaker announced the forthcoming Tuileries to the left.

"Now, that was awesome," Annja huffed out. Bending forward, she pressed her palms to her knees.

"No, stand and stretch back your arms to draw in air," Ascher coached. "And quickly."

The twosome spied the punks as they mounted the bridge. Hasty looks were exchanged. How to fend off the pursuers?

"You take the boat," she said to Ascher. It was key he got to safety. Besides, she could handle a couple of street punks. "We'll split up."

"I cannot leave you, Annja."

"You're not leaving me—you're protecting the map. Now go!"

He understood what she suggested. With a nod, he dashed off, and so did Annja. "Call me when you are safe!" she shouted.

The punks dropped onto the sidewalk like monkeys clambering over a zoo wall.

Ascher made a furious run down the sidewalk beside Annja, and then leaped onto one of the moored boats. He scrambled over a red Smart car tethered to the boat's stern. Timing the moment, Ascher eyed the approaching water bus. With a great leap, he soared and hung in the air for a moment over the curdling white waves that curled out from the boat's bow, then his legs pedaled and he began to descend.

A thunderous roar from the tourists rose as he landed on the boat, clinging to the railing, his legs dangling over the river.

Still racing down the sidewalk, the wall to her left and the river to her right, Annja lured the punks after her. The tour boat veered to the right to go down the left-bank side of the island.

Now she just had to shake the tail.

Or not.

Annja stopped before a stairway that marched up to street level. Walking up the bottom steps, she then turned and faced her pursuers.

The three men, to their credit, didn't so much as pause when Annja produced a sword out of thin air. The first, clad in baggy trousers and a zipped-up sweatshirt, leaped toward her. Annja sliced low, drawing her sword across his knees. He dropped, yelping and collapsing on the bottom step. Blood seeped through the camouflage fabric.

Right behind him, the two remaining men had clasped hands and barreled forward. No weapons in sight. Such dumb determination.

Annja leaped, clearing their heads. She snapped into a roll in midair and landed on the cobbled sidewalk behind them. Since taking possession of Joan's sword, her physical prowess had increased slightly. She could make that run a little faster, hold her breath underwater a little longer and add a few feet to a leap with ease. It wasn't magic. It was something ancient and innate.

Landing solidly, she twisted her shoulder and bent backward to avoid the glimmer of steel that flashed in the air. A stiletto missed her head and pinged the stone wall behind her.

It was never wise to approach a man with a sword—or a woman, for that matter. Yet both thugs again charged her. Her sword sliced the air. Annja felt resistance, blade to bone. She'd cut through the bicep of one of them.

Before she could return the stroke of the blade, the other plowed into her, putting her up against the limestone wall. He actually growled. Annja jammed up her knee, connecting with his side. It wasn't a groin shot, but she'd gotten close to his bladder. Bellowing out a curse, he released her.

Both her ankles were grabbed and she lost balance. The one on the ground had crawled up behind her. Releasing the sword momentarily, she landed the cobblestones on an elbow, but couldn't roll. Pins and needles shot up her arm. He had a tight wrap about her ankles.

The one standing over her muttered something like "Where is the sword?" in French, and wound up for a punch. Annja stretched out her right arm, opening her fingers to receive Joan's sword—

And all went dark.

13

A weird sort of semiconsciousness toyed with her brain. Annja sat upright, but her neck ached for the awkward tilt of her head. Her eyes were not open. She could hear voices. Whispery, but with some real volume to them. Eerie. They were…inside her head?

Had she begun to hear voices such as Joan of Arc had in the fifteenth century? It wasn't entirely ridiculous. Having inherited the martyr's sword, the voices should be a given. Add that to her penchant to talk to herself and she was certifiable.

Get a grip, Annja.

Concentrating, trying to press through the weird fog of her brain, Annja listened keenly.

"I ask for a sword and you bring me a woman. I don't *need* a woman," said an angry yet controlled male voice. "I need the sword."

"Boss, I know her. I've seen her on the TV."

"Oh?"

Annja heard metal sliding across a smooth surface. A few clicks across a keyboard. Must be a laptop on a desk.

"Show me," the first voice said.

The keys clattered. Annja distinctly sensed someone paced before her. Every other beat the creak of leather sounded from low, near the floor. Squeaky shoes. That brought her count to three in the room, besides herself. So far.

The last she remembered was shouting for Ascher to escape—with the map. He had, by leaping to the passing water bus in a remarkable feat. And yet, here she sat. Obviously chivalry had not survived the centuries.

She'd thought taking on three men would be easy, until it had stopped being easy.

After being knocked out she had been taken somewhere. She didn't feel tied up. In fact, she was not, for a twitch of her left foot did not sense bound ankles. And her hands were free, resting on her lap.

Interesting. It could only mean the thugs who'd kidnapped her were present, and probably held enough firepower to make whoever was in charge believe she was secure.

Use the sword.

If she produced her sword and charged them now, she might never discover the mechanics behind this bizarre scheme. If it was a scheme. Whether to trust Ascher still bothered her. He could very well be in the room.

And if any in the room were armed, a thin blade wouldn't do much good when it came to deflecting bullets. Wonder Woman, she was not.

"Ah," the voice that seemed to be the leader said. "I see. Annja Creed."

So much for anonymity.

Now was as good a time as any to let them know she wasn't

out. Annja lifted her head groggily. It didn't feel as though she'd been drugged, just clocked a good one, but the pull in her neck muscles forced her to move slowly.

"We have a celebrity in our midst." The leader strode toward her across a highly polished black marble floor.

The entire room, Annja noticed with a glance, was also walled in black marble. Outfitted with a chrome-and-glass desk and chairs and ultramodern artwork that boasted a few dashes of ink across white canvas.

And then there were the swords, displayed under tiny halogen spotlights. Half a dozen, at least, from her scan. It was difficult to determine their century of make or if they were merely historical reproductions. Probably the real deal.

A man approached, tall, thin and decked out in a gray suit. Diamond cuff links caught a glint of light and flashed violet and red at Annja. Medium-length brown hair waved about his head. It was thick, and though it looked tousled, she wondered did he have to work on it to get it just so? His face was gaunt, not an ounce of fat, every bone a deadly blade. Clear blue eyes were the only spots of color in the entire room, save the diamond flashes. His smile surprised her. It wasn't evil or plotting. He looked normal, like a businessman.

With a million-dollar budget for suits and accessories.

He stalked right up to her, and Annja realized she sat on a sort of love seat with black leather cushions and chrome arms. He put up a shoe on the seat to the left of her thigh and leaned forward over her knees. The spicy scent of his cologne was too appealing for this precarious situation.

Crossing his arms, he looked her over. He smiled the richest smile Annja had ever seen, like whiskey and dark chocolate and cherry pie filling all rolled up together.

Don't fix images of good things to this man. Stay wise. And alert.

"My name is Jacques Lambert," he said.

He didn't sound French. Actually, she wondered if his accent didn't have a touch of Boston to it.

"*Chasing History's Monsters,* eh?" Though soft, his voice hit a nerve in Annja's neck, which twanged worse than the pulled muscle did. "I've never considered Charles de Castelmore a monster. Tell me why you're pursuing the sword for such a show?"

"Not every moment of my life is concerned with the show, Monsieur Lambert."

"Ah, she speaks. And rather eloquently for a popular television personality." Jewel eyes danced across her face, perceptive and ready for the pounce. Blindingly white teeth amped up the deadly allure. "It isn't every day I send my men on a quest for a rare sword and instead am brought a rare beauty."

"Are you still speaking of the sword?" she asked.

"Unfortunately not. Though I wish I were. My men tell me there was a man with you who got away with the treasure."

"Define 'treasure,'" she said.

"Hmm." He stood and glanced to the wall where a silver-and-gold épée, polished to a glimmer, hung point down. "It is long and pointy and hurts when pressed into a person's flesh."

"Sorry, don't have one of those to hand." Yet.

Lambert smirked, and pushed away from the love seat. "I like you, Annja Creed. But not enough to suffer your ill humor."

His eyes were placed close to his nose. Predatory, that position. Annja had always noticed the position of a person's eyes: close to the center meant predator; farther to the edges of the face signified prey. Hers were somewhere between the two.

"You've not got the sword?" he asked.

"It was obvious we hadn't a sword in hand before that ridiculous chase through the Tuileries began. Inept bunch of thugs." Annja cast a glower at the two hoodlums. One stood over the desk beside the laptop. The other loomed to her immediate right, gun in hand. They were not the same men who had pursued her and Ascher. Suits and ties had replaced camo and running shoes.

"But you have it somewhere safe?" Lambert asked.

"Define 'safe.'"

An open palm across her cheek stung much more than her pride. She hadn't seen it coming. The man moved quickly. He returned to leaning over her, huffing once from the exertion of his violence, and gripping the chair arm.

"Safe or not, you have the sword. You were at the dig site, and you accompanied Ascher Vallois home." A smile returned. "I'll need a location to ensure your safe passage out of here."

"And where exactly is here?" She moved her jaw wide open, tonguing her teeth. Nothing loose. "Is this BHDC?"

Lambert straightened. The easy smile tightened, revealing teeth. "You've done your research."

"I am an archaeologist by trade. Research is my thing."

"Ah, so that explains your partnering with Vallois. Though, how much of an archaeologist he is remains open for debate."

"You know the man. That would lead me to guess that you are the one who decided he didn't need both kidneys. Am I right?"

Lambert rubbed his palms together like a child delighted over a toy. "Oh, I really like you, Annja. *Messieurs.*" He gestured to his henchmen. "You may leave. Manny, keep post outside the door."

He waited for the thugs to trundle out. Annja took a moment to study the swords on the wall to her right. Three of them, each displayed under a halogen light. One was a rapier, sixteenth century, if she was not mistaken. Two closest to her position were épées, single-edged damascened blades, and boasting gorgeous hilts encrusted with jewels and gold.

All appeared sharp and ready for use.

"You appreciate a fine sword?" Lambert walked to the wall and touched a blue double-edged blade. "This one is German made. Not the usual S-shaped *quillon* indicative of the maker, but instead a straight bar for protecting the knuckles. The blade bears a *memento mori.*"

"A death promise," Annja said, and Lambert nodded approvingly. "I have trouble believing you took away a man's kidney merely because you wished to display yet another sword on your wall."

"But you discount the intrigue and value of the find, Annja. Most people aren't aware that d'Artagnan was anything but a fictional character in an adventure novel. Find a person who even knows what a musketeer is and I'd be surprised. History is growing thin."

"It's not," she retorted.

"Really? Mention a musketeer nowadays and people look for a candy bar."

He had a point, but a stupid one at that. "History is constantly expanding as we uncover more and more through digs and discoveries. But I can agree that the depth of interest grows shallow," Annja said.

Arms crossed high on his chest, he turned to look over his shoulder at her. "Did I mention I like you?"

"Was that before or after you slapped me?"

Lambert strolled before her. "Can you imagine raising a child now, in these modern times, who resembles the greatest musketeer who ever lived?"

Annja tilted her head forward. He'd been going down an easily followable path, until he got to the child part. What did a child have to do with a stolen sword and her getting the stuffing kicked out of her on the bank of the Seine?

Trying her legs, she realized she could stand and dash out of here. But thugs stood outside the door. She'd sit tight.

"A child?" she asked.

"Doesn't have to be d'Artagnan." Lambert splayed his hands before him as he paced. "Could be Louis XIV or someone more recognizable, like Einstein or George Washington. Those choices would fall to scholars and the educated, I'm sure. The more socially conscious of parents might choose a celebrity, such as Angelina Jolie or George Clooney. The possibilities are endless."

Still not following the man, Annja strained her thoughts. How did Angelina Jolie and Louis XIV fit into the same discussion? And a child who resembled either of the celebrities?

And then it struck her. The research she'd done online. She hadn't been able to fit this quest for a legendary sword to a company that did genetic research. Until now.

"You *were* after the DNA evidence on the sword," she concluded.

"There was evidence?" His shoes tapped the floor in quick clicks as he approached her. "What did you do with it? Christ, I imagine the sample was contaminated beyond belief."

"There was a hair wrapped around the hilt, but the root was not intact. And I'll thank you to have a little respect for my profession. I know how to handle an artifact without contaminating it."

Though she hadn't handled it properly at the dig site, nor after the map had been stolen.

"It could still be there. More of it. Something you overlooked." Lambert again placed his foot on the couch. A bead of sweat clung to his forehead. His confidence had fallen a notch. "I must have that sword! Do you realize what a sample of DNA can become?"

"A new kidney?"

"Ha!" He gripped her by the shoulders, and Annja flexed her fingers to prepare. One wrong move, buddy. "A new life!"

Lambert spun away and paced toward his desk.

Annja stood and, though compelled to reach for her sword, she stilled the urge. She was on the verge of discovering something, and she didn't want to push him back under the rock.

"Life?" She remained standing before the love seat so he wouldn't be tempted to call in his thugs. "Are you talking—" if therapeutic cloning could create a human organ, then what was to stop him from "—human cloning?"

Glee danced in his bold eyes. A wicked, maniacal glee that cut into Annja's gut as if a blade. *He's not all there.* Otherwise he'd be keeping this information close to his vest. She had that thought, and then quickly switched tracks.

"Human cloning is illegal," she said.

"Well." He offered a shrug and a dismissive splay of fingers. "We haven't actually cloned a human."

"But you're trying?"

"I cannot reveal BHDC's inner workings. To do so may, or may not, incriminate me."

"You've given me quite the earful already. A few years ago there was an article in *Scientific American* supposing BHDC had already mastered therapeutic cloning."

"Ah, you have done your research. Points for you, Annja."

"How, exactly, does that work? I don't understand anything beyond the basics."

"What? Therapeutic cloning?"

She nodded. It would be a start, to turn a key that may open further discoveries about BHDC.

"It's all a bunch of scientific mumbo jumbo. But you must consider the possibilities should we develop the technology to create human organs. No longer would we need donor lists. Children now dying in wait of a donor organ would survive."

"And that's all you're using the DNA for?" she asked.

"There is so much one can do with the code of life. Genetics can be traced through family bloodlines through the study of DNA. As you must know," he said, "genetic archaeologists use the process. I find it is most useful in providing proof for claims to family fortunes and proving paternity. Finding a descendant for d'Artagnan's sword? It is very possible. With today's technological advancements we are able to literally trace one's ancestors back to the days of the Romans, if we wish."

"Child's play. Scientists are tracing DNA back to the seven daughters of Eve," Annja said.

"If you believe the theory of the original seven."

"It's not a theory," Annja said. "Belief or not, most police outfits have a connection to DNA labs for forensics testing."

"But not everyone can create a human organ for transplant. It's a tricky but most satisfying accomplishment."

"Do you have…?" *Ascher's kidney growing in a jar,* jumped to Annja's tongue, but she didn't speak it. It creeped her out to imagine a lab jar with a meaty kidney floating inside, awaiting transplant.

On the other hand, to consider all the children and adults who would benefit from such a science truly was a wondrous thing. But wonders tended to be accompanied by hidden pitfalls, obsessions and evils.

"As for cloning," she prompted. "Beyond a mere organ. What about a whole human?"

"Somatic cell nuclear transfer. No one has successfully cloned a human. And if they had, the laws today would keep them from making it public knowledge."

"I thought there was an announcement in the scientific community a few years ago?"

"Ah, yes, that ridiculous Clonaid baby. The Raelian cult, if I recall correctly. They have not been able to produce scientific confirmation of the claim. It was a dupe on the entire world."

"But why—presuming you had the ability to create a clone—a historical figure?"

"Ah. Well, wouldn't you—if you could not have a child, and had decided to go the cloning route—want to be able to choose a historical figure? A little Marie Antoinette, for example. Or an Alfred Einstein or even Thomas Jefferson."

"Have you DNA evidence for all those people?" Annja asked.

"Of course. Along with treasure hunters, I staff genetic archaeologists and an assortment of skilled medical personnel. We're always on the lookout for viable samples."

"That's sick."

"Not at all. That is the future of biohistorical genetics."

"But…I obviously don't understand cloning. Can you use dead DNA?"

"Of course. I'll forego the lengthy scientific explanation, but suffice to say, so long as the sample is viable we can work with it. It's a process to extract the genetic material and synthesize a usable genetic code. But it is worth it."

"Really? There are a lot of customers for babies who resemble historical figures?"

"You would be surprised."

Yes, I would be. What would be the purpose? Flaunting your miniature Marie Antoinette before your friends, when they may merely grin and wonder what you're so proud of. Not many knew what historical figures looked like when they were children. On the other hand, she could imagine the twisted benefits of having a child who looked like a contemporary celebrity. If one were so vain as to wish their child looked like a movie star, would they then use that to profit from it?

"What about the couple who desires a mini-Hitler romping about their feet?" she asked.

"Oh, Annja." Lambert's chuckle rippled a chill along Annja's shoulders. She felt no comfort standing alone in this room with him. Time to start scoping out an escape route.

"You must understand," he said, "that the cloning process would merely produce an identical subject in physicality and appearance. The human brain cannot be cloned. The personality of the subject would not be passed along to the clone. And those couples believing they can clone a lost loved one killed in a car accident will be sorely let down. We attempt to make that very clear in our literature."

"You have literature?"

She had heard quite enough.

The fact Lambert had been so free with his facts led her to believe the exit wasn't going to be shown to her. And she could see no other means to escape unless she crashed through the plate-glass window. How many stories up were they?

"So you'll let me leave?" she asked.

"Of course."

She lifted a cynical brow.

"If you take us to Ascher Vallois. While the sword is key, the treasure map must not be overlooked."

So he knew about the map.

Ascher was probably following it right now. How to read the map? If it was of the underground tunnels, could she find a similar map online to compare it to? Had Ascher had that thought yet?

"I knew it couldn't be a mere sword that motivated you," she said. "You're a weekend treasure hunter, as well?"

"It is hardly a hobby. The profit from our plunder finances BHDC."

"BioHistorical Design Corporation. I get it now. You steal DNA evidence, process it and sell it to the highest bidder. It's—" the realization expanded like a nuclear mushroom in her chest "—identity theft at its most intimate and evasive."

"Oh come, Annja, they don't mind. They're all dead. A stolen hair here, a pilfered molar, perhaps a femur—though it is rather difficult to get viable DNA from bones."

"George Clooney isn't dead," she stated.

"Yet, wherever he goes, he leaves DNA in his wake. A fingerprint, a fallen hair, saliva."

He strode the floor, swinging his arms now. "Besides, you are arguing an impossibility. We're doing nothing wrong in the eyes of the law. Therapeutic cloning is completely aboveboard."

"In Britain. It's still illegal in France."

"Yes, I did once have a lab in Britain, but they aren't keen on pirates. I can't return to that country."

He shrugged. The grin he gave her hid many secrets that she wanted to release. A self-proclaimed pirate?

"Madmen always believe in their ideologies," she said.

"I'm not mad. I am a modern-day pirate, Annja. How else to finance our studies without plunder?"

Now the connection between the map and the cloning was coming together. The treasure was required to finance what must be a cash-sucking foray into the maniacal dreams of a strange future of cloned historical figures socializing with replicated modern-day celebrities.

"Even if I did hand over the map to you," she said, "you'd never be able to navigate it. There's no means to determine direction or even a starting point. A navigational device is missing."

Lambert brushed a finger across his lips as the most amused expression tickled his eyes. "So you are unaware of what you have?"

"I know what I'm missing," she said.

"I see." He turned and marched over to his desk. Annja was a little surprised that he simply left her standing, untied, able to dash away. Possibly he suspected little danger from a woman. Silly man. Hadn't his thugs related their struggles by the river?

A struggle that found you the captive, she chided herself.

"I don't need the map, Annja. I have a copy."

"A copy?" How many had Ascher made?

He typed in some information on the laptop keyboard, and the image of a map appeared on the screen. Annja approached slowly, leaning in to study the image.

"Look familiar?" he asked.

She nodded. It was as if Ascher had scanned the map onto the screen. But he couldn't have had time to do so since acquiring it yesterday morning. Could he?

He'd had time to humidify, copy *and* laminate it.

"Where did you get this?"

"One of my researchers turned it up after an exhaustive search in the stacks of the Bibliothèque Nationale. I'm sure the source was Nicolas Fouquet's journals, though that's not immediately to mind right now. You know the financier kept copies of all Queen Anne's correspondence. Though I am still a bit baffled as to the creator of the map. There is no signature on it, as was the custom."

"Not the queen?" Annja asked.

"Do you think Anne of Austria took the time to scribble out something so elaborate as this?"

Annja traced the jagged corner of the map on the screen. It had to be identical to the map Ascher held.

"Missing the same corner, I presume, as the one you hold. I have to believe whoever designed it did so purposefully. It's not torn, but rather cut. And only with the designer may lie the answers."

This copy was in color. Annja saw now the thick red line. The river or something else?

"You see? We have both been walking the same path. I'm not sure how you got Vallois to side with you, without—"

"Ripping out a kidney?"

"Exactly. Though you are not hard on the eyes. Perhaps he's sleeping with you."

She rolled her eyes at that comment.

"I won't settle for holding the bouquet," Lambert said. "I will have that treasure."

"Who's to say it's even there still? Wherever *there* is. It's been three centuries. The map has obviously been copied once. What proof have you there aren't a dozen more copies lying around? Someone could have claimed the treasure centuries ago."

"You don't seem particularly worried at that prospect. Nor am I," he said.

He slid to sit on the edge of the desk and crossed his arms over his chest.

"This map here is a copy, more than likely made by Nicolas Fouquet. I wager he may have been as confused about how to navigate it as you are. But he did spend three years imprisoned with Charles Castelmore—the sword's owner. Do you think he managed to discover how to read the map during those years?"

Annja crossed her arms, her focus blurring on the laptop screen. Interesting question. And while she did not for one moment feel safe standing next to a man who had sent thugs after her and Ascher, right now it felt as if a colleague had posed a question.

But Fouquet had eventually died imprisoned. Even if he had learned how to read the map, he was never free to follow it. Of course, that didn't rule out lackeys or perhaps even Fouquet's wife.

"You know how to read the map," she tried. "You know who created it?"

"Ninety percent sure." He curled long fingers over the edge of the desk. A little-boy smile dashed his mouth. One who had found many treasures and eagerly sought the next daring adventure. "And I must say, I'm quite surprised you haven't stumbled upon it, as well. But that's all I will say about that."

"Because…even though you know how to read it, you're unable to," she said, working out the possibilities as she spoke. "You're missing the navigational key, as we are. But you know what that key is."

He gave a noncommittal shrug.

"Now you decide to keep incriminating evidence close? I don't understand you, Mr. Lambert."

"That's *monsieur.*"

"You're no more French than I am. What was wrong with the United States? Do they take particular offense to pirates, too?"

"*Monsieur.*" A blond woman poked her head through the door and held out a business card. "There is a man here to see you. Urgent."

Lambert retrieved the business card and read it. "I've not heard of this person."

"He said he has an artifact you may be interested in viewing."

"Did he show you?"

"No, but he's carrying a small wooden box. He seems kind and elderly. A little hunched in the shoulders. Not a threat."

Lambert crossed the room and turned the laptop away from Annja. After a few keystrokes, and an intent observation of the screen, he said, "Very well. Bring him to the adjoining meeting room. I'll be there momentarily."

After the woman left, Lambert crossed the room and pressed his forefinger to a small switch on the wall across from the desk, which Annja hadn't noticed before. It was a biometric reader. A small green light flashed as it read his fingerprint. In response, a six-foot-wide portion of marble wall slid silently upward. Now there was an escape route.

"Sit tight, Annja. There's only one way out, and my pit bull is guarding the exit. I'll return momentarily and we can resume our discussion, yes?"

He didn't wait for a reply. The door slid shut, and the wall appeared to seamlessly rejoin.

Annja turned around. The laptop, still powered up, displayed a view of what looked like a lobby, lined with white overstuffed chairs.

The lobby of BHDC?

She leaned in and touched the mouse.

A secretary walked into camera range and sat down behind a desk, the same blonde who had just announced the visitor's arrival.

Annja hit the back arrow and up popped the image of the map on the monitor. Actual size, her spread hand almost covered it completely. It was an exact copy, even the fleur-de-lis showed at the end of the red line.

But there, along the scanned margin where a black smear showed when the paper must have lifted from the scanner, was a scribble. Not on the actual map, but outside the edge. A notation made by Lambert? He'd wondered about a missing signature from the map's designer, so this could not be it.

Annja tilted her head to read the small, tight letters. "Ma—" She couldn't make out the last letters. Could it be Maquet? As in Auguste Maquet, who cowrote with Alexandre Dumas?

It made sense that Lambert had found a copy in Fouquet's journals. Auguste Maquet, Dumas's collaborator, had discovered that a map existed during his research. And the only way to know that would have been to *see* the actual map. Maquet very likely would have been researching Nicolas Fouquet for *The Three Musketeers,* as well as for *The Man in the Iron Mask,* which, literary scholars conjectured, was based on Fouquet's imprisonment.

That still didn't answer the question of *who* had created the map. Someone Lambert obviously felt could provide the method to navigate the map.

Moving the mouse, Annja clicked on the Internet browser icon. Checking the history tab, the browser opened up to the *Chasing History's Monsters'* Web site. Another click on the back browser brought her to Google, where her name had been entered in the search box.

Lambert obviously hadn't known about her until now. That was a good thing. But not for Ascher Vallois.

Quickly clicking the other desktop icons, Annja searched the applications for incriminating files. She bet Lambert wouldn't leave bait like that lying around. On the other hand, he had been very free with details of BHDC's activities.

Cloning historical figures? It seemed too out there. Bizarre. Morally wrong.

Perhaps he'd spilled because he already knew she would not be leaving this building. Not alive anyway.

That realization made her next decision a no-brainer.

Annja stalked over to the door. She opened the fingers of her right hand and closed them over the sword's grip. She swung the door inward, and stepped out.

The thug growled, but before he could connect fingers to gun grip, Annja swung up a roundhouse and clocked him on the jaw.

It wasn't a knockout hit, but it did send him wobbling to splat against the wall. Holding back the urge to slash him across the chest, she turned and bent to deliver another punch, up under his chin to deaden the mandible nerve, then stepped over his slack body.

She stood in a long hallway of black marble. A few framed swords and various medieval weapons, lit by halogen lights, dotted the length of wall both ways. It was impossible to determine which way was out.

Besides, Annja didn't want to leave yet.

14

Jacques Lambert assessed the white-haired fellow who nodded as he entered the meeting room. The man was distinguished and calm. He felt no hint of apprehension as he'd suspect a treasure hunter or someone with ulterior motives would possess. A cream linen suit did not disguise a powerful build for an elderly gentleman.

He carried a wooden box secured with two rubber bands.

Jacques approached Roux, curious about the box, but more inquisitive about a stranger who seemed to change as a chameleon. In the security video he had appeared rather hunched—as Sabrina had explained—but now, he seemed to have grown at least a foot. Curious.

"My assistant informs me you give your name only as Roux," Jacques said.

"It is my name."

"No first name?"

"Not lately, no."

The men held each other in regard for a moment. Jacques

was expert at sizing up an opponent down the length of a blade. His elder was keen of eye and held himself straight and bold. No attack was imminent. Jacques could not place the man's accent—he wasn't an expert at the many European variations. Whatever it was, his speech was quite formal, almost from another era.

"Why the theatrics?" Jacques asked. "You're not the same man my receptionist decided was a frail, elderly gentleman."

"Perhaps she saw an entirely different side of me," Roux replied.

"Or else you had not wanted her to see you as a threat."

"A man should always put on a considerate face for a woman. They so rarely are given the respect deserved in this patriarchal society."

Hooking a leg up onto the stainless-steel desk, Jacques crossed his arms over his chest. Normally he would not put himself below eye level of an opponent, but he wanted to present a casual front, throw the man off from whatever he was sniffing for.

Knowing the female archaeologist sat in the next room put him on guard. Two unknowns in the same day? That could hardly be coincidence.

"What brings you to my office, Roux? We are a private company. All appointments are by invitation only."

"I realize that."

"As I've said, I cannot guess your reasons for visiting a fertility clinic, sir."

"Fertility? Heavens no. My gentlemen are still quite potent," Roux said.

And yet, he'd been completely unaware of the fact he'd been standing in the waiting room for a fertility clinic, Jacques thought. He tightened his grip on an elbow.

"You see, Mr. Lambert, after recently learning about BHDC, I realized I am in possession of something you might find of particular interest."

Jacques looked at the man straight on. Always meet your opponent's gaze, for there is where the first signal of attack shows. "And you gained your knowledge of BHDC… how?" he asked.

"An anonymous source. Don't ask for names, Lambert— we both know the business you operate treads the borders of lawlessness. I personally care little what you deem moral and just. But I believe I can help you, if you agree to help me."

An offer as such always proved intriguing. But often dangerous.

Jacques was very careful whom he allied himself with. Unfortunately, he hadn't been discerning enough with Ascher Vallois. One would think a knife through the kidney would acquiesce anyone.

The elder gentleman held his head at a tilt, his soft blue eyes unthreatening. Briefly, a flicker of his father's soft yet accusing gaze gripped Jacques with memory.

It's not so simple, Jack. This money is stolen. And even if it was not, it won't help Toby move higher on the donor list. There are rules. We have to wait.

Rules. Ridiculous rules that had allowed an innocent boy to die. Rules had killed his brother.

Ever since, Jack Lambert had made his own rules.

"Mr. Lambert?"

"Hmm? Oh. Go on," Jacques said.

Roux set the box on the conference table and snapped off both rubber bands. "I understand you may have an interest in historical artifacts."

He tilted off the cover and Jacques leaned across the table

to inspect. A musty odor combined with an astringent note rose into the air.

"It is the actual chain-mail hauberk from a prominent historical figure," Roux explained. "Fifteenth century."

"Who told you that?"

"No names come to mind. Have you an interest?"

"Depends on which prominent figure you're offering. Is that blood?"

A brown, flaking stain coated three of the mail links. Viable DNA could rarely be retrieved from ancient blood. Due to oxidation, UV light, environment and other variables, it wasn't a reliable method. Bone or teeth would prove a better source.

"There is blood, but here—" Roux lifted the mail. It made a rattling sound.

Jacques struggled inwardly not to grab the mail away and insist the man handle it with more care.

Roux pointed to a section of the artifact. Embedded within the metal rings, almost as if woven in, were fine hairs. "This is what I thought would most interest you. I count four, possibly five hairs total. A few yet have the roots on them, I believe."

Curiosity piqued, Jacques held out his hand and Roux set the lightweight mail onto his palm. The mesh of rings had apparently been well cared for. There was no rust, no grime embedded within the links, as was usual for chain mail. He was cautious not to completely open up the vest for he wanted to keep an eye on the bloodstain, prevent further flaking.

Indeed, there were hairs twisted about the links. Whoever might have worn this had given a part of his or her very being. And the hair was coiled tight about the rings, ruling out the possibility that Roux had simply woven his own hair into the mail.

"Who did it belong to?" Jacques asked. "A valiant yet nameless knight? One of Charles VII's foot guards? Is there a certificate of provenance? Sir, I only deal with legitimate—"

Roux pressed his knuckles to the desk and leaned forward. His imposing bearing shadowed Jacques. "It was Jeanne d'Arc's coat of mail."

"Jeanne d'Arc?" Jacques stifled his laugh because he did feel a certain amount of respect was owed this enigmatic yet deluded man.

He knew, as most casual historians did, that the only remaining articles believed to belong to the ill-fated martyr were but a few letters she had signed. Her ashes had been burned twice over and then cast into the Seine, though there were some who would claim to possess her charred bones. DNA testing had proved one such bone to be a cat femur.

"You don't believe me?" Roux scooped up the mail and, plucking the box in his other hand, turned for the door.

"Wait!"

The odd man continued all the way to the door before stopping, and he didn't turn around. Not like the usual snake-eyed con artist who would sell a replica to make a fast buck, this man. There was something utterly intense and solid about him. He truly believed what he held was authentic, Jacques realized.

"Have you any proof?" Jacques asked.

Roux swung around and held up the box on a palm. "Only my word."

The compulsion to simply trust struck Jacques at his heart. The child inside him craved the appearance of a nameless yet valiant knight come to rescue him from his annihilated dreams. To bring back Toby.

It's not that simple, Jack. You just can't steal money and expect it to cure your brother!

And here stood a powerful presence that seemed to grasp out and wrap that strange fantasy into Jacques's soul. A protector he and his brother had never had. A man who would vanquish all pirates and stand boldly the victor for all just causes.

"I understand that you do not know me from Moses," Roux stated, "but you'll have to trust me, Mr. Lambert. This mail has never seen a museum or an archaeologist's curiosity, so papers, or whatever you require, have never existed."

"Then how can *you* know it is authentic?"

The elder man summoned a mischievous grin. "It's been handed down through the generations."

That was about the only way around a written provenance. Yet even inherited treasures and artifacts were often validated with a letter or family diary. And who could ever truly know if Great Uncle Charlie was playing a joke on the entire family by claiming ownership of the genuine article?

"This would be quite a feather. The DNA of the Maid of Orléans?"

He realized Roux could have learned about BHDC's genetic research with an Internet search, as had the Creed woman.

Jacques glanced to the wall where the sliding marble door was cleverly concealed. It had been a good fifteen minutes. Did he trust she would sit tight? With Manny guarding the door, she wouldn't get far.

"What do you say, Mr. Lambert? Have you interest?" Roux asked.

"If we can extract a viable sample."

"The hairs?"

"Possible."

"More than possible." Roux crossed the room and again leaned over the desk. "Your breathing has increased and your palms sweat," he stated. "You want this."

Jacques curled his fingers into his moist palms. "I do," he whispered.

"Excellent. I'll leave the chain mail with you. But I must have it back. Will a week prove long enough?"

"Yes. But what do you ask in exchange, Mr. Roux?"

"I'm glad you asked."

He again set the box on the desk, top open, so the chain mail revealed its mystery. Reaching inside his suit coat, he withdrew a plain white envelope. Roux held the envelope up to the fluorescent lights, which did not illuminate the white paper well, although it was enough to see a few curved lines from inside.

"I've also brought along a more recent sample," he said. "This is what I want, Lambert. You may borrow the contents of this box and use it as fits your needs, no small sacrifice on my part, I'll have you know. You will also check this modern sample and verify genetic relation."

"You're saying you think the newer sample is also related to the saint?"

"I'm really not sure. But I trust that if anyone can tell me, it would be you."

Jacques crossed his arms over his chest. Surely this old man was dcluded.

But could it be possible?

He liked having the high-profile figures on file. It was almost comical to witness parents when his administrative facilitator told them they could have a child who looked like a favored historical figure. Who really knew what Joan of Arc looked like? Yet the belief that her personality would manifest in a clone was a detail he never discounted.

That misguided belief was the strongest selling point for BHDC.

Jacques leaned toward the man. "Give me a few days. I'll call you."

"No phone numbers." Roux laid the envelope on the table. "I'll return next Wednesday. Thank you for your time, Mr. Lambert. Best of luck with the treasure hunt."

He left the room, and couldn't see Jacques choke on his own breath. He knew about the sword and the map? Or did he simply know BHDC sought treasure worldwide?

No, Jacques kept that information close to his vest. No Internet search was going to turn up such incriminating evidence. Which could only mean, this Roux was somehow associated with Ascher Vallois.

Or…the Creed woman.

Flipping open his cell phone, Jacques connected to his secretary's console. He punched in the three-digit alert code. Sabrina would know what to do.

Roux would not notice his escort home.

Nineteenth century

AUGUSTE MAQUET SAT across the room from the man who had given him entry to the writing world by taking his first play in hand and signing his name to the title page, Alexandre Dumas.

They had collaborated on many titles since then, and—so long as he got paid—Auguste was not insulted that his name did not appear on any of the published book covers. He knew Alexandre Dumas was the name the publishers wanted to sell, and the name the reading public wanted to buy.

They were currently halfway through the first in what Alexandre deemed could become a long and multiedition series about three of King Louis XIII's musketeers, and the young Gascon soldier who won his way into the hearts of them all.

Auguste had done all the field research and spent many a day in the dusty study room of the library taking down notes from legal reports, historical memoirs, and recopying maps and assorted indices and references to events and occasions that would give authenticity to their adventure stories.

Historical figures were utilized copiously; actual history was not.

Neither Auguste nor Alexandre was too concerned that history must be twisted, the dates altered, the occasional anachronistic prop used, in order to scribble out a dashing good read. With the flair of a rapier-armed swashbuckler, Auguste wrote up the initial outline, and then handed it over to Alexandre to flesh out and make wordy—for they were paid by the sentence.

"Interesting about the map, eh?" Auguste tapped his notebook where he had made a perfect copy of the map found in Nicolas Fouquet's files in the Bibliothèque Nationale. "I wonder if the treasure was ever claimed?"

Alexandre looked up from his writing desk, a rare pause during one of his marathon sessions. Breadcrumbs sifted from his belly onto the blue pages he'd been writing on. "Couldn't have been claimed by Castelmore—he died indebted."

"Fouquet?"

"Possible. He may have sent someone after it while he lived out his days in prison. No matter. It cannot be there now. You think to follow that map? When you are sure there is a missing navigational device?"

Auguste shrugged. "If the sword could be found…" He lifted the pen-and-ink drawing of the Val-de-Grâce cathedral. There was something about the cathedral. A connection. "I have an idea where the starting point may be."

Alexandre wiped away the crumbs and dipped his quill into the ink bottle.

"Send some young men down into the tunnels. Have them clatter about. Myself, I'm quite sure it is long gone. Likely d'Artagnan's sons found it. It makes the most sense. They had little upon their father's death, and I suspect Charlotte was rather miserable. But surely she did hand over the sword to her children."

"But where would they have obtained the navigational device? What was that device?" Auguste asked.

"My friend, are you troubling over a new plot or personal whimsies?"

Auguste sighed. Alexandre wasn't a slave driver, but he did have a work ethic that would not allow for meandering when one should have his nose to the paper. "Hand me the gold paper. I'll begin the draft on that Monte Cristo idea."

"Another treasure story. My good man, I sincerely believe you may journey down beneath the city for a look about yourself."

"No Parisian catacombs in Monte Cristo's story. Something more adventurous…What about an island near Elba?"

"Napoleon's exile? Hmm, yes, I like that. Perhaps some place close, in the Mediterranean. If! The island of château d'If. I like that very much. A treasure to right wrongs?"

"Oh, indeed. The hero must have been wronged by…"

"His closest friend," Alexandre provided.

"Yes, and seek vengeance."

"But he mustn't be the harbinger of such vengeance, merely the catalyst."

Auguste nodded, picking up his pen and began to make notes. "It shall be done."

15

A mace, a halberd, a longbow. They were a few of the weapons hanging on the wall outside Lambert's office. All thirteenth to fifteenth century, Annja surmised with but a cursory glance over them. Farther along were swords: a saber, a broadsword, a rapier with swept-basket hilt that was most definitely seventeenth century.

It was quite the collection. But she hadn't time for appreciation.

At the end of the long hallway, Annja slipped through an unlocked door. She found herself in another nondescript hallway. If Lambert was going to leave her alone, then she would wander. She wanted information.

Down the hall to her right, a glass door showed a view of a building across the street. An exit. To her left stretched another hallway.

Annja went right.

Twenty feet from what she guessed was the reception area, she paused and slid up against an inset door, and listened. Two women spoke in comfortable tones. One was telling the other she was a little late for her appointment, and the other reassured her it was fine. The one Annja guessed to be a receptionist directed the other to take a seat and the doctor would be right with her.

Doctor?

What would a genetic research—?

Of course there would be medical personnel here, she thought. But why patients?

Wanting to dash to the waiting room for a peek, Annja's attention veered down the hallway in the direction she had come. A man in a white lab coat walked toward her, his head down and attention focused on a stack of manila files cradled in one arm.

Pressing herself tighter against the door, set into the frame about eight inches, Annja started summoning excuses for why she was standing there, obviously not looking very patient-like, when the doctor turned into another room. The door, on hydraulic hinges, hung open briefly to reveal a stairwell, and then snapped shut.

Scanning down the hall to each direction, Annja then scampered over to the door. It wasn't marked. A biometric scanner positioned on the wall near the handle blinked red—then suddenly it turned green.

The door pushed open.

Annja, hidden by the steel door, dodged a look around it. The person in a white lab coat headed toward the reception area. She slipped around and sneaked inside the stairwell as the hydraulics eased the door shut.

Cinder-block walls enclosed the stairwell. A fire extinguisher hung behind the door. The stairs didn't go down, so she stepped lightly up two short flights to the next floor.

There was no window on the steel door. Caution slowed her motions. Biting the edge of her lip, she pressed the hydraulic bar and peered out. She saw low lighting on the plain white walls and a glossy linoleum floor. There was no one in sight. Her intuition suggested it was probably a private floor.

Slinking down the hallway, she noted biometric scanners outside every windowless door she passed. The feeling that she crept toward doom skittered up her spine.

At the same time, a scurry of excitement pushed her onward. Digging for bones was fun. But skulking for secrets was a thrill. And while she was no expert sleuth, her experience with asking questions about artifacts and discovery of their origins could help her here. It was all about the who, what and why.

Ten feet ahead, the hallway turned both left and right. Pressing herself close to the wall, Annja peered around one corner. The coast was clear. And down the other direction a door opened.

Annja crossed the hall and pressed herself against the opposite wall. She listened, and heard footsteps, softening as they walked away from her.

She dared a look around the corner. Another hydraulic door was halfway closed. The back of another person wearing a lab coat walked away from her.

Dashing around the corner, Annja didn't think she'd manage to catch the door, so she willed her sword to hand. Plunging the tip into the crack of space between door and frame, she caught it.

The person who'd left the room stopped, about thirty feet up the hall.

Breathing through her nose, Annja tilted the sword outward to open up the door so she could fit her fingers inside. Pulling it open, she slipped inside as the person turned around.

Had she been seen? Not sure if the person had made her—or they could be heading back to this room for something forgotten—Annja remained by the door, back to it, and hands pressed flat to the wall.

She counted ten seconds. Heartbeats pulsed madly in her ears.

Closing her eyes did not help to increase her hearing. She couldn't hear beyond the swish of the overhead fans. Aware of the temperature change, Annja shrugged a hand up her sleeveless arm.

A minute passed. Reasoning that if someone was returning it would have happened by now, Annja turned her focus to the room she stood in.

Scanning the four upper corners of the ceiling, she sighted two cameras. She hadn't assumed she was walking around unnoticed. Perhaps Lambert watched her on his laptop at this very moment. This would be a quick reconnaissance.

The room was twenty feet wide and about twice as long. Three aisles of silver metal file cabinets stretched before her. To even begin to guess which would offer the most intriguing information would take too long.

She needed visuals. Hard evidence. She wasn't sure what she expected to find. Clones? Bodies suspended by wires and fed through intravenous tubes? Jars with fetuses preserved in alcohol?

"You don't see *that* many movies," she muttered.

Turning to inspect the wall behind her, Annja noted a particular case of steel file cabinets to her right. It was the only standing file with a lock. And yet the top drawer was open about half an inch.

"Like candy left out for a child."

Stepping lightly, she gave the nearest camera one last

glance, and then tugged open the top drawer of the file cabinet. It was stuffed with manila folders and neatly filed documents.

She scanned the file tabs. Each was marked with a six-digit number. Two or three letters preceded some of the numbers. A holographic device the size of a dime ended each label. She guessed it must be a scannable recording device. She wasn't up on advanced technology, but nowadays, anything was possible.

A clear label, like Cloned Humans, would have been helpful, but utterly ridiculous.

She tugged out one file and scanned the first page inside. There were no names, only case numbers, which matched the file tabs. Lists of medical abbreviations read like hieroglyphics to her. Yet hieroglyphics she could eventually decipher. This, not so much.

"'Genetic markers,'" she read aloud one of the only lines she could understand. "'Matches verified.'" More indecipherable abbreviations and codes.

Another file, followed by others, each offering the same impossible-to-discern evidence. The sixth file slowed Annja's pace and she read further.

"Implantation date? Now this is interesting."

"'Subject, gravida 1, implanted on 08/14/07. In vitro successful. Embryonic and fetal development normal.'"

She scanned down the page, glossing over all the stuff she couldn't understand. There were comments about general health noted on three different dates, which Annja assumed coincided with doctor's visits at BHDC.

"'Gestation premature at thirty-three weeks. Cesarean delivery.'" At the very bottom were measurements and weight. And the designation—female. "A baby?"

And yet, the final notation disturbed her the most. "'Survived sixty-eight minutes. Complications due to—'"

The door to the room slammed open. Annja shoved the file back into the drawer.

"I've been expecting company," she said. Reaching out to her right, she curled her grip around a reassuring solidness. "What took you so long?"

WHEN HE RETURNED to find his office empty, Jacques rushed to the door, only to find it wouldn't open. Something large lay on the other side, blocking his exit. His downed man.

Dispatching security, Jacques then went to his desk and tapped in a few commands on the laptop to activate the security program. He had access to all of the building's cameras from his command station.

"She knocked out my biggest guard, and now she's infiltrated the records room." He pounded the desktop. "Just who are you, Annja Creed?"

Switching to full screen, he found the correct camera. Annja stood with her back to him, rifling through a file drawer. The most important one. The information contained in that file cabinet would threaten his future, his very dream for a future.

Jacques ran a hand over his hair. Fine perspiration formed at his temples. A lump rose in his throat. "How did she get into that? How did she even gain access to the third floor?"

Jaw held tight, he resisted pounding the computer monitor. He'd been so eager to acquire the DNA evidence that Roux offered, he'd grown overconfident of his hold on his uninvited visitor in this room.

The video showed Annja turning suddenly. The top of Theo's head showed at the bottom of the surveillance video.

And then the most remarkable thing occurred.

Theo drew his pistol to aim, but the woman brought a sword down across his forearm, disarming him.

A sword?

"Where the hell did she get that? From my collection?"

But she hadn't held it a moment ago. Both of her hands had been flying through his private files. Unless she'd stashed it beside her somewhere…

"But—" Jacques tapped a finger on his lower lip. She didn't bend to retrieve it. It is almost as if…it appeared from out of nowhere. "Impossible."

She swung again, bringing the sword tip to Theo's throat, and pressing him backward. They left camera range, and Jacques switched to another view.

He did not recognize the weapon she wielded as one from his collection. It was double-edged, utilitarian and looked… medieval, but that was about all he could determine from the grainy security feed.

Would she slay Theo on camera? She must be aware she was being videotaped. Surveillance cameras were mounted in plain sight in the records room.

"Who is this woman? I thought she was a television personality."

The blade slashed. Annja swung up her free left fist, and clocked Theo under the jaw. As the behemoth security guard fell, Jacques saw the delicate line of blood across his throat. She had not cut to kill, but merely to threaten.

He focused on the sword—no, definitely not from his collection. She swung it high, prepared to strike again, but when her victim hit the floor, she lowered her right arm, sword in hand—

It was gone.

The weapon had literally vanished from her grasp. It had not fallen to the floor. She had not sheathed it behind her back or at her hip. Nor had she set it aside.

It was gone.

And Annja Creed made her escape.

Too stunned to react quickly, Jacques murmured, "What a remarkable weapon. If it really does come from out of nowhere…"

He swung around the desk and marched to the door. "I must have that sword."

16

Annja ran through the reception area, giving a frantic wave to the receptionist, who rose, moving around the steel desk, but was yanked abruptly to a stop as her headset was still attached to the telephone.

She noted one woman seated in the reception room on a couch. Young, blond and sporting a big belly. Pushing through the front door, Annja scanned down the street to the left. No traffic, not a single car parked on the street. To the right, the back of a woman in a navy-blue dress swayed in the midday sun.

Veering to the right and slowing to a fast walk, Annja quickly paralleled the woman, turning to offer her a smile. She received a glowing smile in return. The woman rubbed a hand over her generous belly.

Annja continued walking. Two pregnant women?

Where the hell was BHDC? Turning and searching the cityscape, she couldn't pick out any familiar landmarks, which was normally easy in Paris.

To her right, the angry rush of traffic revealed the *périphé-*

rique circled close by. It was the main freeway that enclosed the city. That meant she was somewhere near the outskirts of the city proper.

A cross street ahead offered two cafés and a magazine shop. A man walking a dog paused to buy a newspaper from an outdoor vendor.

Annja slid a look back toward BHDC—no thugs yet. The pregnant woman sent her another smile. Annja made a dash for the magazine shop.

Once inside, she offered a *"bonjour"* to the man behind the counter, then picked up a glossy copy of *Vogue* and pretended to read it, while she kept her focus outside. The pregnant woman strolled without a care, and she turned down the street, perhaps to go into one of the cafés.

Now someone did emerge from the BHDC building. Not Jacques Lambert, but a tall man holding a pistol in plain sight. He looked both ways, then headed the opposite direction Annja had taken.

"Idiot," she muttered. Returning the magazine to its stack, Annja decided she was in need of a cup of coffee.

THE PREGNANT WOMAN in the navy dress met a girlfriend in a coffee shop that boasted decadent truffles behind a curved glass counter. She acknowledged Annja with a bright smile as she entered. Annja gave a little wave as if to say "Ah, such a coincidence, we just saw each other on the street," and then went to the counter and ordered a coffee with three creams.

On interior surveillance of her surroundings she noted the aisle behind the counter stretched back to a door, propped open, most likely to a courtyard where a trash bin was kept. It could be contained, but she was betting money that it opened to an alley. An escape route, should it come to that.

While she waited for the sales clerk to retrieve a fresh carton of cream, Annja read the small placard on the front of the register. It featured a picture of a cathedral she recognized, but couldn't quite name at the moment. Tour Mansart's Greatest Works it advertised.

"Mansart," she muttered. "Why does that…?"

"Mademoiselle?" The clerk handed her a cup.

"What cathedral is this?" she asked, pointing to the advertisement.

"Ah?" The clerk reached around and peeled the taped notice from the register. "Oh, this expired last week. It is a tour of François Mansart's works. This is Val-de-Grâce."

"Right, the cathedral that Queen Anne had commissioned so she could baptize her son?" That was about all Annja recalled of the historical monument.

"Exactly. I am an admirer of the architect, so I posted the tour. You have been to Val-de-Grâce?"

"No. So he was seventeenth century?"

"Oui. Designed many famous sites and mansions until Mazarin had him publicly ridiculed by declaring him wildly extravagant and to be having an affair with the queen. None of it was correct. But he suffered for it, and never worked again. Pity. So many wonderful things he could have yet created."

"Mansart and Queen Anne," Annja said under her breath. She took a sip of the coffee, and glanced to check her pregnant woman was still there. "Mansart?" she said.

Instead of Maquet.

Could that have been the word Lambert had scrawled along his copy of the map? Historically, the architect fit into the picture. Too well.

"Do you know anything about the tunnels that run under the city?" she asked, making the query light and not too serious.

The clerk shrugged. "I know that Mansart had to reinforce many of the tunnels beneath Val-de-Grâce due to cave-ins during the construction. Paris sits upon a complex network of tunnels. I am surprised the whole city does not collapse!"

"Don't tell that to those who ride the Metro," Annja said with a laugh. She offered a tilt of her coffee cup and a thankful nod. "Very interesting to consider. *Merci*."

She took a chair two tables away from the chattering women and placed her back to them to maintain a good view of the street before her. Lambert's thug could double back and check out this end of the street. At least she hoped he did. What kind of thug was he if he didn't?

So. Mansart. This could be a lead. But she couldn't do anything about it until she got back to her car and her laptop.

The coffee served to zap her consciousness sharply. After being knocked out and transported—and then what she'd seen in the BHDC building—Annja wasn't sure it hadn't all been a weird nightmare.

She took another sip of the cream-whitened brew. No, she was thinking clearly. She'd read horrible things in the files back at BHDC. And the woman sitting not ten feet away from her had probably come from the building. Was she being seen by a BHDC doctor? Did they operate an actual fertility clinic?

Annja found it hard to believe biopirates could be so generous. That's what they were—evil men stealing genetic material from unsuspecting women. The fertility clinic was a front. Had to be. It provided a means to their research.

Was the woman chatting in animated glee with her friend a guinea pig?

"It's such a treasure." The pregnant woman's words carried over to Annja. "Michel and I have been trying for years. Such marvels medicine can perform."

Her friend agreed, and the two shared a giggle.

Annja swallowed back a huge rise in her throat. Yes, a baby would be a treasure to an infertile couple. But what kind of baby was she carrying? A clone? A mini-Marie Antoinette?

"Have you picked out names?" the friend asked.

A few more giggles.

If BHDC experimented with cloning they would need stem cells. Stem cells were not easy to come by, and illegal if gained through improper means and methods.

Though it was a guess, and a wild one at that, she scared herself with her thoughts. Did BHDC harvest eggs from infertile mothers, with the promise of fertility treatments? Perhaps a few eggs were set aside and used for cloning research. The mother would never miss them.

That made Annja wonder if BHDC actually did perform fertility treatments. Why bother after they'd gotten the stem cells they sought?

But there were pregnant women coming out of the woodwork around the place. Was that their payment for participating in a research they could never know was illegal?

"Are they carrying clones?" Annja muttered over her coffee cup.

The files she'd scanned had detailed failed births and infants dying but moments—sixty-eight minutes—after birth. BHDC was a clone factory of sorts. And they hadn't yet mastered their trade.

ANNJA PUT DISTANCE between herself and BHDC. The street where the café sat ended at what appeared to be a cathedral. It made perfect sense. There were hundreds of churches and cathedrals in the city.

She walked toward the cathedral, hoping to orient herself from there. The scent of the river carried through the air, so the Seine must be close. Perhaps a few blocks away, though the French didn't call them blocks.

The street veered to the left and right to circle the cathedral. Annja stopped at the corner across from the courtyard. For the first time she spotted a street sign.

"Rue Jeanne d'Arc," she read the sign. "Who would have thought?"

The utter serendipity of the moment struck her, and she smiled. "I guess I just have to accept the fact that I'll always be where I should be. Cool."

An open-air market edged the courtyard before the cathedral, which she now saw was Notre-Dame-de-la-Gare. Our Lady of the Station. Probably the cathedral had little to do with Joan of Arc, but, compelled, Annja walked forward and took the steps until she found herself standing inside the dark quiet of the grand structure.

The air held an ancient and musty aroma. Looking back outside toward the market, a wistful wonder overcame Annja for what it must have been like to be so young, and so determined to fulfill a holy quest whispered by God. It had to have been too much for Joan, for one so young. She had faced her destiny fiercely.

"As I should mine," Annja said.

She held out her right hand, opening it to receive the sword, but did not will it to this realm of reality where she stood. There was no need. The knowing was all Annja required to feel the power of it. Immense power hummed in the sword. Ancient wisdom, united with desperate determination. A bold confidence seasoned with the barest desire for the soul's freedom. And always, valor.

"I have not been subjected to half so many horrors and trials of endurance as she must have experienced. I can do this. For as long as I must," she pledged.

Clasping her hand over her heart, Annja looked through to the sanctuary. Vast arches and the vaulted ceiling made her so small. She did not enter. But she did whisper what felt like a prayer for the unborn child in the belly of the woman she had watched in the café.

"I pray it's not one of Jacques Lambert's experiments." And then she crossed herself, as she had not done for a long time.

The nuns from her New Orleans orphanage would be so proud.

Stepping back outside, she figured there must be a Metro station close by. Scanning the neighborhood, she saw a familiar site to her right. The library.

Not far from where she stood, the familiar four book-shaped buildings of the Bibliothèque Nationale appeared just over the building tops.

Skipping down the cathedral steps, Annja fixed her path to rue Charcot and headed toward the library. She thought she probably had enough change in her pocket to gain access. And her reader card should be on file. She'd gone through the obligatory interview with a librarian a few years ago to get that. The library was very particular about whom they allowed to access their information.

Keeping a keen eye to her periphery, Annja picked up her pace.

Jacques Lambert would not allow her such an easy escape, she felt sure. The cameras had recorded her rifling through documents. And her fighting the thug with a sword that she'd summoned out of thin air.

If only she'd had time to nab some of the paperwork. It was

up to her to get evidence into the hands of the proper authorities before the bad guys caught her first.

Yes, bad guys, she thought. BHDC was attempting to clone humans. The documents she had read proved that. She couldn't guess how many fetuses had been destroyed or damaged in the process. And what about actual births? The one file spoke of cesarean delivery. She wasn't a medical genius but she knew enough to know that what was going on there was a bad thing.

But where to go? Without evidence, would the French police jump on this and take immediate action? Who was she to decide what was the best option? Would Roux know what to do?

She'd tried his cell phone, but Henshaw said he was out. Her next-best choice, but probably useless considering she wasn't in the States, was Bart McGilly.

Annja dialed his number.

"Hey, Annja, long time no hear. The connection isn't good. Where are you?" Bart asked.

"Paris," she replied.

"City of love. I wish I was there."

And she wished he was, too.

"I have a dilemma and was hoping you might have some words of wisdom." She relayed the entire adventure to him and what she'd seen at the BHDC offices.

To his credit, he didn't tell her she was in over her head. That was Bart. They were friends first, and always. Though she sometimes suspected he considered her more of a little sister. She could never quite place him as a brother. He was too attractive for that.

"I don't know how the European laws operate, Annja, I'm sorry. I'd suggest you go to the police with your suspicions but without hard evidence, it could be difficult. They're more likely to nod their heads politely and scoot you out the door."

"That's what I thought. But if I can get evidence?"

"Then you go to the police, go directly to the police, do not pass go, do not collect two hundred dollars. Because I suspect if you find evidence, you'll also find a hell of a lot of bad luck. You watch your back, Annja."

"Always do." She hung up, not feeling any more sure of the situation, but also relieved just from talking to a friendly voice.

While she was tucking her phone away, it rang.

She checked caller ID. It wasn't an unidentified number, so it wouldn't be Lambert. Ascher Vallois? Last she'd seen, he'd been hightailing it away from her, map in hand.

So you are unaware of what you have?

Lambert's insinuation haunted her. What *did* she have? The navigation device? But what was it? Would looking into François Mansart answer that question?

She crossed a street that stretched before the massive library.

"What have you gotten yourself into?" she asked herself as she found a shady spot and sat down on a public bench to answer the call. "Hello."

"Annja, you are not harmed?"

The urgency in Ascher's voice was completely feigned. If he had really been concerned he would have stuck around to help her fend off the bad guys.

On the other hand, she was thankful he'd gotten away, and he had been the one to encourage him to do so. Not that the map mattered to Lambert, but she felt sure, had he gotten Ascher in hand, he may have been less another kidney right now.

"As little as possible," she replied. "And what of you? I won't even ask if the map is intact. Rain, wind or flood could not destroy that hermetically sealed artifact."

"Get over it, Annja. It's a copy. Where are you?"

"Just outside the Bibliothèque Nationale."

"So I have been jumping boats and fleeing bad guys while you have had your feet up reading books?"

Oh, the fool. Annja squeezed a fist so hard her fingernails dug into her palm. "I haven't gone inside yet. Been a little too busy to get any reading done."

"Where have you been?"

"Inside BHDC."

"What?" Was he really so surprised that the thugs back at the river could have overwhelmed her and taken her captive?

Maybe. The man had far too much confidence in her. It should have never gone down this way, but Annja was thankful that her capture had allowed her to learn more about BHDC.

"We need to talk, Vallois, and I need to take another look at that map," she said.

"I'm staying in the Fifth Arrondissement, in a cozy hotel kitty-corner to Notre-Dame."

"Is my rental car still parked out there?"

"It is still there."

"Good. I'll be there…soon." She had no idea how long it would take at the library, or if they'd even allow her admittance. "I might stop and get something to eat on my way. I'm starving."

"No, I will feed you, Annja. Please, it is the very least I can do," he said.

It *was* the very least. Patting a few loose strands of her hair from her face, she briefly wondered how awful she looked after a day of fighting, capture and escape, and then decided she didn't care.

"I'll be there in a few hours. Don't go anywhere."

"Will you bring the rapier?"

"I don't have time to get to it right now. It's safe, Ascher. It's…"

Lambert was still eager to get the sword, even knowing the

DNA evidence was no longer useable. He collected swords, but that didn't make obtaining it worth critically wounding a man. So there must be something about the sword….

You are unaware of what you have.

"Annja?"

"I changed my mind. I'm going to get the rapier. I'll meet you at your hotel in about four hours?"

"Excellent. I will have food."

17

The reading room was charmingly quiet and the perfect way to unwind after the day she had been through. Annja chose a table toward the corner of the room and near a window, and thanked the librarian when she arrived ten minutes later with a cloth-covered box tied with thin canvas ribbon.

"Must be a group project?" the librarian said in French as she set the box before Annja on the table.

"Why do you ask?"

"This is the second time in less than a fortnight I've retrieved this information." She smiled, and Annja caught a glint of wild waiting for escape in the pupils of her soft blue eyes, disguised behind proverbial thick black-rimmed glasses. "François Mansart is a popular man this month."

"Yes, a project," Annja agreed, sliding a hand over the aquamarine cover of the box. "Do you recall the person who previously requested this material? Man or woman?"

"A woman," she verified. "I did not get her name. She requested Nicolas Fouquet, as well, if I recall correctly."

"A study in seventeenth-century scapegoats," Annja provided. "Both were persecuted by Cardinal Mazarin."

"Let me know if you'd like me to bring out the information for Fouquet. We do close in a little over an hour. Good luck."

Luck? She'd need an act of God to find something within an hour. Unless the work had already been done for her. If whoever had previously requested this information had been on the same quest Annja followed, the pertinent information could be on the top.

Annja set the cover of the box aside and peered into the depths. She hadn't requested any of the larger architectural drawings that could be viewed only by microfiche. The map, if it was in the library's possession, should be the same size as the one she and Ascher had found in the sword.

"And if someone was here recently…" One of Lambert's hired treasure hunters, she suspected.

Pulling on the soft white gloves the library had provided, Annja glanced toward the glass-enclosed office where three librarians worked. Two sets of eyes studied her. To be expected.

Carefully, she began to sort through the contents, which included small sketches of buildings, a few garden designs, but nothing completed that would lend to an actual draft of building designs.

She expected that the documents should be laid in the order they were last viewed. But it appeared as though they were not. In fact, they were ordered by sketches, then a few letters, which she did not take the time to read, and then… "This is it."

The document she touched pushed the breath from her lungs.

Annja drew out the small paper, about half the size of normal notebook paper. She recognized the design drawn in detail with black ink.

"The Batz-Castelmore coat of arms."

The three-dimensional drawing displayed the coat of arms upon a round disk, which curved over to form thick edges. Immediately, she knew what she held. An exact reproduction of the pommel fit to the rapier Queen Anne had gifted to d'Artagnan.

Or perhaps the original design for the pommel.

"Mansart designed the rapier? Curious."

Though the man was never originally a trained architect—relatives taught him stonemasonry—she did not see any evidence that he designed weapons in this collection.

"Anything is possible. The man designed a freaking cathedral—he can make a small decorative rapier," she muttered.

To the left of the drawing a simple jagged circle had been drawn, the same size as the pommel, perhaps a few millimeters smaller in circumference. Annja traced the jags, unsure what it signified, but sensing the answers lay in her hands.

Bending over the table, she stared at the picture. If she looked long enough would the truth reveal itself, as if lemon oil were applied to secret handwriting? Why had the whole process of navigating the map been made so difficult?

"Difficult to one who doesn't know the secret. The queen probably handed d'Artagnan the sword and said, 'By the way, this is how you use it.'" Which would have led him to riches. However, Annja knew better. "Or not."

Glancing inside the box, she sorted through a few more documents, and nearly let out a whoop when she touched the map.

"Here it is," she gasped.

She held an exact version of the very map she and Ascher had found. Including the same missing corner.

"This must be the original. Or, one of two originals?"

If Mansart had indeed drawn the map, he would perhaps see to making a copy for himself. And then there was the copy that Lambert had said he'd found in Fouquet's files. Of course the financier would have made a copy of this bit of intriguing evidence to come into the queen's hands.

Though, Annja recalled her conversation with Jacques Lambert—he hadn't been sure the map had been found in Fouquet's files. Perhaps his treasure hunter, a woman, had been in here less than two weeks earlier? She'd found this map in Mansart's files and hadn't documented its origin, or Lambert hadn't cared, once he'd had the map in hand.

Standing straight and rotating her neck, Annja worked out a few kinks. As if preparing for the big challenge, she drew in a few breaths and shook out her arms and fingers.

Keenly observed by three sets of eyes, she repressed a smirk and leaned over both documents, placed side by side.

They were definitely created by the same hand. The drawing style was crisp, clean, and the methods of shading utilized a small pen-point stippling that was exact on both documents.

And suddenly Annja noticed the obvious.

She placed the drawing of the pommel over the map. Moving the right side that contained the simple jagged-line circle over the missing corner on the map proved it fit exactly.

Flipping back and forth between the two, Annja determined the jags on the circle could be rotated to match perfectly the jagged edges of what she'd originally thought to be a torn edge. But it wasn't torn; it had been carefully cut to fit as if a jigsaw.

"Incredible."

She had a match. But what had she matched?

Sliding the pommel drawing so the actual design lay over the torn corner, Annja now looked at the coat of arms, upside down. And there, at the bottom of the curve, directly below the point of the herald, was the letter *N*.

"North."

She traced her finger around the pommel. "West and east and south!" she said.

Wincing, Annja clenched her fingers over the edge of the table in an attempt to keep from looking toward the glass office. Three pairs of eyes admonished her for her outburst, she felt sure.

The door creaked open. She was busted.

But it didn't matter. She had figured it out.

"Mademoiselle?"

"Sorry. Got a little excited." She gestured to the drawings. "I don't suppose I can make a copy?"

"You've little time to hand copy the documents now. Perhaps you can return tomorrow?"

Right. No photocopying privileges here. But she didn't need a copy, because she had the real thing.

"I think I have what I need. *Merci.*"

IT APPEARED Roux was just returning home as Annja pulled up the circular drive before his mansion. He paused on the stairs and turned to wave at her.

Parking and rushing out to meet him, Annja decided an explanation about her less than chic condition wasn't necessary. He'd seen it before, and if he did comment it would be trite.

"Find your treasure?" he asked, inviting her in and following as she marched toward his den. "You're in a hurry, Annja."

"I'm racing against BHDC to find this treasure, Roux. And I just figured out the key piece in the puzzle. Where's d'Artagnan's rapier?"

"Still in my study on the desk where you left it," he said.

"You didn't lock it away? This house is not burglar proof. I remember well the time it was broken into by crazed monks."

"I've enhanced my security since the Brotherhood of the

ilent Rain. But you're right, I've been busy. There it is. Safe
nd sound."

She lifted the rapier by the hilt and tilted the blade
downward. If Lambert still wanted the sword—even though
e had a copy of the map—then something about it must be
valuable. The worth of it as an artifact would never bring
more than a few thousand euros. Maybe tens of thousands.
Chump change to an organization like BHDC.

She tilted the hilt to inspect the pommel.

Roux joined her. His presence put her to unexpected ease,
he first time today she'd released her tight shoulders to
breathe out an exhale. If she could afford a few moments to
o some yoga poses, she should. A little downward-facing dog
would stretch out her back muscles.

"I'm sure the musketeer never wielded that blade in a
uel," he commented over Annja's shoulder. "It was a prize
e valued, to be sure."

"Why wouldn't a musketeer, who was very obviously
trapped for cash, and constantly in debt, *not* seek to claim
he riches he held in his very hands? Have I been foolish to
elieve very few are even aware of the treasure, when perhaps
 has been pursued through the centuries by curious treasure
unters?" Annja asked.

"Would there not have been mention of it in a historical text
r included with the treasure-hunting sites online if that were
he case?" Roux said.

"Perhaps." She'd checked the major treasure hunting sites,
uch as GeoCache and Treasurenet.com. Nothing on d'Artag-
an's sword.

She glided her fingers in admiration over one flat side of
he blade. It was much thinner and more flexible than her own
word. Not a weapon designed for battle. This was a gentle-

man's sword, designed more for show than duel. Though certainly the tip was sharp and would go nicely through a man's torso, if needed.

"Why would the queen give the man a map without a key?" Annja wondered. "It doesn't make sense."

"Unless the key was to hand?"

She met Roux's blue eyes. They glittered with mischief. "Yes, to hand." She tilted the hilt toward him to display the pommel. "Take a look."

Roux tilted the pommel upward with a touch of his finger. "What am I looking at?"

Annja took a look herself and saw the crest was still crusted with dirt. Tracing her fingernail along the raised crest impressed into the pommel, she cleaned out some of the dirt still embedded within the heavy gold disk. What she needed was a small brush archaeologists used to clean away fine particles. But the appearance of a small *N* along the outer rim gave her a thrill.

"I don't understand why a corporation focused on genetic cloning would have an interest in an ancient sword," Roux commented. "The value is not so great—ah."

"They finance their endeavors with the treasure," Annja finished his thought. "They are pirates, swooping in to steal treasure and literally stealing historical identities from the grave. Lambert staffs biopirates as a means to finance his twisted studies."

"Twisted?"

"I uncovered horrible evidence that they are attempting to clone humans."

"Babies in jars?"

She smirked. "Not quite, but close."

Roux appeared appropriately horrified, and swept a palm over his mouth.

"I followed a pregnant woman from the place."

"You were there?" he asked.

"Yes, just now. But I have no tangible evidence. Why else would a pregnant woman be seen by a doctor at such a place? I think she's carrying a clone."

"Human cloning isn't possible," Roux said.

"It's not *legitimately* possible. Trust me, I'm a major skeptic, but I have a feeling the attempt to create human clones occurs more frequently than we'd like to believe. Yet who will admit they are involved in such research? That is, until the experiments actually work. In the meantime, humans are suffering for the research."

"But I thought the cloning process merely involved extracting the DNA from embryos. Less than a week old?"

"Two weeks actually. And that is only for therapeutic cloning. The embryo never grows to be born. I found evidence that BHDC has actually been seeing their experiments to the birth stage. They're killing babies, Roux."

"But to kill them makes so little sense. If they are experimenting…?"

"Not killing them purposely, the cloned child is born, then does not survive beyond— well, I saw one file that put the survival to sixty-eight minutes before the infant stopped breathing from complications."

"What sort of complications?" Roux asked.

"I don't know. I didn't have time to read it all. Complications from the cloning process, I assume. It's not perfected, which is why it's illegal, and beyond the legalities of it, it's morally wrong."

Suddenly overcome by a strange wave of emotion, Annja pressed her palm over the sword hilt and closed her eyes. A thick hollow nagged inside her throat. "It's so wrong. Isn't it?"

"It is," Roux said. He placed a hand on her shoulder, a tender attempt at consoling her. "Why don't you sit down?"

"No time. I'm to meet Ascher in the city. I think I was followed, as it is. See here?"

Roux nodded as she drew her fingertip around the pommel, tracing the worn impression of the directions of the map.

"A compass. My dear, I think you've found your way to reading the map."

"And all it took was a cup of coffee and an old tourist flyer."

She screwed off the pommel from the hilt and set down the rapier on the desk behind her. "Lock that up. I'm taking this with me."

"Will I require reinforcements to stand in your wake?" he called to Annja's retreating back.

She smiled at his playful, yet knowing, assessment of the situation. "You may."

Pulling open the front door, she dodged as the whoosh of an arrow skimmed her head.

18

"Increased security, eh?" Annja said to no one in particular. She kicked the door closed, pressed her shoulders to it—then decided that wasn't a good idea.

As she dodged to the right, the force of an explosion hitting the door sent wood splinters as big as her arm flying in all directions. Flames ignited the remnants of the wood door. Embers sifted into the foyer in a rain of orange bits.

Annja landed on the marble floor in a face-forward sprawl. She heard Roux order Henshaw to go for the automatic weapons.

"Are you all right, Annja?"

"Peachy!"

"What was that? A grenade?"

"Felt like it. Must have been an RPG."

Rolling to her back, she decided whoever had shot the grenade would come next. Springing up, she took a crouching, ready position aside the flaming doorway. Joan's sword arrived from out of the otherwhere, fitting to her grip.

No, my sword, she thought determinedly. It's no longer hers.

Roux moved around the opposite side of the door. He brandished a machine gun, and had found himself a Kevlar flak jacket. The room was still fuzzy with the dust of the shattered door.

"I've got the front," she said. "You go around back and check the perimeter."

"Will do," he said.

The barrel of a sniper rifle appeared in the doorway. Annja held back defense until she saw the elbow of the gun wielder. He turned toward her. Clad in black from head to combat boots, his eyes were revealed in a thin slash across his face mask.

Before he had time to react to Annja's position, she drew the sword in a sweep across his gut. The rifle clattered across the marble floor, skidding over the rubble of charred wood and ash. Blood pooled quickly beneath his clutching fingers. The man dropped to his knees, yelped and sprawled to his side. He wasn't dead, but that wound was going to leave a mark.

"You should really knock before entering," Annja said as she stepped over the body. "It's the polite thing to do."

She slid up against the opposite wall and swung a look outside. All clear. Only her rental parked in the driveway. She returned to position, shoulders and hips against the wall.

Drawing the sword up and pressing the flat of the blade against her forehead, she closed her eyes and exhaled. Never in a million years would she have imagined such a life. Defending herself against men who wanted to kill her? But now that she was living it, she did it with relish.

She'd been gifted a sword that secreted a great treasure. And it wasn't a gift she intended to ever ignore.

Focusing, she concentrated on picking up activity outside. Movement. Footsteps.

With an intensity of calm that bordered on meditation, she

connected with sounds outside. Beyond the crackle of flame that quickly reduced to simmering embers in the door, wind brushed through the yew hedges that lined Roux's front yard, listing the stiff branches against the brick exterior of the house. The hazy darkness would not reveal snipers hidden in the shrubs that lined the drive. She wasn't for putting herself out in the open as an easy target.

A glance to the man lying to her right showed he wore a headset. A minuscule red light flashed near his temple. There were others.

The scuff of footsteps moved up the limestone steps that fronted the mansion.

Moving her elbow up to bring the sword horizontal, blade tip tilted down, Annja prepared. Slowly, she exhaled. A deep breath carefully drawn, loosened her muscles to the point of readiness.

The footsteps moved cautiously. And now the rub of clothing focused Annja's hearing. Nylon, windbreaker type of fabric that moved in sharp swishes.

Overhead, the dull patter of automatic rifle fire did not break her concentration. Roux must be up on the roof. The man could take care of himself.

Where was Henshaw? The butler had previously proved he could fend for himself. Annja instantly abandoned worry over him.

The footsteps doubled pace. The toe of a combat boot broached the threshold. Annja swung around. The gunman had but a second to register her position. A red laser beam bobbled across her chest. She spun and drew her sword arm in a wide arc, while twisting her body out of the rifle's line of fire.

She slashed the gunman across the clavicle, avoiding the carotid artery—she didn't want him dead. Warm droplets of blood hailed her hand and wrist.

Gripping the hilt tighter than usual, she fisted the stock of the rifle with the coiled base of her hand, the sword pommel clacking against black steel. The gun fell. Annja kicked the weapon across the floor, away from the fallen shooter.

The gunman lunged for her neck. The sword slice had served little more than to aggravate him.

Thanks to her martial-arts training, close combat didn't give her cause to blink. Releasing the sword from her grip sent it away. Annja brought up a knee and connected with a kidney. The man grunted and doubled over, but the impact couldn't be too deadly for the heavy flak jacket protecting his organs. But his position allowed her to kick up with her other knee, smashing it into his nose. Cartilage crunched. He let out a French oath.

Meanwhile Annja kept a keen eye out the front door. No other gunmen in sight. That didn't mean there weren't snipers in the foliage along the driveway. Had they taken out the guard at the gate? There was no other way in, unless they'd scaled the iron gates.

Swiping a bloodied hand across her cheek cleared the hair from her face.

Swinging around behind her opponent, Annja gripped the back of his nylon jacket. Out of the corner of her eye, she spied a large object drop from above, outside.

A man landed sprawled across the manicured lawn. One point for Roux, or maybe Henshaw.

Swinging her attacker up and using his weight to increase impact, Annja crushed his face into the door frame. He pushed back, forcing her up against the opposite side of the frame. Wood splinters from the shattered door dug into Annja's shoulder. She wore no protective gear, just the T-shirt and khaki shorts.

Groping for his face, Annja dug her fingers into anything soft. She landed both eye sockets. To touch another person's eyeballs gave her the creeps, but it was either that or lose this fight.

He bent forward, and Annja, now clinging to his body, legs wrapped about his waist, dug in deeper. Her aggressor fell to his knees and collapsed, moaning and grabbing at his face.

Annja stood. Gripping a hank of his hair, she crushed his face into the limestone step, and used her hiking boot crammed against his jaw to keep him down. She demanded, "Who sent you?" she shouted.

He replied in French that she could do something nasty with herself.

So, in French, Annja repeated, "Are you with BHDC? Did Lambert send you?"

Yet more French oaths. This one obviously didn't care that she had a mystery to solve, and usually when one gets his face smashed bloody that doesn't mean it's going to go all that well. She didn't even want to see what his eyeballs were doing. In or out?

"Ms. Creed?" Henshaw appeared in the doorway, wielding a semiautomatic in one hand and what might have been a confiscated crossbow in the other.

"Got things covered, Henshaw." She lifted the sniper's face and gave it one last shove against the step, which succeeded in knocking him out. "Where's Roux?"

"Gathering the intruders."

"There's one on the lawn he missed," she commented as she stepped over the fallen gunman and inspected the crossbow Henshaw handed to her.

"The one on the lawn is mine."

"Nice one, Henshaw. Let's get them tied up and see if Roux can get them to talk."

SHE LEFT ROUX to handle the five thugs who had invaded his home. One was dead. A fall from a four-story rooftop generally did result in death. Three others were injured badly, and Roux intended to deliver them to an undisclosed aqueduct in the center of Paris, in the vicinity of a hospital—should they choose to seek medical attention—but the final man he kept for interrogation.

Annja did not question his neglect to call the authorities. Report a break-in? That would prompt too many questions Roux, and Annja, would rather not consider. Any man who had walked this earth for five hundred years must maintain a certain anonymity with local authorities.

Annja had to explain that she suspected she'd been followed after her kidnapping.

"They held you against your will? Just this afternoon?"

"I'm free. They left me alone and I was able to escape."

"Alone? Hmm, yes, I suppose. Good for you."

Good old Roux, always concerned, but never quite sure how to express that feeling, she thought. He seemed nervous. As if he wanted to say more, but he did not. The last time Annja had seen him so roused by events he had just returned from a forty-eight-hour Texas Hold 'Em tournament.

"I'll see what I can prod out of him," Roux offered with a glint to his eye.

As Annja left, the carpentry crew Henshaw had called to fix the demolished front door pulled up the drive. He'd found a work crew immediately. It was a wonder what money could buy

She had been careful driving to Roux's estate. She'd kept watch the entire trip. Yet there was no doubt she'd been followed from BHDC by Lambert's thugs. And further, there could be little doubt Lambert felt threatened by her now that she'd infiltrated his files and knew he was involved in human cloning.

THE RIDE INTO PARIS WAS uneventful, and again Annja kept a keen eye for a tail. She parked again near Notre-Dame, since the tight streets in the Fifth Arrondissement rarely offered parking spaces, and some were even marked only for pedestrians. Ascher's hotel was tucked in a cozy little corner above a touristy restaurant that featured, as scrawled in chalk on a board sitting on the sidewalk, Les Cuisses De Grenouilles.

Smirking, Annja recalled her first adventure with frog legs. No, they did not taste like chicken. And even the French were averse to eating them. It was strictly a tourist spectacle.

Ascher greeted her at the door with a kiss to both cheeks. "You're late."

"Had a matter to take care of at a friend's house," Annja said.

"You look a mess, Annja. That is your normal look, eh?"

"And here I thought you were all about the flirtation," Annja bantered back. "Is that how you pick up women? Comment on their disarray?"

"A disheveled woman is a gorgeous thing."

He tried to be light, but he shook his head and apologized, offering the end of the bed to sit.

The room was not much larger than the bed. A narrow aisle between the bed and the window led to an even narrower door, which she presumed was the bathroom. Probably no larger than a shower, toilet and sink. What was it about the Europeans that they didn't attach their showerheads to the wall? It was so difficult to wash one's hair when having to struggle with that.

"Did you get food?" she asked. Important things first. Annja sat on the bed, then stretched out an arm and lay on her side. "I'm starving."

Ascher set a bag on the bed. Grease stained the brown paper. It smelled wonderful.

"It's an hour old, so probably not hot."

"Doesn't matter, as long as it's not frog legs."

"No, not those awful things. From the Greek restaurant down the alley," he said. "There are more Greek restaurants in the fifth than French, you know that?"

"I don't care, so long as it's edible." Annja pulled out a heavy-paper-wrapped gyro and bit into the tepid concoction. Marinated pork and a mild, creamy garlic sauce. Delicious. A stack of thick *pommes frites* marinated in grease sat at the bottom of the bag. "You're not going to eat?" she asked.

"I did already. Thirsty?"

He offered a chilled bottle, but there were no glasses.

"D'Artagnan's favorite," Annja said, studying the label. "I'm game."

Armagnac was a single distilled malt brandy that, besides being the famous musketeer's drink of choice, had also been used by apothecaries as a disinfectant in the seventeenth century.

She took a swig. Annja wasn't a big drinker, and had nothing to compare this to. It burned the roof of her mouth, as any good disinfectant should, but not for long.

"You like?"

She nodded. The burn rose in her throat and she managed a hoarse "Sure."

"If I had the proper goblets, then you could truly appreciate the fullness of this exquisite brandy. Smell the pepper and the apricots." He wavered his fingers over the narrow bottle neck, then slugged back a swallow. "But this is how d'Artagnan would have indulged—straight from the bottle!"

His enthusiasm warmed her. Certainly he was a man of gusto and extreme fascinations. She could picture Ascher Vallois striding the cobbled roads of the seventeenth century, gentleman's rapier at his hip and a musketeer's tabard swinging, the silver lace catching the eyes of passing ladies.

He would most definitely seduce them with his charm and impressive dueling skills. And once within the privacy of her boudoir? The man would have been a lady-killer.

A gray sweater fit tight across Ascher's abs, and dark trousers showed off the incredible quads that he'd obviously earned jumping over obstacles as a *traceur*. Of course, mountain biking and rock climbing didn't hurt to enhance the overall package, she felt sure.

Yeah, he offered a complete package. Handsome, talented and athletic. What woman wouldn't swoon to his charms?

Even after he'd committed a small betrayal in the interest of keeping his life?

She noted he took her in from head to toe, and the smirk that curved his lips. "What's up, Vallois?"

"You should eat more before you drink too much," he said.

"I can handle my drink. Just like I can handle my men," she said.

Okay, so that last part wasn't entirely true. She could handle a man wielding a pistol, coming at her with death in his eyes, but a sexy Frenchman set on seduction? She was out of her league.

But when had such a position of lacking skill ever scared her off?

She took another swallow. The Armagnac had ceased to burn. Now it warmed her belly and relaxed her. No wonder d'Artagnan had liked this stuff. "Not bad."

"Ah, the American way of summarizing a truly exquisite find. If I could say the same about you, Annja, it would be a pitiful reflection upon the French male. Not bad? *Non,* you are exquisite this evening."

"Thank you, but I know I look as though I've been through the wringer, because I have."

"Tell me everything that happened after we parted on the Seine."

She twisted to face him. "Are you here on official business for BHDC, or are you here acting for yourself?"

"Annja, I work for no one but myself," he said.

"I don't believe it."

"But you must. Why else would I have called you, Annja? I was worried about you, that you may not have fared well with those men chasing us."

"I didn't do so well. In fact, as you were floating away down the Seine, I was being knocked out and carried to BHDC."

"You were captured?" He slid a hand over hers, which startled her, so she pulled away and nearly knocked over the bottle in the process.

Chill, Annja. Have another drink.

"How did you get away?" Ascher asked. "Did they let you go?"

"Not exactly. I made a run for it. And they followed me to the home of a trusted ally. Much gunfire ensued. And a bit of nasty eye gouging."

Annja inspected her fingernails. They were lined with half moons of dirt and blood.

She took another swig of brandy.

"Annja, I had no idea the star of *Chasing History's Monsters* lived such an adventurous life. Do you get paid for risking your life?"

Not when she should be on vacation. Nor did she receive financial reward for any of the situations she had found herself in that involved fighting off thugs and saving the world. But she was occasionally able to use the experience as work related and write off the flight and hotel room. She doubted her producer, Doug Morrell, would approve of this adventure as fodder for one of the shows.

"Ascher, just…I'm not sure if I'm ready to tell you everything right now."

"I understand. There is a loss of trust between us. I must earn it back. But you believe that I have been truthful with you now? About the danger BHDC presents?"

"Yes, they are dangerous, but in a creepy, twisted scientific way. This has become much more than a simple pleasure dig."

"*Oui.* I'm so sorry, Annja. I did not mean for you to become involved in something so strange."

He lay on the bed and stretched his arms up and behind his head. The stretch revealed his abs. Annja lingered for a moment on the sight. A man had to be disciplined to develop a body like his. She liked that about him. For every fault, he matched it with a surprising positive.

"I cannot, for the life of me, have imagined it would result in your being kidnapped. How can I make this up to you?"

"Hand over the map," she said. And then she shook her head. "No. I'm sorry, too. This was your dig. You are as much a victim of BHDC, if not more so."

Her eyes strayed higher on his torso. The rucked-up sweater revealed the scar where his kidney had once been. It was small, about an inch. It must be where the blade exited, because she'd seen the long scar on his back. Damn, that must have hurt.

"I have no right to waltz in and walk off with something that means as much to you as it does to me," she offered. "But can I trust that we both want to keep the map from Lambert's hands?"

Ascher nodded. "We are in accord."

"Not that it matters anymore." She finished the gyro and

dug to the bottom of the bag for a few remaining fries. "I know what it is about the rapier that Lambert wants."

"Of course, the map. Did you bring along the rapier?"

"Part of it," she said.

Ascher choked on a swig of Armagnac.

"The map is not what Lambert wants. Because he's got a copy," Annja said.

"He does?" Ascher sat up, jostling the paper bag and Annja.

She slid off the bed and stepped into the little bathroom to wash her hands.

"Scanned and saved on his laptop," she called out. "It's a match to the one we have. Seems Nicolas Fouquet made copies of all Queen Anne's correspondence. Lambert has been researching the same archives we have, only he discovered the original map. Or an original copy."

Studying her face in the mirror, she decided she had seen herself looking much worse. Was that a bruise at the edge of her jaw? Must be from Lambert's slap. Heh. She'd battled thugs and avoided grenade and gunfire, and yet a simple slap succeeded in marking her.

"That makes sense," Ascher said as she returned to the confines of the bedroom. "I read about Fouquet's fastidious records in my studies. So the copy, is it missing—?"

"The same as ours. The lower left corner where a navigational key might normally be found. And after viewing the scan, which was much clearer than your black-and-white copy, I began to wonder if it was designed that way, with the piece missing. Which led me to the Bibliothèque Nationale, on François Mansart's trail."

"Mansart? The seventeenth-century architect? Annja?"

She stopped, midwobble, and caught herself against the door frame. "What?"

"You should sit down. You don't look well."

"Was that stuff old?" She eyed the almost empty bottle. Empty? "Christ, Ascher, I think you really did get me drunk."

"Nonsense, Annja, you drank but half the bottle."

"Half? Yikes," she said as she sat in the only chair in the room.

"You do not indulge often?"

"Diet Coke is more my speed. So what was I saying?" The room had begun to spin. The movement challenged her. She did not like to be out of control of her senses. "Mansart," she whispered. "The library. Hand me my backpack, will you?"

She tugged out the laptop and attempted to power up. No WiFi. And did it matter? All she really wanted to do was sleep.

Ascher finished the Armagnac and set the bottle on the floor. "Do you ever take a moment, Annja? You are always on the go, focused on the adventure. You are welcome to shower here. Perhaps I could massage your shoulders for you."

"Ascher, let the dog loose, okay?"

"I do not understand."

"The cad," she explained further. "He doesn't have a chance with me, so take off the leash and let him roam elsewhere."

"My flirtations did not scare you off from meeting me, so you must have appreciated them," he said.

She shrugged, not willing to agree, but knowing he was right. Their online conversations had served to fill a missing part of her that she didn't have the time to pursue in the real world, at least not in real time. The missing part? A relationship.

Sure, a boyfriend might understand her job required much world travel. But how many men would understand when she couldn't talk about the extracurricular activities that saw her fighting evil? Hey, honey, I'm home. I killed a bunch of bad guys and saved the world today. Supper ready?

The idea of such a relationship made her smirk. She

wondered what it would be like married to a superhero. Not that she considered herself super or a hero.

"Annja, if I were trying to seduce you right now, I'd be over there, whispering into your ear and touching your brandy-stained lips," Ascher said.

Annja drew a tongue along her lower lip. Despite the huge sandwich she had consumed—rather, devoured—she could still taste the Armagnac glazing her lips. Wasn't a full stomach conducive to warding off a good drunk? Why did she feel so woozy?

"Yes, that plump, chewable lip," Ascher said.

So watching her gobble down food hadn't put him off? The man was either blind or desperate. She sensed he had moved to the end of the bed, and glanced away from the laptop screen to find he offered another bottle of the wicked brew.

"Ascher, I'm the one who should be getting *you* drunk so I can steal the map from you."

"You wouldn't steal a thing, Annja. I know you better than you do yourself."

He was right. It wasn't fair, but he was right. At least on the matter of stealing. Not her scene.

"You can have it." He slid off the bed to stand, yet still they were about half a foot apart. "I want to see how adventurous a woman you are."

Warmth spread all over her body, making her loose, relaxed and open. It was time to start drinking ice water.

"Do you know what BHDC is involved in?"

Ascher shrugged. "Cloning human body parts. Did you see my kidney while you were there?"

"Wouldn't have been surprised if I had. Lambert heads a corporation dedicated to biohistorical research. They claim the DNA from famous figures and...I don't know. I can' imagine that you could clone a historical figure. But they collect the DNA anyway."

"DNA pirates? Such exotic mischief."

"Mischief? I thought it was the Brits who were masters of understatement. It is morally wrong. They've done experiments, Ascher. They've attempted to clone humans."

"You have proof?" he asked.

She didn't have tangible proof. Oh, to have pocketed one of the documents she'd read in BHDC's files.

"Of course." Ascher nodded. "Trust yet to be earned. I will never stop trying to seduce you, Annja. But I respect you. Maybe, it is, I want you to seduce me, eh? We Frenchmen do have our own fantasies about the American woman."

Annja leaned closer to him and said, "I've never seduced a man in my life."

"Then I will be your first. You are doing an excellent job so far."

"I haven't done a thing," she said.

"The way you devoured that meal made me wish you were devouring me."

"I think I'll take you up on that offer of a shower now."

His expression changed so quickly, Annja knew she had said something wrong.

19

Jacques had put a tail on Annja Creed, though he wasn't sure he shouldn't do the fieldwork himself after all the mishaps. He'd heard back from the crew who had followed Roux out of Paris to the old man's mansion. Four men went down, with one dead. Reports told that a woman had assisted Roux.

So Roux and Annja Creed worked together?

How, and why? Had Roux arrived in his office to distract him with the decoy coat of chain mail while Creed sneaked around BHDC? It was possible. But that would mean the mail did not belong to Joan of Arc, which disturbed him more.

If it was genuine, then he couldn't imagine why Roux would put forth something so valuable, without then expecting Annja to find something in return.

And whom was the mysterious modern sample from?

His men had allowed a woman—who had entered the facility without a weapon—to get away. Though how she'd gotten the sword she'd used to defeat Theo was another mystery. One he would solve.

And then there was Ascher Vallois. He and Creed were working together, though *why* was another frustrating question.

Annja Creed certainly had her allies in Paris.

"Such an enigma, that woman."

She hosted a popular television show about monsters. Jacques had downloaded a few episodes to watch. She wasn't as voluptuous or vacuous as the blond hostess, Kristie something-or-other, but she was more credible. She worked a lot of historical detail into her stories and featured short interviews with scientists, historians, archaeologists and other experts to verify her research. The woman was no slouch.

Jacques could not figure out her interest in d'Artagnan's sword, and, ultimately, the treasure. It didn't seem a feasible show topic; there were no monsters involved in the musketeer's history. Was it merely her fascination for history?

"Idiot! Of course, anyone would have an interest in the prospect of treasure," he told himself.

BHDC thrived because of found treasure. It was their sole means of finance. And the best way to obtain it? Stalk the serious treasure hunters and swoop in when the booty was brought up. Mad Bloody Jack was still riding the seas, even without the trusty Evil Gentleman Tobias at his side.

Jacques owed much to his brother's memory.

From the moment Toby had breathed his last breath, Jack had begun to dream, imagine and design his own future—a future without sickness. He took science courses and advanced biology classes offered in high school. Then he'd met Andrew Harrison, his head geneticist, in his second year of college. Andrew had turned him on to the possibility that DNA manipulation could serve the human race.

Therapeutic cloning became his passion, to create life for those in need. Genetic cloning had been a natural progression, a sideline to his goal. And it paid the bills. Most of them. But until BHDC could show proof they'd actually successfully cloned a human, their clients would remain the few and desperate.

So plunder was needed to finance the bulk of expenses.

And while he should step back and allow the spoils to the victors—there were bigger caches of plunder to be claimed elsewhere—Jacques Lambert could no longer risk *not* following through. Both Vallois and Creed knew too much.

Hell, he'd spilled information when she'd been in his office. He'd come off as intelligent, in possession of knowledge very few could have. Jacques had never spent much time around an attractive woman. He never had the leisure to date or consider a relationship. Did a pretty woman so easily loosen his lips?

And now Creed had looked upon sensitive documents. He couldn't be sure exactly which ones she'd read, but all the papers in the locked file were for no eyes but his own and those of the research lab.

Perhaps it was time to pack up and move on. Britain's cloning laws were much more lenient than they were in France. Though there was his difficulty with Tony Blair in 2002. The former prime minister did not take kindly to bio-pirates. Jacques Lambert couldn't easily waltz back into England without MI-5 sniffing onto his trail.

"Jacques." He smirked at the moniker and wrapped his arms across his chest. "Jack, boy, you've come so far, don't let them bring you down now. You are so close. Toby would be proud. Father will be suitably shown up. Old bastard. I have what it takes to change the world. To make a difference. And I will."

But first, he had to devise a backup plan. A means to keep

Annja Creed from going to the authorities. And the only plan that made sense involved shutting her up for good. It wouldn't be easy. She was a celebrity. And crafty.

The intercom buzzed and, noticing it was a line from the lab, Jacques clicked on. "Yes?"

"I've begun to synthesize the samples you sent down," Andrew Harrison said. His head genetic engineer was a keen scientist with a bold daring that Jacques appreciated. Andrew had lost a sister due to lack of donor for a heart transplant. They understood one another.

"Where you able to extract DNA from the chain mail?"

"It appears so. I won't know for another twenty-four hours. I've put a rush on the job, as you requested."

Jacques knew it took time to synthesize and isolate DNA, but the PCR process did run quite smoothly, and billions of copies of the DNA strand could be produced.

"You're doing the other sample at the same time?"

"Of course. I'll ring you as soon as I've results."

"Good. Thank you, Andrew. You are indispensable."

Jacques clicked off.

He had surrounded himself with a very small but trusted team of colleagues. Jacques needed no one else to keep BHDC running smoothly, albeit out of sight of the law. And to protect him from curious eyes. They all had lost someone to medicine's lack of concern. First do no harm? Rare was the surgeon or medical practitioner who honored that code.

On the other hand, Annja Creed was the sort of adventurous, intelligent woman he could use on his team. She could prove an asset. If he could show her a reason to want to join his quest.

"Time to look up your history, Annja. Do you have relatives you'd die to protect? If you do, I will find them."

IT WAS GENEROUS of Ascher to rent her a room, and not expect that she'd want to share with him, Annja thought.

Head still spinning from the brandy, she headed immediately for the shower. After she'd soaped away the past forty-eight hours of adventure, she wrapped one of the hotel's thick terry robes around her body and made a beeline for her backpack.

The shower refreshed her, but she still felt woozy. However, there were things she needed to get processed before the alcohol completely stole her thoughts.

She tugged out her notebook and began to write down everything she could remember from the files at BHDC. There had been a lot of indecipherable medical terminology, and even the few sentences and terms she had recognized had been difficult to piece into understanding.

Yet the overall, albeit slightly blurry, picture pointed to human cloning.

It disturbed her to recall the woman she had listened to in the café as she'd chatted with a friend about the upcoming birth of her baby. If there was a clone in her belly, did she know? Had she freely entered into a contract with BHDC in order to gain a child she may have pined over for years because of infertility? And if so, had she ordered a little Marie Antoinette or perhaps gone the modern route and applied for a Brad Pitt?

And if the mother had knowingly gone into the process, had she been informed that cloning wasn't a mastered science? That no successful birth had survived beyond a few minutes? And should it actually survive, that the possibility of her having a baby who would grow to resemble whom she hoped, was impossible? And that she would not be getting a clone that would think and act like the original?

Annja couldn't imagine that any woman would take that

risk. To volunteer to be a guinea pig for cloning? No sane woman would do such a thing, knowing the results would lead to premature delivery and/or complications leading to death.

And with the news stations occasionally reporting on how organs could be cloned—but not humans—who would believe BHDC's cloning scheme could work?

On the other hand, innocent people were duped out of thousands daily by false Nigerian widows' Internet scams.

Annja sighed. People were that gullible, and always would be.

She had to believe the pregnant woman was being used by Jacques Lambert to further his experiments *without* knowledge of the risks.

"Poor girl," she murmured. "Can't imagine what it must be like to want a baby so badly."

Doing a quick sketch, Annja worked the woman's face onto a page in her notebook. She should have followed her from the café, gotten some solid information, like a license plate number or even a name.

This had become too big, Annja realized. When innocent humans were involved, she had to seek help from authorities. But without a name of the mother or a shred of tangible evidence against BHDC she felt lost.

Roux had been no help whatsoever.

Pressing her fingers to her temples, she winced at the pounding ache that only increased in volume. "No more armagnac for this girl."

ANNJA WOKE when she heard a rap at her door. The indomitable Frenchman must be standing outside. For a moment she considered ignoring him, but she really didn't have the time to waste.

Yet she already had. Realizing she'd fallen asleep, Annja glanced to the window. Daylight shone in.

She opened the door.

"Come in, Ascher. Why didn't you wake me?"

"It was almost two when we finished talking last night. And you looked as though you needed to sleep off the brandy." He entered, holding the laminated map before him as a sort of peace offering. She took it from him and spread it upon her notebook.

"It's only seven now," he offered. "You haven't lost much time."

"With Lambert's goons lurking about every corner, I think time is irrelevant. It's stealth we need. And a new perspective," she said.

"You have the navigational device?" Ascher sat on the chair near the window and crossed an ankle over his opposite knee. He was wearing jeans and leather jacket today. And rubber boots that climbed past his knees. Interesting fashion statement.

"I do." She dug in her backpack for the pommel.

"Ah! I knew it!" he declared triumphantly. "You've had it all along, since last night. You didn't want to tell me, but it slipped out now when I casually mentioned it."

Caught. But not sorry for the deception. Though she was feeling the ache of her drinking binge. Not a binge, just a few swallows. She was definitely a lightweight.

Annja shoved the backpack away on the bed. "Just for that, I'm going to keep you in the dark a bit longer. You dressed for some mucking about?"

"If we go underground, boots are necessary. You can purchase some down the street at the *supermarché*."

A visit to a French supermarket was always a treat. They stocked everything from food and clothing to houseware.

and pharmaceuticals. Sort of like a Kmart, but with cool things like wine and cigars. A few aspirins were all she really craved.

And some wisdom.

"Ascher, what would you do if you knew a woman was in trouble, but hadn't proof of it, and weren't sure which authorities to contact?"

"I'm assuming we're not discussing Annja Creed," he said with a grin behind his steepled fingers.

"I followed a pregnant woman from BHDC. If she's carrying a clone, she, well…does she need to know? If I'm wrong, it would be ridiculous to say as much to her. But even if I'm not wrong, what could she do about it? She was huge. Probably ready to give birth any day now."

"You are positive they are cloning?"

"I read the files. Here are my notes."

She pushed the notebook toward him, but he remained in the chair.

"I believe you, Annja. I've been stabbed and swabbed, in proof. I would only try to keep close watch on the woman. Ensure she receives the best medical care. And…try to keep Lambert from her."

"I'm surprised she's not under some kind of BHDC house arrest, lock and key, as it is. Course, that would alert her that not all was as a normal birth should be. She must be completely oblivious. And in a short time, she'll give birth, and when the baby dies, they'll probably make up some excuse. Complications of some sort. She'll never know she was being used as an experiment. God, I feel so helpless."

"Not a common feeling for you, I imagine," Ascher said.

"No, it's not." Annja tossed the pommel once and caught it. Helpless for now. But she would keep the woman's welfare in mind. Maybe Bart would have some ideas for her. "So let's see if this works."

"The pommel?" Ascher looked confused.

"The key," she said, savoring the reveal when she saw his surprise.

"That's it? We had it all along?" Ascher joined her on the bed and observed as she laid the sword pommel over the missing corner of the map. She rotated it, not sure which way was correct.

"It's a compass," Ascher said in an awe-filled gasp. "The navigational device has always been with the sword. So clever!"

"I discovered a drawing of this very pommel in François Mansart's papers at the library. I couldn't make a copy, but I didn't need to."

The heavy gold piece was cool on her palm, a chunk of history that still made her giddy to think about it. She turned over the pommel and traced the threaded column, which fit the piece onto the sword hilt. "Do you think d'Artagnan knew this was the way to read the map?" she asked.

"Possible. But why then put the map back in the hilt if he had found the treasure?"

"That is the question we'll never have answered. See here, this jagged line on the underside," she said.

Along the rim of the pommel a finely etched line jagged a complete circle. It matched the drawing exactly. First glance could assume it was merely a random line, perhaps an unsmoothed mark the goldsmith ignored. One side of the circle consisted of short straight lines, crenellated, as if a medieval tower.

As he leaned in, Ascher's head blocked her light source from the tiny window. The warmth of his presence, the closeness of him, startled Annja.

A handsome Frenchman was sitting too close for comfort and smelling too good for her better judgment. Vacations should involve fun activities. Hunting for an infamous sword. Picnics. Laughing. Sex with a handsome treasure hunter.

"What?" His eyes darted back and forth. "Annja?"

"Huh?" Giving her head a mental shake to jar the debauched thoughts from her brain, Annja then pressed Ascher back with two fingers to his shoulder. "You're blocking my light. Hand me the map."

Studying the underside of the pommel against the map, she determined the pommel fit exactly upon the serrated corner.

"You've done it," Ascher whispered. "North is that way, and—we've got to secure it so we can follow it."

"I've got a better idea." Annja reached into her backpack and retrieved a Sharpie marker. Positioning the pommel just so, she then marked out the four points of the compass right on the lamination.

"So where do we start? We still have not figured how this is positioned to the Louvre or the river," Ascher said.

Annja tugged her laptop from the backpack. The hotel did not offer WiFi, but she thought to give it another go. Sometimes if it was a windless day…and she was two floors lower than previously…

"What are you looking up now?"

"I was going to check a hunch, but the hotel doesn't offer WiFi. Though I do have a WiFi vampire program. And, if the restaurant below offers it…"

"Vampires?"

"It's a WiFi detection program. If there's a signal in the area, I might be able to tap into it."

The program scanned for a signal—and found one. Within minutes she was online.

"My guess is it's not on the Right Bank," she said. She typed in a search for Mansart. "When did Mansart design Val-de-Grâce?"

"Mid-1600s. You think? But yes. Anne of Austria commissioned the cathedral from him. There is a connection. What made you think of Mansart?"

"There was a notation on Lambert's copy of the map. I think it might have been a conjecture. Here." Annja scrolled down a page on the architect that Wikipedia brought up, and read aloud portions relating to the creation of the Val-de-Grâce cathedral. "Mansart was surprised when construction began that there were numerous cave-ins. Limestone quarries beneath the building site had to be filled to support the church."

She looked to Ascher. "He had to have spent some time underground, in the tunnels. Who better to hide the map and a trail to the treasure?"

"I understand. So you think it is under the cathedral?"

She pulled up a map of the Left Bank, circa seventeenth century. The two of them studied the ancient map alongside the map they'd discovered inside d'Artagnan's sword.

"Turn it to the right," Ascher directed. "Yes."

The streets aligned. Or rather, the landmarks aligned to the larger blocks of space on the map, and some of the tunnels exactly matched the streets.

"It is on the Left Bank," Ascher said. "I think this is Val de-Grâce right here. And here, this larger space, the Luxembourg Gardens, surely. Which means the red line is not actually the Seine, as I'd originally guessed…."

"I think it's the path to the treasure. And here, the fleur de-lis, which we believe is the X that marks the spot," Annja noted, "is to the west of the gardens. Close to the Seventh Arrondissement?"

"Yes, perhaps. Not so far as the Invalides. There would be some tunnels directly beneath a street. This is boulevard Montparnasse, I'm sure. If we go down close to the cathedral and find a street marker, we should be able to follow this."

"Well, then, I think we've got ourselves a treasure hunt, Monsieur Vallois."

"I think you are a genius, Miss Creed."

Ascher slid his hand around behind her neck, his fingers gliding up into her hair, and pulled her close for a kiss.

And she kissed him back. It felt right to surrender to a moment of success. They'd figured it out. *X* finally marked a real and tangible spot.

"All right, Frenchman, that's enough," she said. Though it was bittersweet to stop the kiss. The world wouldn't be completely right until she got some aspirin and some breakfast. "We've got work to do."

"Treasure hunting?"

"Shopping first."

20

"Where are we headed?" Annja scanned the streets as they walked along the parked cars fitted closer together than a stack of Oreo cookies. "Wasn't the manhole down the road as good as any other?"

Ascher chuckled. He'd slung a leather backpack over his broad shoulders, and walked briskly. His rubber soles shucked along the cobbled street. "We mustn't be quite so bold, Annja, though I do admire your fortitude. There is an entrance to the underground ahead. I know the owner."

"Someone *owns* an illegal entrance?"

"Oui." He flashed her an innocuous smile, and led onward. "You will see!"

At the end of the Luxembourg Gardens, and out of eyesight of Val-de-Grâce, was where Ascher said they could enter the underground. If they had placed the church correctly on the map—the treasure was not there—but perhaps closer to the east border of the Seventh Arrondissement. They should start closer to the end, but it was the only entrance Ascher wa

'amiliar with. To find someone who knew otherwise would
ake too much time.

And if there were any thugs on their trail, the diversion
would prove necessary.

The cheese shop smelled pungent and stinky. The air of it
immediately overwhelmed Annja's olfactories. Good thing the
aspirin she'd purchased at the *supermarché* had worked fast.

A rotund woman in a utilitarian brown dress that matched her
eyes greeted Ascher. The woman bussed both of Annja's cheeks
and made it clear she was delighted to meet her. Then she bustled
off behind the counter, calling gaily to Ascher in French that she
must have assumed the American girl couldn't understand.

"She's going to let you taste the goat's cheese," he said.

"I got that," she said with an angled smirk.

"It's fresh made and my favorite."

"I'm not much for cheese." Feeling as though she'd just
been introduced to a boyfriend's mother, Annja pushed down
the nervous clench in her gut. "Why are we in a cheese shop?
I thought we had some spelunking to do?"

"We do. I'll return shortly." Ascher then slanted back and
slid a hand along Annja's neck and leaned in close. "Whatever
he hands you, taste. I promise you won't regret it."

He slipped behind the counter and disappeared, leaving
Annja with the weird thought that Ascher and the woman were
allied, and she was right now preparing a slice of poisoned
cheese. Take the American girl out of the picture. Ascher
finds the treasure, and she goes home in a coffin.

She swished a hand along the back of her neck where
Ascher had touched her. Thoughts of their kiss in the hotel
surfaced. Nice. If only this vacation had really been a
vacation, she might have been more leisurely with him—hell,

sex wasn't out of the question. But not with so many unanswered questions threatening more than her own well-being.

The initial olfactory attack of the premises had begun to wear off. Now Annja noted the musty-wood scent that must be a cheese, but could be the old walls and floor. The counter boasted a gorgeous butcher block with a thick slab of rosy granite laid over the top.

To her right a wall of pickled vegetables seeped a vinegar aroma into the atmosphere. Green string beans, whole eggs and sliced carrots were just a few of the jarred concoctions.

Adjusting her backpack, she shifted the weight of her supplies. She now wore gray rubber boots that climbed to her knees, jeans and a windbreaker jacket over her T-shirt. Knowing there was a helmet with headlamp in her bag, she surrendered to the excitement of the quest.

"All for one," she murmured. "And one for all."

Tracing a finger along a gold fleur-de-lis stitched into a folded tea cloth, she mused, "Did you really allow a queen's treasure to slip through your fingers, d'Artagnan?"

What would the musketeer have done with jewels and riches?

"Probably buy a few rounds at the local tavern for his regiment and invest in those exploding grenades he desired." She smiled and leaned over a table of assorted cheeses to inspect.

"You try?" The woman reappeared, and rumbled across the creaking wood floor in her sensible, sturdy leather shoes. "*Chèvre.*" She thrust a cheese knife laden with a hunk of gooey white substance toward Annja.

The cheese knife lifted expectantly, and behind the hand a pair of eager brown eyes waited.

"Oh, why not?" To refuse would be beyond rude. Annja took the cheese and popped it in her mouth, impulsively closing her eyes as she chewed. Initially tangy, she could detect the flavor of goat's milk. It was firm but creamy on her tongue. *This isn't so bad. Actually, it's quite good.* "*Tres bien,*" she said.

When she opened her eyes the woman had already returned to the counter and was slicing off another hunk of something pale yellow streaked with blue veins.

"Oh, no, I mustn't," Annja said in French. Not anything with mold in it. Not so soon after her Armagnac hangover. "Really, one new cheese a day is my limit."

Ascher popped his head out from a door behind the counter. "Come along, Annja. *La vie sous-terraine!*"

Skirting the proffered hunk of cheese, Annja slipped through the door, which immediately opened on a flight of dangerously narrow wood steps, the edges of which were rounded, likely from centuries of shoes and feet.

"It is good, *oui?*" Ascher called up to her.

"It was gouda," Annja tried, and smiled to herself.

The joke went over the Frenchman's head faster than a sniper's bullet. She should never attempt her goofy sense of humor more than once in a great while.

Annja stepped onto the earth floor of a small cellar lined with walls of stacked cheeses. Down here the smell was not so pungent, but perhaps that was only because her nose had adjusted. Or it could be the dirt walls balanced out the smell with a thick, earthy, moist scent.

A naked lightbulb hanging from an electrical cord tied with thin strips of what looked like cheesecloth to the overhead beam glowed over their shoulders.

Her heart sped up. She'd once spelunked Ellison's Cave in Georgia. It boasted one of the longest vertical drops in the country, over a thousand feet. Quite the rush. Yet the darkness and sensory deprivation always initially unnerved her. Soon enough, though, she got her climbing legs and it was all good.

Cheeses of all shapes and colors perched on wooden shelves in the cool darkness. Wooden-handled tools with silver corkscrews and long curved knives hung on hooks. A caliper, a wooden hoop and a stack of mesh cheesecloth sat on another shelf. She had no idea of any of their uses—tools of the trade.

The creak of a wood bar shifted across iron latches. A squat little man, a match to the cheese woman—he even wore an apron fashioned from the same brown cloth the woman had worn—removed three wooden bars from a small door hinged to a wall that would have made a perfect hobbit entrance.

"This guy has his own private entrance to the underground tunnels," Annja said. "Awesome."

"Doorways like this exist all over the city," Ascher offered.

She knew that from some of the historical texts she'd read on Paris. Most were decrepit old stairways, crumbling or closed off decades ago with homemade brickwork. The city bolted all manholes, and any official entrance to the underground tunnels through government buildings required keys, some of which, she had heard, crafty tunnel explorers had obtained for their midnight visits to such places as Notre-Dame, the Conciergerie and a few noted museums.

"Many residents had secret escape tunnels during the German occupation," Ascher explained. "And before that, well, there has always been reason for people to hide, or run, and secret away from those above ground."

"To hide a spy during the Revolution or a medieval horse thief," Annja said.

"*Oui,* can you imagine? I enjoy tinkering around in these tunnels with fellow cataphiles, but to be pursued with your life in danger, and forced to go underground? It must have been frightening."

"You come here often?" Annja asked.

He cocked his head into a suggestive tilt. Gascon charm crinkled the sun-browned flesh at the corners of his eyes. "It is the first time I've brought along a woman."

"Should I consider this a date?"

The old man smiled up at Annja, though she could tell he didn't understand the English they used.

"It would please me if you would," Ascher said. "But now tell me, is it often you allow men to escort you into creepy dark places?"

Annja gave the question smirking consideration. "It happens more often than you might think," she said.

The door sprang open and, though she expected an eerie cold breeze, she felt nothing, save the increased beat of her heart. Adventure waited.

Ascher slapped the cheesemaker across the shoulder, and, turning to hand Annja his backpack, he then stepped through the doorway—and dropped out of sight.

Peering inside, her hands clinging to the iron-framed doorway, Annja looked down. A brilliant flash blinded her. Ascher had turned on a small flashlight. There were no steps, not even an iron ladder such as a city tunnel would install for access.

"Jump!" he called.

"Right behind you!"

Into the unknown, she fell, and landed in a crouch, ready to roll to take the brunt of her landing, but finding it wasn't quite as far as she'd originally judged.

Their backpacks dropped at their feet. *"Bonne chance!"* the old man called.

The sound of the iron door slammed shut above, sealing them in what felt and looked like a tomb.

Drawing out the helmet from her backpack, Annja flicked on the headlamp and flashed it around. The thickness of the dark cut off the beam three feet in every direction.

When a person went spelunking they must always chose a trusted friend or guide to share the adventure. Did she trust Ascher?

Yes. Strangely…yes.

The walls were no more than arm's reach to each side of her, and the ceiling loomed a foot above her head.

"Cozy," she muttered, "in a lung-squeezing, heart-pounding kind of way."

Annja had read about the forbidden passages that traced over five hundred miles of labyrinthine paths beneath the city during some of her research on Paris. The tunnels dated back to Roman times and were expanded further in the seventeenth and eighteenth centuries. The Val-de-Grâce tunnels, which Mansart had had to reinforce, dated from the rococo time period.

The tunnels varied in width and height from huge, paved sections that one could drive an army tank through, to the smallest wormholes that a man had to literally slither through, and pray that cheeseburger he'd had for lunch didn't find him stuck in the middle like an entombed mole.

Despite the illegality of it, an entire community lived beneath the city in gypsum and limestone quarries. Cataphiles, they were called, and this was their secret kingdom. There was even a cata-cop force, created in the mid-twentieth century, to police them.

Ascher's hair brushed her wrist.

He bent and unzipped his pack. A second later a pale yellow beam rushed across Annja's hiking boots. It was redirected into her face. His helmet and worklight. She followed suit, strapping on her own yellow helmet. It was the only color besides pink that fit her head. Not much of a choice, but she wasn't worried about fashion down here.

"Just how far down does it all go?" she asked.

"There are perhaps seven levels. Some areas descend three hundred yards. You will get dirty, Annja."

"Good," she said.

She caught a glimpse of the contents before he slung the backpack over one shoulder and tilted that quizzical Frenchman's smirk at her.

"You plan on spending a lot of time down here? What's inside your pack?"

"Gloves, multitool, a leaf knife, snacks."

"Snacks?"

"Annja, we embark upon a journey now. Into the bowels of Paris."

She flashed the light along the walls. The flash fell across blue-and-red rubber pipes. Must be part of the plumbing system. Bowels, indeed. "Aren't we already there?"

"Not even close," he said.

"But the map. It's very simple. We follow the red line."

"Only because there were not so many tunnels in the seventeenth century as there are now. We'll have to discover the old paths by means of the newer ones."

It made sense. "Hand me the map," she said, "and let's get started."

"We'll take the utility tunnels until we come to an opening to the depths. This level closest to the street is probably not seventeenth century. Where's your compass?" he asked.

Annja leaned close and placed the pommel on top of the map, to verify the markings she had already made. They had a basic idea where on the map they had descended. The cheese shop was but a few blocks west from Val-de-Grâce.

"What an appropriately macabre place for the queen to leave a treasure," she said.

Of course, the aqueducts and underground passages had been utilized to transport criminals, or the occasional king who wished to avoid persecution by his starving subjects. Had Louis XVI gone under during the Fronde, would he and his queen, Marie Antoinette, have kept their heads? Probably not. Entombed prematurely in a graveyard of tunnels seemed the more likely result.

"What do you think so far?" Ascher said as he began to walk.

"Too soon to ask. You've spent a lot of time down here?"

"I've been in the catacombs, beyond the small portion that is marked out for tourist consumption."

"How'd you manage that? Or do I even want to know?"

"It's all about who you know and what year wine you bring as a bribe."

"I see. I didn't bring the cheese-maker wine."

"No, but I give his son fencing lessons on the weekends. Have for years. The boy is entering junior competitions this year. I believe he will do well."

"You like teaching fencing or the kids more?"

"Both. I enjoy watching a young mind grasp a concept and growing with it. Children are much more malleable than adults, open to new ideas, but as well, they are more determined. Eager for a challenge."

"Ascher, I do believe you've just impressed me."

"What about you, Annja? Are there children in your future?"

Now, that question was too left field to even consider.

"Let's get moving, Vallois."

"*Oui.*" He walked ahead. "We should pay attention to where we are going."

Like leaving a trail of cheese crumbs?

"I've got an idea." Annja swung down her backpack and dug out her digital camera. "This way we won't attract any rats."

"Ah, yes. We can take pictures at each turn. I will point in the direction for our return."

"Pose," she said.

Ascher did pose, knees bent and cocky French smile. He pointed back the way they'd walked. Annja snapped a shot.

Together, the twosome turned to the left, orienting themselves, and comparing their position against Ascher's handheld compass. It took a few moments, each of them tracing their fingers over the laminated map and guessing at their position, when they finally decided on a point of origin.

"We shouldn't have too far to go," Annja said.

"Horizontally. We've yet to go vertically," Ascher pointed out.

"Lead on, then. I'm not getting any younger."

"You are young and beautiful," he said.

"And you, I'm keeping an eye on. I want to find that treasure and get out of here."

"You don't like spending time with me in a dark, romantic cave?"

"Buddy, if this is your idea of romantic, I can tell you right now, we've got no future."

"Come along." He made to put an arm around her shoulder, but Annja walked forward, leading the way.

"I'm very romantic," he said. "You haven't seen anything yet, baby."

Annja rolled her eyes at his attempt to Americanize the moniker of "baby," and quickened her pace over what was becoming rougher terrain. The ceiling had lowered about half a foot, leaving about a hand's width of space between it and her head.

Thankfully, they'd yet to find water. That could only mean dank, stinking sewer water. And possibly rats. Rats she could handle. But she wouldn't be disappointed by their absence. There were still miles of caves to explore.

"Mr. Romantic," she muttered, finding the sound of her voice a comfort. "Like stealing a girl's treasure map is so romantic. Must be I don't understand a Frenchman's charm."

"It wasn't so much that I wanted to steal it from you. You're too pretty to want to hurt—" Ascher knelt and tapped an iron slab.

"And yet you did steal it," Annja said.

"Self-preservation," he explained. "Snap a shot of this, Annja."

She did so, and he posed pointing in the direction they had walked, and would want to walk when they needed to back-track to get out of there.

He lifted the iron, which appeared more a door, and flashed the light down inside.

"Hold this." He handed her the light, slid his legs into the shaft and lowered himself in a lunge, until he hung by his fin-gertips. He dropped. A few seconds passed before Annja heard him hit ground. "Come on, Annja!"

Flashing the light, it flicked across his face. It was probably a good ten feet straight down. The walls behind him were rough-hewn stone.

Ascher called to her again. Peering down the hole, she saw he made a beckoning gesture with a hand.

"Catch!" she called, and dropped her backpack.

The tunnel she knelt in grew dark as a starless sky. Annja couldn't see her hand before her face. For that split second she became aware of the gravity of this excursion. Should their batteries run out, they would be lost.

Below, the sweep of the headlight beam reassured.

The leap left her stumbling to right herself against the wall, until a warm hand slid around her stomach and pulled her upright.

"Okay?" he asked.

"Of course."

Ascher shoved the backpack into her hands, and then adjusted her headlamp. "There are cata-cops all over. And there's a hefty fine if you're caught down here," he warned.

"You know quite a bit about the seedy underbelly of the city." She followed as Ascher started one way then stopped. "I guess that shouldn't surprise me, you being a thief and all."

"Will I ever live that down?"

"I'll drop it. I'm not one to hold a grudge," she said.

He stepped into a dark pathway that ran north and south. The tunnel was narrow, so that two could not walk side by side, but the ceiling was much higher, which gave a claustrophobic-like atmosphere, yet whispered cool air over the crown of her head.

Annja snapped a picture. "Look there." She beamed her light onto a plaque that had been cast in stone. It read in French:

Crazy that you are, why
Do you promise yourself to live
A long time, you who cannot
Count on a single day.

"Just what I needed to read." Annja studied the map to avert the creepy shudder the poem had stirred in her. "The map is crinkled here. Difficult to tell without smoothing it, and that's impossible because someone laminated it."

"You Americans and your implied anger." Ascher took off to the right, and didn't bother to wait for her.

For a moment, Annja stood there in the junction, headlamp beam not illuminating Ascher's path. There was something so wrong about the man, and yet, so utterly right.

She liked spending time with him. He met every challenge this adventure had presented with head-on glee. And despite a character flaw of thievery—which Annja must admit was induced by the threat of death—he was genuinely charming. He'd been overly flirtatious with her online, but now, the man beneath the cyber surface had risen to shine. She would definitely miss the man after they'd completed their quest.

Ascher made a sound. And it wasn't a good one. Most similar to losing one's breath. Having it choked away?

"Ascher?"

21

Seventeenth century

Blazing torchlight crept along the ceiling of the low limestone tunnel. Ribald laughter and feminine giggles hit the dull stone and dropped the echo immediately.

Pressing a lace-trimmed handkerchief to his perspiring brow, François Mansart turned to face his merry brigade of revelers and threw out his arms in declaration. "To the queen!"

"To the queen!" they shouted out behind him.

A particularly buxom maiden stumbled into François. Her bosom crushed against his arm and he dipped his head to kiss her right there. She let out a squeal, tinged with wine and lust. He scooped her up closer, waded his fingers through layers of voluminous fabric and gave her derriere a squeeze.

"Watch those torches!" another maid shouted from behind him.

The queen's maid. A perfectly staunch and lacking-in-humor bit of lace and overtightened stays. She hadn't cracked a grin since they'd entered the darkened underground tunnel, nor had she taken a drop of wine or beer.

"Can we hurry onward?" she said to François, pushing past him and becoming entangled in the skirts of the wench he held. "I desperately want out from here!"

"Yes, yes, I wish you gone, as well."

Queen Anne had designated the uptight wench as her personal envoy to the cache she wished placed in the tunnel. Just behind her two of the queen's footmen carried a chest about the size of a footstool, and locked with a brass mechanism.

He could only imagine what lay inside. Many more times the small gift he'd been given for drafting a map to this elusive hiding spot. He suspected Anne sought to hide her affairs from Cardinal Mazarin. The Italian had a leering eye always focused on the queen. François pitied her.

Mazarin had played his own cruel game against François, recently accusing him of wild extravagance and machinations against the crown. He wasn't sure how much longer he'd have the Val-de-Grâce project should the king be swayed to side with the cardinal.

So he'd agreed to help the queen. She wasn't a critical political ally, but she did have the king's ear. Anne had not given details, beyond that she wished it safely hidden away, but findable. And yet, the find must be a quest, not easily gained.

François had gotten the notion to tuck away the treasure after the miserable experience constructing the cathedral. It was still under construction. They'd only completed reinforcing the tunnels beneath the building site a fortnight earlier. Dirty, sweaty work. That he could determine. François was merely the architect.

"Look there! A macabre temple of death!"

Half of the revelers split from François and veered right,

into the small chamber he'd noted the previous week. Completely lined in skulls and femurs, a sort of makeshift temple had been erected. He suspected unsavory sorts used it for devil worship. He'd detected candle wax and perhaps a drop of blood on the surface of the stone dais. He'd leave the drunken party to it.

Hugging the amorous wench to his side, he proceeded onward after the queen's maid. Perhaps after the treasure had been laid, he could convince the woman to loosen up her stays and put caution aside.

Two wenches, one for each hand. Now that stirred his appetites.

Present day

ANNJA DASHED DOWN the passageway, bending as the stone ceiling angled a sudden lurch downward. Rubble on the floor consisted of pebbles, chunks of rough limestone fallen from the wall and the occasional bone. Putting aside dread—because the adventure was far too thrilling—she climbed a steep rise, and then the pathway tilted down forty-five degrees.

Momentum moving her briskly, her headlamp glittered across two sets of eyes.

Two men shouted French obscenities as they struggled with one another. Ascher's backpack slammed against the floor at Annja's rubber boots. His helmet followed. A beam of light glared up into her face.

From what she could determine, the other guy was young, a teenager, and had long dreadlocked hair. Definitely not a cata-cop. But then, what did she know? Maybe the police tried to blend with the underground life.

He clawed at Ascher with dirty fingers and kneed him in the thigh. No, policemen did not act like that.

Sliding her hand inside Ascher's backpack, Annja pulled out the folded leaf dagger she'd noticed earlier and opened it up. Using caution—she would allow Ascher to handle this one, as long as he was able—she kept a keen eye on the action. If the boy was high on drugs, he could possess remarkable strength, and may not feel his injuries as Ascher would.

Ascher delivered a punch below the kid's rib cage. A kidney shot. The boy bounced against the limestone wall behind him, arms splayed out. Annja's headlamp highlighted the track marks littering his inner arms. With a growling sneer, the kid barreled right back into Ascher.

It was plain to Annja that Ascher was doing his best not to harm the boy—who now appeared much younger than her original guess, perhaps only fifteen or sixteen.

They exchanged oaths and the kid declared Ascher a dirty cockroach, the epitome of French curses.

This was getting nowhere fast.

Removing her lighted headgear and nestling it into Ascher's backpack so it spotlighted the brawl, Annja waited as the two struggled. Finally the boy's back spun to her.

She jumped, hooking her arms over his shoulders, and clamping her thighs around his hips for hold. The boy slammed her back against the curved dirt wall. Annja choked on falling bits of dirt and stone.

Dagger firmly in hand, she had the sense not to use it. She could cut him fatally. And how to get emergency help down here? But she had dislodged the attacker from Ascher.

"It is you who attracts this danger to me!" Ascher hissed. And then he chuckled.

Adrenaline flushing his system made his eyes wild with

menace. Dancing like a prize fighter from foot to foot, he wound up and then punched the boy in the gut. The force banged the kid's head back into Annja's throat. Breath chuffed from her lungs.

"Me?" She let her hand fall and poked the dagger into the boy's thigh. He fell to his knees and Annja slunk away. "You're the bad-luck charm, Frenchman."

The boy beat at his bleeding thigh and fisted a mad gesture at Annja. She wielded the dagger before her in a threatening move. She jumped to dodge the kid's spit.

Ascher leaned in and with one good punch knocked the kid's lights out. He knelt there, momentarily frozen, and then dropped forward onto his face.

"Toxico," Ascher said. He toed the kid's shoulder. "Drug addict."

"It's the drugs that make him so violent," Annja said. "It's not his fault. I didn't cut him too deeply, did I?"

"A flesh wound," Ascher said after he'd examined it. "He could have killed you."

"I could have killed him."

"But you did not." Ascher swiped a palm across his face. Adrenalized from the challenge, he bounced still, ready for more action.

"He was more a threat to himself than us," Annja said.

She replaced her helmet. Rolling her shoulder forward worked at an ache in her shoulder blade. She'd hit the wall hard, but didn't sense any injuries. "I want to put some distance between us and him. If we're lucky, your cata-cops will get to him before he wakes. What?"

"Miss Creed, you do not cease to amaze me."

She followed his glance to the kid sprawled in the darkness. "Not only are you talented in standing against thugs with guns, and accomplishing *parkour* at the drop of a hat, but you seem to slip from danger like a rat and can protect yourself with your physical prowess, as well. What can't you do, Annja? Tell me, because you put me to shame with your talents."

"There are a lot of things I can't do," she said.

"You must name one. Please, anything to make me feel as if there's the smallest need for my presence should danger again strike."

She cast a small smile to the side so his headlight wouldn't beam upon it. He desperately needed to gain some macho points, and not appear as someone who needed to be rescued by a woman.

Annja wasn't about false confidence. The man was an athlete. He'd had a bad bit of luck with the drug addict. Toeing the rounded ball end of what was possibly a femur, she decided tossing him a bone wasn't entirely beneath her.

"I can't hit a baseball to save my life."

Ascher perked, but a smile didn't quite curve his mouth.

"I don't know the first thing about engines and cars," she added. "I like to drive them, but how to fix them? Forget it."

"I'll take that," he said. Bending to retrieve his supplies, he managed a wink in her direction as he slapped on his helmet.

Annja walked onward, digital camera ready for another navigational picture. "Do you hear that?"

Ascher swiped a hand over his face. Blood trickled from his nose, which he wiped away with the back of his hand. "Music?"

"Not far ahead."

"Be careful, Annja. If the kid came from wherever the music is—"

"Could be an underground rave," she finished, and marched onward.

Around the corner and shuffling through a narrow tunnel

three feet in diameter, the twosome came upon a huge sheet of plastic draped over an opening about ten feet high by four feet wide. Red-and-green lights flashed on the other side in rhythm to an erratic techno beat that lost its tone in the thick earth walls and did not carry beyond a muffled base thump.

Annja approached slowly, and peeked through the dirty plastic sheeting. The room was narrow and dark, save for the flashing lights. Dancing bodies packed the contained area. Fists rose high to pump in time with the beat. Sloshes of alcohol from plastic cups sprinkled the crowd. Most heads were shaved bald. Combat attire and the flash of blades at hip, ankle and torso cautioned her.

"Looks like all men," she whispered.

The warmth of Ascher's body pressed alongside Annja's arm as he peered in along with her. "Supremacists. You don't want to go in there, Annja."

"Aryans?"

"*Oui.* Not a crowd you want to introduce yourself to." Ascher tugged her away from the plastic sheeting and pressed her against the wall. "We're going this way."

"I don't think so."

A new voice spoke. Annja recognized it instantly.

22

"You are a difficult woman to track, Mademoiselle Creed."

"Oh yeah?" The sight of Jacques Lambert's face sent Annja's heart plummeting. Though she hadn't entirely ruled out being tracked. "Apparently not difficult enough."

"I employ the best trackers in the country. We've been on your trail since the cheese shop."

Annja sucked in a breath. She prayed the owner and his wife were unharmed.

"And Monsieur Vallois." Jacques Lambert nodded to Ascher, the headlight beam catching him under the nose and momentarily spookifying him. "You guard that right side well, eh?"

"I do not like you," Ascher growled.

And Annja had to agree. But for the moment she was more concerned about taking in the periphery. Beyond the immediate glow of the flashlights and headbeams, she counted six men, suited in overalls and night-vision goggles. Each wielded a semiautomatic with a tiny red blinking LED at the stock.

"You will do the honor of leading the way," Lambert said to Annja. "Unless you wish to attend the party?"

The raucous vibrations of the techno beat warned Annja there may be worse trouble behind the plastic sheeting than Lambert and his men may offer.

"We've not completely deciphered the map," she offered. "We're still tracking it, taking odd turns and coming up against dead ends. There are ten times more tunnels now than there were in the seventeenth century."

"I'm in no hurry," Lambert said, before turning to one of his men. "But you'll do me the privilege of holding the weapon Monsieur Vallois has in his boot?"

Ascher bent and took out the blade. It was the one Annja had lost when they'd battled the drugged-up teenager. He dangled it, tip down, and one of the dark goons lunged from behind Lambert to swipe it.

"And what of you, Annja Creed?"

She met Lambert's eerie gaze. "I don't have any weapons."

"Visible," he said.

He'd seen her use the sword in the file room. It was on the surveillance tape. A tape she should be keen to get at. The last thing she needed was a leak to the press that one of the stars of *Chasing History's Monsters* might herself be a monster who wielded a magical sword. Wouldn't Doug Morrell have a heyday with that?

Briefly, she wondered if Roux might be able to infiltrate BHDC to steal the tape. The man had certain skills that continued to befuddle her, yet she would utilize them whenever she could.

"You can search me," she offered, holding her arms out to her sides. "If it'll make you feel better."

"Not necessary," he said, though the same goon who'd

stepped forward for Ascher's knife had already stepped up to cop a free feel. "Step back, Theo. Let's be to it."

AN HOUR LATER, and after passing through many, twisting tunnels, Annja wondered if they were completely lost. They'd descended another thirty or forty feet deeper through makeshift steps and holes that literally dropped from one dark realm to the next. If they hadn't had the map, she might grow old and die down here. Cataphiles could add her bones to the walls. She would become a literal fixture in Parisian history.

A discomfiting thought.

And if she were not holding the map, she might wonder if Ascher was leading them astray. There were moments they both studied the map and he suggested a direction completely opposite to where Annja felt they should go. Yet she deferred to his knowledge; he had the most experience in the Paris underground.

She took comfort having Ascher close, and trusted he did not ally himself with BHDC. He may not necessarily be on her side, but he did want the same thing she wanted—to keep the treasure out of Lambert's hands.

The air grew thicker the farther down they traveled. Annja could feel the icy darkness out to her side, where her headlamp did not beam.

She wanted to find the treasure and get the hell out of here. A goose chase in this hellacious labyrinth was not tops on her list.

Their next pause, at a T in the tunnels, found her and Ascher disagreeing about yet another turn.

Was he purposefully agreeing to go on a course he knew was wrong?

"Oh, stop it," she murmured under her breath. She had decided to trust Ascher. Enough said.

They passed through tunnels nearly fifty feet wide and twelve feet high. These had been used during the German occupation when Hitler had driven tanks below to hide or ambush.

They bent and shuffled through tunnels three feet high and no wider.

When Ascher suggested they squeeze through a tunnel about a foot square, Lambert adamantly refused. Though it would have served a means for their escape, Annja was more than a little relieved. Not her favorite way to die, entombed within a worm tunnel like a giant, well, worm.

Not that she hadn't been in equally tight squeezes when on digs. She'd been trapped in a sandy trench dug into Highborough Hill when doing a segment on the Saxon deities for *Chasing History's Monsters*. Good thing she wasn't truly claustrophobic. But then she'd had a crew of trusted colleagues to help her out of trouble.

Now it was every man for himself.

They had been underground almost three hours. Ascher had said the batteries would last for six. Or should. Annja crossed her fingers on that one.

They now walked a narrow tunnel lined in yellowed skulls and leg bones. The stacked bones were placed in a definite pattern. Three rows of leg bones, the ball-like lateral and medial condyles pointing out to form a knobby line, and then a row of skulls, most facing outward to display empty eye sockets, and the occasional disturbing hole in the forehead that, Annja decided, could only be from a sharp weapon. It was possible these were from a former cemetery.

Running her fingers lightly over the cold, smooth bones, Annja fancied which ones might have been soldiers and had given their lives for their country. Or were most victims of a cruel plague or unclean living conditions? A particular skull, still with all its teeth, grimaced at her.

There was something scratched into the limestone. She flashed her light over it. The date 1670 was very clear, but the mark below it was not. A circle with an indistinguishable letter inside it. A stonecutter's mark. Cool. She snapped a picture.

"Perhaps we are beneath Saint Ignace," Ascher suggested softly. "It must be, to judge from our turns and the distance we've walked."

"Which arrondissement?"

"Saint Ignace is in the seventh. A small but gorgeous church," he said. "Can you smell the quicklime?"

It had been poured over the rotting bodies to extinguish the putrid smell, and though at the time they hadn't known it would kill germs, it had.

So they were in the seventh. One of the ritzier neighborhoods in Paris, it boasted the Eiffel Tower. Interestingly, its high-class status was not apparent from beneath. But they had to be close; this was where she and Ascher had determined the treasure might be found.

The tunnel they traversed ended abruptly at a wall of skulls. A design had been worked with the bones of former Parisian residents. A large circle, two skulls thick in outline, expanded about five feet in diameter before them, and filling in the non-circle parts were thousands of femurs. In the center of the heart was a small plaque.

"Did we take a wrong turn?" Lambert wondered. He commandeered the map and swept the flashlight over it. The beam flickered.

"You're running out of juice," Ascher said slyly.

"We've got reserves." Lambert was quick to cut him off.

"It appears as if the end, the glorious *X* marks the spot, is ahead. Through that wall."

"This could be a new addition created by stray bones. The cataphiles are always putting up new walls and tearing down old ones," Ascher noted. "They haul cement blocks and jackhammers down here." He tapped the wall of bone before him.

Annja leaned against the wall and listened, as Ascher did, while he tapped. "No, it's original. These skulls are tight and the debris solid, like mortar," she said.

"Very possible. For as old as these tunnels are, they could contain any number of blocked-up passages. Either by necessity or because they were dangerous."

Annja brushed her fingers over the plaque, which was thick with dust. There was something engraved on it.

Their heads turned away from the intrusive flashlights over their shoulders, Ascher whispered, "As soon as we get the treasure, we will overtake them, *oui?*"

"Seven against two. I like those odds."

"I like a woman who can get behind those odds."

"What's the holdup?" Lambert called. "Push it down!"

"There's a plaque," Annja said.

She bent before the small piece of stone and beamed her flashlight over the small French words. *Selon Mes Mérites.* Hmm… "As I deserve?" she whispered.

An appropriate saying for anyone who may have found a treasure, but not for a treasure left behind. Her heart sank. They were too late. Or this was the wrong *X* marks the spot.

"Perhaps we should retrace our footsteps," Annja offered. She beamed her headlamp down the direction they had come. The sandy floor glinted with fine mica particles as if crushed diamonds. "We may have taken a wrong turn."

"You're not looking at all the options," Lambert said.

"Which are?"

"Break down the wall."

"I will not damage a historical structure," Annja said. "Such destruction is worse than theft and piracy."

Lambert looked to one of his men.

The man with shoulders as solid as a Mack truck, took a bouncing step back, prepared, and as he lunged forward, Annja dashed in to push him away. "Are you insane? You will destroy history!"

"Annja, be careful," Ascher warned.

Lambert beamed his flashlight down the passageway. "You don't think the ravers we passed haven't destroyed enough already?"

"Bloody pirate," she spit out.

"Mad Bloody Jack thanks you kindly, *mademoiselle*."

Why she was allowing herself to get so worked up must have something to do with being entombed for hours under duress, she thought. Annja kicked the rubble-littered floor with her heel.

"Do whatever," she snapped.

Lambert lifted a hand and gestured. "Theo!"

Another of the thugs charged the wall, and this time Annja allowed it. It was either that or more arguing, which would only result in her defeat.

The thug bent up a knee and connected with the wall of skulls, foot flat and thick heel of a combat boot torquing to dig into any give that may result.

While the entire wall didn't come crumbling down, the force of the impact did push in two skulls and dislodge the plaque. The flat stone piece teetered forward and fell.

Compelled to rush for the piece, Annja missed catching it. It didn't break upon landing the dirt floor. Small thanks for that.

Musty quicklime dust scented the air. It was a familiar smell to Annja, that of ancient times best regarded with reverence and not the blatant disregard Lambert inflicted with his greed.

Icy cold air gushed from the enclosed section of tunnel, streaming over Annja's nose and cheeks. Angry ghosts of history.

If only.

As Theo dragged himself upright and brushed off his hands, another thug began to pull out the skulls.

"Careful," Lambert instructed from over their shoulders. "One wrong skull and the whole thing could come down."

"Isn't that what you want?" Annja asked.

"Not if it's connected to a wall we need to get back out of here."

"Let me do it." Annja shoved aside the thug. She might be able to limit the destruction some. Fitting her fingers through two eyeholes, she carefully rocked at an ancient skull. "I'm going to hell for this."

"They are long dead," Lambert said over her shoulder. "Their souls don't care what you do with their bones now."

He'd said something similar about stealing DNA from dead historical figures. The man was utterly mad. He thought he was serving mankind, but instead he destroyed it.

"You should respect the dead, no matter their state," Annja muttered, and proceeded to carefully extract the skulls.

The actual wall was only three skulls thick, equal to the length of the femurs, which were tightly stacked about the skull circle. Once Annja removed the skulls that curved along the top of the circle, the femurs loosened, and the structure slowly collapsed.

She jumped back to avoid the dust of centuries' dead.

A warm hand gripped her arm from behind. She didn't startle, because the touch wasn't rough. Ascher silently conveyed his presence. And she took some relief in his being there. Not completed surrounded by the enemy, then. But a little lost as to what would happen next.

And what if there was a treasure? That would mean she and Ascher no longer held value to Lambert. And a tunnel full of bones was the last place Annja wanted to die.

Lambert leaned inside the hole and poked in a flashlight. He popped back out and handed Annja the flashlight. "Ladies first. It's a small room, about four feet long by three feet high."

"I'd rather watch." Annja crossed her arms firmly. She'd gone to the limits with helping these crooks.

Lambert nodded to one of his men. He moved swiftly, wrapping an arm about Ascher's neck in a chokehold. Shoving the barrel of his weapon into his left side elicited a pained moan from Ascher. The side where he'd lost a kidney a few weeks earlier.

Regarding her calmly, Lambert said softly. "I was unable to uncover relatives or close allies who would mean something to you, Annja. But I suspect Vallois should serve to prick a personal nerve or two."

"Give me the damn flashlight." Annja grabbed it from Lambert and stepped through the hole. Coffin-like and musty, the surroundings were familiar, and yet this was the first time she'd been inside a room completely constructed of bones.

Lambert's head popped inside her hiding spot. "Your lover awaits your victory, my warrior Creed."

"He's not my lover."

"You often kiss friends so passionately?"

When had she—? The only time she and Ascher had—

Had there been spies in the hotel? How could they have witnessed that kiss without—they must have been observing through the window with a sniper scope.

Damn. That Lambert had knowledge of her every move disturbed her on a level she couldn't even comprehend.

Ignoring her silent horror, Lambert slid inside the nook and nestled his body close, his thigh fitting against hers. "So, what do we have here?"

She hated that this awful man knew so much about her every move.

"Seems a secret room," she commented. "Possibly it was bricked up with the skulls shortly after the treasure was hidden here. Of course, the plaque dates to the wrong century."

"We've come to the *X* on the map—or rather, the fleur-de-lis. It's the right place," Lambert said.

"I can't imagine why Mansart would make it so difficult."

"Ah, you hit on the Mansart connection."

"Thanks to your map."

"Glad to be of assistance. You are keen and perceptive. You know, Annja, we would work well together."

"I don't work for madmen."

"Ouch."

She tried to move her leg away from his, but there was nowhere else to put it.

Annja scanned the room, lined with skeletons. Like a tiny cove that might have once been designed as a rest stop within the greater labyrinth? The tenor of her heartbeat grew more apparent. The air, a mixture of dirt particles and desiccated bone dust, formed a cloud at the back of her throat. Muffling. Not a place she wanted to stay in too long.

Most especially not with Jacques Lambert crouching too close for comfort.

"Wouldn't it have been easier to place the treasure below the Louvre," she wondered aloud, "in the aqueducts?"

"Very busy waterways, those aqueducts. Especially in the

seventeenth and eighteenth centuries. I've no idea, myself, why the great secrecy and ridiculous treasure hunt, but obviously someone wanted to make it difficult. Perhaps so the reward might be appreciated all the more?"

Annja sighed and pressed the back of her head against the wall of skulls. Her eyes circling the space, she tried to envision a drunken crew of musketeers tramping about beneath the city, oil lamps held high and boisterous laughter echoing off the stone walls. It would have been an adventure that should have appealed to d'Artagnan. And perhaps that was what the queen intended.

Lambert slapped her thigh. "This is cozy, *oui?*"

"Take your hand off me."

He gave her leg a squeeze before clasping his hands together about his knees.

"Let me see that map again," she said.

If there were any place that might have an *X* on it, this little nook had to be it.

"I'm surprised at you," Lambert said with a snap of his finger against the map. "Lamination? That's not very proper for an archaeologist, is it?"

"Implanting cloned embryos in unassuming mothers' wombs. That's not very proper for a geneticist, is it?"

"Touché. But I wager you think you know something that isn't at all what it really is."

"I guess differently. Explain the pregnant women in you waiting room?"

"I cannot. Not to you. To explain genetic engineering would make your head spin."

"I got me some learning in college. I can even balance my checkbook. Try me."

"Annja." A tilt of his head flashed a bright beam of light into her face, so he pushed back his helmet to sit at the back f his head. The headlamp splashed light across the ceiling f their intimate cove. "As I've already attempted to explain, BHDC offers a very particular service. We trace genetics and amily bloodlines through DNA. Most useful in providing roof for claims to family fortunes and treasure."

"That you then swoop in to steal," Annja said.

"As any good pirate would, my dear."

"I don't get you, Lambert. All this for what?"

He sighed and adjusted his position so he sat in a half turn oward Annja. "All I have ever done in my life has been only or my brother."

"Your brother?"

"My twin. He died when I was seven."

"And you think you can bring him back by cloning him?"

"Not at all. It would not be my brother, but a physical copy f him. Mentally, the cloned version would be his own person."

"Then I don't understand."

"Had technology been more advanced thirty years ago, the medical community might have been able to grow a new liver or my brother instead of allowing him to suffer and die because y family hadn't the money to pay for a replacement."

"People can't actually buy replacement livers, can they? Most certainly not thirty years ago," Annja said.

"Technology can do remarkable things, Annja. But no, hen we were children, sadly the technological advances ere few. Yet, even when I got the money for an operation my ther said Toby had to wait on the list. The list! Do you know ow long donation lists are? To land at the top of a donor list an take years. Sometimes those waiting for a donated organ ever get them. The recipient might die before it happens."

"But it's how things are. Did you expect your brother could mp to the top of the list with money?"

"I was only seven, Annja. I expected the world."

"But you know better now."

Or perhaps not. The man's eyes managed to widen and reduce him to a mere boy, staring helplessly at her, awaiting a dream he could never have. Losing a sibling at so young an age must have irreversibly altered his logic.

"We are not God," Annja said. "Accidents and disease while tragic, happen for a reason. Maybe we shouldn't be so quick to fix everything? It is the way the world is."

"But it doesn't have to be that way." Dropping the little-boy facade, and clenching a fist, Lambert's tone grew sharper. "Therapeutic cloning is a remarkable science. Kidneys can be cloned. Livers, the spleen and skin grafts and bone marrow for implanting. No longer should there be a requirement for a *list*."

"I can understand your heartbreak. I really can." Annja realized she'd placed her hand on his knee. The urge to snap it away was more fleeting than her understanding. "And I can see the value of therapeutic cloning. But that doesn't justify human cloning. There is no medical necessity to cloning a human being. It's illegal for a reason."

"It is a natural progression from the therapeutic cloning. It is the future, Annja. Just think of the factories we could populate with worker drones. We'd no longer have to rely on immigrants and overseas alliances."

"That's—" Twisted, she thought.

"Cloning will prove a big moneymaker. You can't imagine the funds our research sucks up."

"I can't and I won't. There's only one way to create life and that's as it should be. Besides, thus far you've only destroyed life and will continue to do so. You must stop."

"Every new technology takes much experimentation to get things right."

The evidence of which had been documented in the files back at BHDC.

"How many babies—fully birthed babies—have you destroyed?" she asked angrily.

"You're not a very friendly woman, are you?"

"Answer the question."

Lambert sighed. "I have no idea. Is it so wrong to offer hope to a couple who suffer infertility?"

"Hope? I followed a pregnant woman from BHDC. She was so…excited. She called it a treasure."

"Isn't a child a treasure?"

"You know that baby won't live. Then what happens to their hope?"

"Actually, I don't know that. This could be the time it survives. Our first successful clone. Science is all about trial and error."

"You'd never allow the mother to keep the child," Annja said.

He sighed. He was not about to answer that one.

Annja felt sick to her stomach. She tasted dirt in her mouth. A fine perspiration riddled her hairline. Time was going away fast.

"I seek only to right wrongs that could have been avoided," he said softly.

She felt him settle against the wall beside her. Relaxing. Not a bad position for her enemy to be in. Though she couldn't draw out the sword in this tight space.

"I began to pursue therapeutic cloning to honor Toby's death. Genetic cloning naturally followed. I only want to help people, Annja—can't you understand that?"

"Human cloning helps absolutely no one. It only gives false hope to traumatized parents and ill-informed couples with dreams of designing their own children."

"If you were given the choice of birthing a child destined to defects that could incapacitate it for life, or one that was perfect and even possessed of genes designed to combat adult illnesses such as cancers and debilitating disease, which would you choose?"

"I'd take the child God decided should be mine," Annja said.

Lambert chuffed. "You do not strike me as a particularly religious woman, Annja."

There was no sense in arguing with the criminally insane. Nor in defending her latent religious beliefs.

"Hold the flashlight, will you?" She shuffled to her knees.

Starting by pressing her knuckles against the wall above them, Annja felt for any skull that would give.

"Maybe there's a secret-passage skull?" Lambert provided in a macabre tone. "You push it and it opens into the treasure."

"You actually expect we'll find treasure? It's been two and a half centuries. If there's one copy of the map, there may be others."

The small tinkle of a cell phone alerted Annja. "You actually get service down here?"

"Surprising. We must be close to a buried electrical line." Lambert flipped open his phone and spoke. "Yes?" A pause. He looked to Annja. Nodding, he replied. "Interesting. And you matched it to the hair sample inside the envelope? The connection is bad. I'll be in touch."

He signed off and shuffled his position, moving a foot up along the wall, so it rested right in front of where Annja had planned to next tap.

"Move your foot. Or wait. Press again, against that skull. Yes, right there."

With pressure from Lambert's boot the skull shattered like smashing open a Christmas cracker.

Eager to see what lay beyond, she peered into the hole. Inside was an obvious shelf, or cache to hide something. But her headlamp didn't beam across shiny gold Louis d'Or coins, or ropes of pearls tangled about glittering diamonds and rubies, and—

"What is it?" Lambert insisted. He nudged closer, trying to get a look, and their heads bonked. "Let me see."

Not about to give up her spot, Annja reached inside and groped around. The nook went back a way. She couldn't feel a wall to end it. "I don't feel anything except dust and rubble."

"Did you find it?" Ascher shouted from outside the nook. His last word was abruptly cut off.

"Call off your goons," Annja said. "Haven't you done the man enough harm already?"

"He is expendable," Lambert said.

"As I am?"

"Your status has recently changed. I'd like to keep you alive. Ever consider working for a biohistorical research company, Mademoiselle Creed? I employ all sorts, including archaeologists and treasure hunters."

"And goons and thugs?"

"Your profession is not so free of criminals as you might believe, Annja."

"I know that. Pirates abound in the archaeological trade. Present company included."

"I thank you for the consideration. No treasure inside?"

She reached inside again, but pressed her cheek aside the wall of skulls, keeping a keen eye to Lambert.

"Maybe someone has already claimed it?" Lambert offered.

"You mean d'Artagnan? He died a pauper. Though it's very possible Alexandre Dumas found it."

"I thought he was quite in debt when he died, as well?"

"Yes, to his partner, Auguste Maquet." She twisted her arm and patted along the ceiling of the small area. "Wait. I feel something. It's a box."

"Maybe a small chest containing diamonds or certificates to land and title and vast riches?"

"To finance your deadly research?"

"It bothers me not at all that you consider me a pirate. It is what I do well, and one should always strive to do that which they excel at."

For a moment, Annja considered doing what she did well—laying men flat with her sword—but the space was too small to move a three-foot-long battle sword, and honestly, she didn't want to kill the man. He deserved to be punished by the legal system. And if attention could be shone on his corrupt experimentation, perhaps policing such a crime would be increased.

Her fingers stretched over what felt like a metal box. It was cool and the curved edges felt ornamental. A thick coating of what could only be dust felt like a pelt of fur. Gripping it, she tugged. Initially it didn't move, but, stretching her arm and squishing her cheek against the wall—make that some medieval villager's bony cheek—she was able to finally pull it free.

"Pull me out," she said to Lambert.

He put an arm around her waist. She hadn't realized how cold she was until she felt the warmth of another hugging her. Lambert pulled her back.

The box, firmly grasped, took out another skull as she tugged it free and settled back against a soft surface to clutch it to her chest.

"This is nice," Lambert commented. "The two of us, alone in the dark."

Annja jabbed an elbow backward, catching him in the ribs. His breath chuffed out across the back of her neck. "There's no lock. I think it'll open easily."

23

Clinging desperately to the box as Lambert tried to tug it away from her, Annja realized she acted much like a child struggling to keep a prize from the bully. So she released the box, and Lambert shuffled out into the tunnel.

Ascher's yelp echoed. Annja crawled from the nook to see her partner in adventure fall to his knees and collapse, arms sprawled before his head. Blood trickled from his skull, but he was moving. His helmet lay on the dirt floor. One of the thugs crushed the headlamp with a thick rubber boot heel.

"You want to walk out of here with me?" Lambert extended a waiting hand to Annja. A twisted messiah of genetically altered future bots, he glowed from the surrounding beams of light.

"Is that some kind of stupid pickup line?"

"Either that or I leave you behind with this one." He toed Ascher's rubber boot. "In the dark."

A glance to the side confirmed her backpack sat untouched where she'd dropped it earlier. But her headlamp was not where she had left it just outside the nook.

"The only darkness I fear is that which shadows your reasoning, Lambert."

"Very poetic," Lambert said. "Maybe you'll get lucky and stumble onto the rave. I'm sure a gorgeous young woman is just the thing to get their aggressive male hormones charged."

"I'll take my chances," Annja said.

"I can sweeten the offer."

"Doubtful."

Lambert noted the abandoned headlamp near the wall just as Annja did. He signaled to one of his men, and again, a vicious stomp crushed out the light. Now only the beams from Lambert's goons crisscrossed the cove they stood in.

He approached Annja slowly, treasure box clutched before his waist.

"Whatever is in there?" Annja prompted. "I'm not interested."

"This? No, this little prize is not up for trade." His approach blocked the light, shadowing his face. Standing toe-to-toe with Annja, he leaned in to whisper beside her cheek. "What say I tell you some surprising information I've learned about your history?"

"My…"

Her history? That she'd been orphaned and had grown up in New Orleans. Hadn't missed the Catholic school she'd attended since the day she'd walked out, yet still thought of Sister Mary Annabelle, who was tough as nails and had taught Annja a sound mind makes for a sound body. That she wasn't much for friendships and doubted she'd ever have time for a real family.

"I prefer a cold, dark, creepy tunnel to your company," she said.

Annja stood before the opening of the nook. Foremost was Ascher's safety. No treasure was worth a man's life.

Lambert leaned in, the box clasped to his chest. "Where

did you get that sword, Annja? The one I saw you draw from out of nowhere in the file room to threaten Theo? Did *she* will it to you? Or…are you she?"

It was chillingly apparent to Annja who Lambert thought *she* was.

"I've got no relatives to will me a thing. And you must have been hallucinating. There are dozens of swords in your office building. You didn't see me steal the one from your display?"

"Why do you lie? To protect that?" He looked to Ascher, still prone, and who groaned but, wisely, didn't make any sudden moves.

"Why do you run, Lambert? You think there's treasure in that box? Open it now and let us all take a look."

"Ha, ha. You are curious." Lambert shook the box near his ear. Nothing rattled from inside. He then pressed it to his cheek. Predatory eyes sought Annja's compliance. "But not curious enough to join me?"

"Guess not." She made show of leaning over Ascher to inspect for wounds.

"What if I make it your only choice?" Lambert snapped a finger. One of his men placed a small-caliber pistol into his waiting palm. "Move aside, Mademoiselle Creed."

He was going to shoot Ascher. And Annja reacted in a different manner than the bearer of Joan's sword should. She threw herself across Ascher, putting her hand on his shoulder and protecting his body with her own.

"Well, that rules out a kill shot. Not to be dissuaded…" Lambert pulled the trigger.

Ascher let out a yelp. His body clenched, but Annja held firm, not about to give Lambert a better target. He must have taken a bullet in the leg, from what she could determine.

"Stupid woman." Lambert gestured to his troops. "Kill him!

Torn from Ascher's prone body, Annja kicked at her attacker's hands and managed to toe a pistol grip and send it flying.

The self-proclaimed pirate called out, "But not her!"

Though she'd been dragged off Ascher, Annja was free for a moment. She lunged backward, her body again landing across Ascher's back. Calling up the sword, she slashed at the first man who dived toward her. The blade tip hooked the edge of his goggles and tore them from his face.

A gun fired. The bullet ricocheted with a dull ping. One of the men hissed to be cautious, Lambert wanted her alive.

Lambert fled with two men in tow. That left four for Annja. She liked those odds.

"Play dead," she whispered in English to Ascher, and then flipped herself upright to stand before her challengers.

Four beams of light danced over her. Her sword glinted brightly. While they vacillated in a plan of action, Annja leaped forward, slicing across the upper thighs of two of the men who stood close together.

They went down, while another gunshot echoed in the close confines of the tunnel. An ancient skull near her feet took the bullet and shattered in a spray of bone and dust.

Another shot was fired. One of the thugs dropped.

Annja glanced to where Ascher lay, but he'd moved. He'd crawled to sit up along the wall. He had fired the shot from an abandoned pistol.

But now he'd brought attention to his position, and all light beams shifted to the wounded Frenchman by the wall.

Annja spun and, using an outstretched arm to torque up her speed, she hit the first man, who bled from the thighs. The impact was hard. She chuffed out her breath. The man toppled and his body plowed down the other two next to him.

"Always did have a knack for dominoes," Annja muttered.

The wounded man twisted at the waist and gripped Annja's ankle.

She drew her sword across his wrist, slicing to the bone. Another shot sounded and one of the headlamps blinked out. A shot for Ascher. Good aim. So the Gascon did have a knack for self-preservation.

The remaining unwounded thug ran down the passageway in the direction they had come.

She knew she should go after him, but she was more concerned with Ascher's wound. Retrieving the pistol from the man who was still alive and sprawled at her feet, she checked the magazine. Empty. She tossed the gun into the nook where the box had been found.

At that moment, the headlamp on the fallen thug's helmet blinked out. The darkness held a lingering flash of gray until her eyes adjusted.

Annja looked in the direction of the passage. She could still see the headlamp on their fleeing thug bobbing along the walls.

"We don't have much time," she said.

Remembering his position, she plunged to the floor where Ascher sat, and immediately found the wound, even in the blinding darkness.

Ascher swore.

A bullet had entered his thigh above his knee. And there an exit wound. It was a clean shot. The small-caliber bullet hadn't torn up too much flesh. The knee was still functional. And it hadn't hit an artery, for the blood did not gush. But still required immediate attention.

As the light swiftly faded, Annja tore at her T-shirt. ripped up the center, which wasn't what she was going for. was impossible to remove a strip from around the bottom. S she shucked off her jacket, and removed the shirt. The chill cave air tickled across her bare flesh.

"Are you getting naked for me?" Ascher wondered weakly.

"Not important right now, buddy."

She sensed his head nodded. Perhaps he was losing consciousness.

Tying the shirt tight over the wound would staunch the flow of blood. But in the dark, she could only fumble about and likely do more damage than good.

Tugging on her jacket and zipping it up, she then slapped Ascher's face. "Stay awake. We've got to move. Now. While I can still track the light. Ascher!"

The distant light blinked out. The man must have turned a corner.

Had Annja not been touching Ascher she might have panicked. Even the most experienced spelunkers and cave explorers cannot deny the feeling of doom that seems to squeeze their heart should they suddenly find themselves entombed in utter blackness.

Drawing in a breath through her nose, Annja pressed a palm over her heartbeats. Thudding like horse hooves on dirt.

"Do not panic," she said. The sound of her own voice pushed away some of the apprehension.

She dived for her backpack to Ascher's right, and shuffled through it. The digital camera chirped on, but switching it to view mode didn't provide the ambient light she had hoped for. Without a flashlight or headlamp they were in trouble.

"Annja…" Ascher moaned, the echoes bouncing off the curved stone walls.

"Are you okay?" Stupid question. "I've bandaged your leg. Doesn't feel like an artery was hit. Can you walk? We need to move."

"Leave me. I'm…dying."

"You are so not dying." She pushed him up against the wall by the shoulder. "Did they stab you in the other kidney?"

"No."

"Then you're walking out of here."

"Annja, I'll slow you down. It hurts terribly. You. Go." He gripped her forearm, rather firmly for a dying man. But then, what did she know about stuff like that? "Just…come closer, Annja. I need…to say something."

"Say it." She leaned closer until she felt his huffing breaths upon her cheek. "Then we're out of here."

"Will you…kiss a man before he dies?"

Still flirting even when he may be bleeding out. This was one hell of a Frenchman.

"You are not dying. And the faster we get you help, the more chance we have of saving the leg."

"Saving the— I'm hit?"

"You don't feel it?" Annja asked.

That meant he could be going into shock. Annja swung another open-palm slap through the darkness and connected with his skull. "Stay alert, Frenchman. And let me help you up. They've taken the flashlights, but I still have the camera."

"You want to photograph my death?"

"Don't be morbid, Vallois."

"No, you leave me. Go! It is far better than life, knowing I was not able to defend your honor."

"Now you're starting to sound like one of Dumas's musketeers."

"You see? I am delirious. Death creeps slowly over my eyelids."

"Give me a break. And don't touch the wound. Your hands are dirty. We need to keep it clean as possible."

"I will die before the infection kills me."

"I could pee on it," Annja said.

"You—what? Annja, I don't want you to—"

"That makes two of us. But urine is a great disinfectant. I'll leave that to you. You've got better aim, as it is. Don't worry, Ascher, you'll survive."

Because to confess that she wasn't sure about the wound—if he would bleed out, and not make it to the surface alive—just wasn't in the script.

She leaned in, not seeing his face, but she could smell his sea-breeze aftershave and the salty tang of perspiration. Touching his chin, she drew her fingers up, reading his bloodied and bruised features. They had worked him over while she'd been in the nook with Lambert.

"Annja, what are you doing?"

"If a kiss will get you on your feet, then I'll do it."

So she did. A fast, hard kiss right to his mouth. Any other time, and any other place…

"There. You feeing less death-like?"

Using Annja and the wall, Ascher pushed himself upright. He swayed, but slapped a hand onto her shoulder. "You have revived me. Another?"

"When we hit topside."

"Promise?"

She sighed and hooked an arm across his back to point him in the right direction. "Promise. Now move. I can get us down the path to the turn. From there, I'm hoping we'll see a light."

Annja supported Ascher as he shuffled along beside her. His body weight hung over her right shoulder. He bounced n his good left leg.

"Hurry!"

To his credit, Ascher did scramble. Rushing blindly through the darkness, Annja concentrated on keeping her path straight. The ground was uneven, pocked with cobblestones and loose pebbles, but it didn't trip her up. The camera strap was dangling about her wrist; she wouldn't attempt to use it for light and risk running the batteries low.

She judged the distance from the thug disappearing to be less than one hundred yards. She and Ascher had to have breached half that length. The chill atmosphere began to creep up the back of her neck. Without the clingy cotton T-shirt, the nylon brushing her skin raised goose bumps. She didn't relish wandering about in the darkness. And to run into the rave again was not her idea of a rescue.

It was entirely feasible that a person—even without a grievous gunshot wound—could become disoriented and lost down here. For a very long time. And if lack of direction wasn't enough, total blackness didn't help, either. She figured it wouldn't take long for a person to go mad in such a predicament. Blindly stumbling about, the ruins of cemeteries and bones at their feet.

Slamming into a wall, she let go of Ascher and put up her palms to catch herself from wobbling backward. Ascher slid to the ground beside her, clutching her leg. She didn't step out of his grasp. They must keep contact.

A turn to the left and then the right did not reveal a light. The thug couldn't have gone far. Though it was very possible he could have slipped down a hole to a lower level.

The only way out demanded they go up. And unless an iron ladder leading up to a manhole was close by, the thug would have to trace the same path they'd originally followed. And how could he without a map or the digital pictures she'd held as a lifeline?

Annja closed her eyes, though it seemed pointless in this pitch darkness. She listened. Her heart raced. Breath came quickly.

But there.

Faint echoes of movement. Not a crowd. Maybe a single person.

She bent and felt for Ascher's face. Leaning against his ear, she whispered. "Sit still. Don't move. I'm going ahead. Not far."

"No," he said.

"I won't leave without you," she reassured. Slipping the camera into his hand, she closed his fingers over it. Then she stepped over his legs.

"Annja." His sorrowful cry almost made her turn back.

He'd be fine. With luck, he'd pass out. The pain must be excruciating. Her immediate fear was shock. He was cool, but not alarmingly so. His pulse raced, though. No time must be wasted. Once the body cooled and the victim began to shake—combined with blood loss—shock was not far off.

Stepping slowly, using her left hand to guide her along the cool stone wall, Annja moved through the darkness. It enveloped her so snugly she might be at the bottom of the sea. She recalled they had passed through a few long tunnels before finally landing the treasure. So far she'd only traversed one.

Each step she marked carefully and painstakingly so as not to crunch any loose pebbles and alert anyone who may be listening. She could still hear Ascher's breathing, punctuated with intermittent moans.

Sensing a solid force loomed just ahead, she put out her hand, stopped and listened. No sound. Not breath. Not movement. It had to be a wall. She pressed her palm forward and her fingers splayed across rock dusted with crumbling bits of soil.

And then she heard it. A small click. Metal against metal. Just to her right. She was not alone.

24

Drawing her semiclasped right hand before her, Annja willed the sword out from the otherwhere. It arrived, solid and reassuring in her grip. But she did not draw it *en garde*. Instead, she stood there in the utter darkness, head tilted down and to the right to listen. The sword she held blade pointed toward her feet, elbow slightly crooked.

She grew so silent her own heartbeat thudded loudly in her ears. No good. She had to hear everything.

Drawing in a breath cleared out the thunderous pound of her life, and in that moment, she drew up the sword. A glint of green light flashed on the blade. She ducked, curling her body down and to the right. A bullet just missed her shoulder.

Now the laser green headlight attached to a man's head bobbed wildly as he jumped into view. Annja lunged backward and slipped around the rough-hewn stone corner. He fired twice. Both bullets ricocheted off the wall two feet from her shoulder. Stone chips pinged her cheek.

To her left she heard Ascher swear.

Digging the toe of her rubber boot into the loose rubble, Annja pushed around the corner and slashed the blade once, but blindly. It met resistance. The slither of steel slicing through fabric preceded a cry of pain. Metal clattered across loose pebbles. He'd dropped the pistol.

The headlamp flashed in her eyes, blinding her. Pummeled against the chest, Annja caught the man as he charged her with his fists. Breaths chuffed out. Her shoulders met the wall in a crunch of vertebrae. He gripped her right wrist so she could not control the sword. She released it back to the otherwhere.

The taste of blood swirled on her tongue. She must have bitten her lip when she'd collided with the wall.

Kicking, she managed to knee her aggressor inexpertly, catching the side of his kneecap. It was enough to detach him from her. The headlamp beam zigzagged across the quarried limestone ceiling.

Annja called back her sword, and making swift work on a man she felt would kill her rather than allow her life, she stabbed the double-edged blade into his chest. In the glow of the green light, his body convulsed once, and his muscles relaxed.

Holding the sword hilt with a firm grip, she leaned over and tugged the headlamp from his head. Then she patted him down, claiming a small flashlight from inside his vest pocket and the pistol, which lay near his head. A 9 mm Ruger, it still had two rounds in the clip.

Pulling the headlamp on over her forehead, she then stood. Tugging out the sword from the insistent suction of his flesh, with a sweep of her hand to fling off the blood, she then dismissed it from this realm.

Ascher let out a hoot when she returned to him. The green headlamp highlighted him like the bizarre night-video clips Annja had filmed previously for *Chasing History's Monsters*.

He stood against the wall, supporting himself with both hands, and his right leg dragging.

A flash of the headlamp across his face revealed beads of sweat on brow, cheekbones and upper lip. Yet a slap of her palm to his forehead found him clammy. Shock?

"I don't know how you do it," he said. "But I am thankful that you can do it. Why does not *Chasing History's Monsters* bring to light your skills beyond standing before a camera and tromping through old castles?"

"I have no television-worthy skills, Vallois. You're delusional."

"Perhaps for a show like the American *Survivor?* You can stand your own against some of the toughest men."

"Yeah? But I'm not big on munching bugs. How's the leg?"

"I am standing. But not for long."

She bent to inspect her makeshift bandage. It wasn't as soaked with blood as she might have expected. Not a bad thing, but not consistent with his condition. They needed to find a way out fast.

"I am very thirsty," Ascher said.

"To be expected. Your body is working hard to keep you upright."

"You think you can find a way out?" he asked.

"Let me see the camera."

Cycling through about a dozen shots—the first few marked by Jacques Lambert when he and his crew had been with them, for they were in reverse order—Annja landed a picture of the wall right behind them. "We're back in business. This way."

She'd have to take him past the dead man. Ascher would see the gaping hole in his chest. There was a question she didn't favor answering.

"No questions, and I promise d'Artagnan's rapier is yours," she said.

"You mean it?"

"You intend to donate it to the museum in Lupiac?"

"Without the treasure, it holds no value for me."

"Yeah, but what treasure? It was just a box, Ascher. And it didn't feel like there was anything inside it, nothing rattling around."

"Y-you didn't look?"

She touched his face. He was shivering. If she could keep him talking, and walking at the same time…

"Lambert snatched it from me before I had a chance." She hooked a shoulder under Ascher's arm and helped him walk with the wall to support his opposite side. "I thought I'd come here for a treasure hunt, but now I'm thinking that was just the lure to lead me to the real trouble."

"BHDC? But I had no idea, Annja."

"I believe you. The universe works in strange ways. Sometimes it draws me to where I should be, even when the reason isn't immediately apparent. But this time it pulled the rug right out from under me."

"But it was a g-good adventure, yes?"

"It's not over yet. Come on, Ascher, you can do this."

They rounded the corner, and Annja stepped over the fallen goon. She held her head high, directing the headlamp across the walls, so Ascher could only make out the outline of the man to step over him. The light didn't fall on the bloody hole in his chest.

AN HOUR LATER, thanks to the photos they'd taken, they surfaced through the cellar of the cheese shop. The owner and his wife were shaken, but not harmed. The old man apologized profusely that he'd allowed the big nasty men through the secret doorway, but Annja reassured him it wasn't his fault.

They hadn't any time to drink a bottle of wine and have some cheese. Ascher needed immediate medical attention. The shop owner called for a cab.

Annja stood out front waiting the car. Ascher sat near her feet on the curb, his body slumped against a street sign pole. "There's a hospital on the island," she said. "I'll take you there, and—"

"And get rid of the deadweight?" He tugged the knotted T-shirt tighter about his thigh and winced.

"For a while. I can't have you drop dead before the adventure is resolved, can I?"

Sitting next to him, she stretched her legs out onto the street, bobbing the toes of her rubber boots together. Ascher, in a remarkable recovery from his waning strength, clutched her by the back of the head—and kissed her.

It wasn't a fast, hard morsel, like she'd given him below-ground to get him to move. This one took its time, and thoroughly impressed her. For a man half-dead, he certainly could curl a girl's toes.

"Thank you, Annja. I am sorry to have gotten you into this mess," he said.

"Nothing I'm not accustomed to. In fact, I might have been let down had this adventure been anything less."

And then she returned the kiss, because some adventures were not to be denied.

ANNJA LEFT ASCHER at the casualty ward in the Hôtel-Dieu on the main island, and in the capable hands of a lovely blond nurse whose giggles had made the indomitable Gascon blush.

Night had arrived, and she had never been happier to revel in the gray illumination a big city gave off. No more pitch-black tunnels for her. At least, not for as long as she could prevent it.

Tossing the pommel of d'Artagnan's sword up and down in her palm, she stood at the corner of a street paralleling the Seine, pondering her next move.

She knew exactly where to find Jacques Lambert. And if he was smart, BHDC would be entirely cleared out of incriminating evidence by now. But the man wasn't that smart, and she suspected he felt as if he'd gotten away with murder.

Because he did it daily.

"Not on my watch."

25

he news of her husband's death shook her more than she xpected it to. They had dissolved the marriage years ago. And truth, while the vows had been honored, she had never felt arried to the man who had flitted in and out of her life as if nuisance insect. Though he had attracted with his muske- er's tunic and a bold honor that gleamed from him as if gold. man of impeccable standards—military standards.

Yes, he had been a tender lover, and there was no denying loved his children. But his very soul had been promised to e king long before she had entered his life.

He had never been completely hers.

Charlotte-Anne should have known when she'd decided to arry a soldier that she could never be first in his life. Only ter military, the king, the queen, his troops—and then even e enemy troops—did she manage to toe a place in the line his affections.

And now he was gone. A man who had given her two fin
sons, and a few precious moments of joy.

The journey from Chalon to Paris required she rent a coac
and endure half a day on the road. In the carriage, ill sprung an
without glass windows, she suffered the interminable five-hou
journey only by force of will. She had to return to the plac
where they once shared their lives. For one last breath of the ai
And to claim a small piece of the musketeer who left her alon
to raise their children, without thought to support said family

Not that she wasn't well enough off. Charlotte-Anne d
Chanlecy, dame de Saint-Croix, had certainly married belov
her station. A family stipend would see her through her en
days, but it would not provide for her sons' futures.

Would there be anything left from their father's military lif
to provide them a start? She doubted it.

Her poor boys. They had not seen their father for seve
years. And now they would never see him. Yet, they bot
desired to serve the military. Already the eldest sought to joi
the guards. Charlotte wished them a better life, but she kne
their father's desire for adventure ran in their veins as molte
lava creeps across the scorched earth.

That same inner fire had attracted Charlotte to Charles.

An inventory had been made of Charles de Castelmore
home on the quai Malaquais. Charlotte had been given a li
by the auditor and told all items would go to pay off debtor
When she inquired if there was a small trinket she could kee
she was told to speak to one of the king's guards. A sma
cache of d'Artagnan's personal items was being held with th
prefect of police until the king signed off on the musketeer
death certificate.

That very same evening, Charlotte was granted an audien
with the king. She dressed in her finest, and even allowe

erself to feel a flutter of anticipation. In all the years she had
een married to the king's favorite, somehow she had never
een invited to court. Her husband, most uncomfortable
round courts and fanfare, hadn't bothered to see that invita-
on secured.

Now she would be granted what she had been owed. But
he felt no such desire to return to the glamour of Louis's court
fter the audience. His Highness had gifted her with the trinket
he'd requested, stating cryptically, "This is the second time
ve have given this to a Castelmore. Make it stick."

Now, clutching the gold-hilt rapier at her side, Charlotte
wayed as the coach took her away from the royal palace
oward an inn at the edge of Paris where she would stay the
ight before returning to Chalon.

She had not begged, but a real tear had come to her eye
hen she'd bowed before Louis and Queen Anne and re-
uested a piece of her husband's possessions for memory. It
as the queen who had instructed Colbert to retrieve the
apier for Charlotte, stating quite firmly that it should be given
o his sons, for it was well-known that Charlotte had re-
ounced all common property upon her divorce with Charles.

Thanking the royals profusely, Charlotte then left the palace,
ith every intention of gifting the rapier to her sons. It was a
ere sword. Decorative. Dangerous to consider brandishing at
e vanguard. Why Charles had not sold it stymied her. And yet,
gift from the king and queen he would surely revere.

The gold hilt might bring a pretty price, but his boys would
cide that, if they so chose.

A private family estate sat in the thick woods north of the
ugustine convent in Chalon. There Charlotte retired, hoping
never look upon another handsome soldier with seduction
his lips, a promise in his eyes and adventure in his heart.

Over the years, the rapier was tucked away into a cove in the wall near the hearth for safekeeping. Upon Charlotte' death, the cove remained untouched and forgotten. He youngest son had been forced to sell his mother's estate to provide for his own family.

D'Artagnan's eldest son died without progeny, while hi youngest produced two sons. Both boys died without children being the last descendants of Charles de Castelmore d'Artagnan

Present day

ANNJA COULDN'T LET things stand as they did. Not withou the treasure. Not without *knowing* if there was a treasure.

If treasure did exist, it didn't belong to BHDC, nor was meant to subsidize cloning research. Lambert had gone to far. She would make the modern-day Frankenstein answer fo the lives of the babies he had created and who had the quickly perished in the name of his twisted science.

Standing before the nondescript redbrick facade of BHDC Annja summoned courage.

Yes, she had to summon it. Just because she possessed sword that would help her to defeat the bad guys didn't mea she wasn't reluctant, if at times wisely fearful of the situatio she got involved in.

Biopiracy was far out of her realm of understanding Jacques Lambert may not be a man who threatened to destro the world, but with his selfish experiments he crippled th future of the world, one small human life at a time.

"Oh, hell, what is that?"

Up on the third floor, a window glowed strangely again the night sky. Almost as if it reflected the setting sun, golde and fiery— She knew what it was. Fire.

"He's destroying the evidence."

All her life Annja had had dreams about fire. She'd never been caught in a burning building or had any incidents involving fire. There was no explanation for the dreams.

"More like nightmares," she muttered.

Yet now the pace of her heartbeat brought her to that moment of struggling lucidity that followed after waking from such a nightmare. It wasn't an explanation so much as a knowing.

Your history. Her history. Joan of Arc was burned at the stake as a martyr. The two of you are connected.

With the sword, had she inherited the nightmares?

Breathing deeply from her stomach, Annja then let it all gush out. Focus. She wouldn't allow what wasn't real to bring her down, to cloud her thoughts. She needed to act. And fast.

Nothing would stop her from learning the truth and seeing justice done. "I can do this."

She marched up to the building where ten-foot-high brushed-steel doors guarded the entrance. No signs or plaques identified the place. It was locked—no surprise.

"Wonder who is inside? Just Lambert? A crew of pistol-wielding thugs?"

Hopefully, no pregnant mothers. If they implanted fertilized eggs into women here, then they very likely brought them back for the birth. There must be a clinic or hospital section in the building. Innocent women could be trapped inside.

Shaking the door, Annja guessed the solid steel would require forceful encouragement. Glancing over her shoulder to check her periphery—the street was quiet, the café down the road dark and the windows covered with bright words advertising the specials.

She summoned the sword.

The blade wouldn't serve to break the narrow glass windows set into the steel, but a firm stroke of the hilt straight down onto the biometric scanner cracked off the cover and exposed wires that short-circuited in tiny pops.

Smashing the pommel repeatedly into the exposed box, Annja was rewarded when the door clicked. It didn't open smoothly, yet she was able to ram her shoulder against the steel and push the door inside.

Releasing the sword from this world, Annja stepped quickly through the reception area and down the hallway that displayed ancient swords, rapiers and knives. A Gothic mace taunted beneath a halogen beam. Caltrops—medieval throwing stars used to take down horses—flaunted deadly iron points. None were encased in glass.

She didn't need any of them.

Arriving at the door to Lambert's office, Annja lifted a leg and kicked near the biometric lock. Still wearing the rubber boots, she felt the impact keenly. She hadn't expected it to fall inward, thinking surely the lock and steel mechanism would hold firmly—but one good kick did bring the whole thing down.

Inside, Jacques Lambert leaned against a desk, his ankles crossed casually and his palms to the black marble edge of the desk behind him.

"I've been expecting you, Annja Creed."

"Really." She stepped across the threshold and, while keeping her distance, maintained a peripheral view of the doorway. "Where's your fiddle, Nero?"

"You saw? There's no smoke, is there? It's contained. Third floor only. You've forced me to take measures."

"Imagine that, you having to take measures."

"Didn't take you long to find your way out from the dark labyrinths that snake beneath our city. Pity about the treasure hunter."

"He's still alive. Not for lack of your attempts. Your goon was ordered to kill, wasn't he?"

"Of course. I don't do anything halfway, Annja—you should know that by now. But your death was not ordered. You hold great value to me."

"Charmed, I'm sure."

There were no lights on in the room, save the small halogens highlighting the swords on the wall. As it was, they provided enough light to show the maniacal glimmer in Lambert's eyes.

Annja had encountered many a power-crazed villain, most very intelligent and reasonable of mind. A villain could never get far without skill and intelligence. But the truly frightening opponents were those who got sucked in by one small twisted desire, and ran with it.

"Speaking of my goons. Did you leave the body behind to rot?"

Annja wasn't sure how to report the death, or to what authorities. Aboveground police or the cata-cops? She wasn't keen on allowing innocent cataphiles to stumble upon a rotting corpse. "Taken care of." Or would be soon enough, she hoped.

She glanced around Lambert's arm. "Is that the box?"

He reached behind his back and slid a small white box into view. It had been too dark in the tunnels to know more than that it was a box and light colored, possibly metal. But now she saw it was wood, painted white. A beam of light fell across the decorative flourishes carved along the edges and the base. It was ornate, but it struck Annja that the design was not fitting of the period. Something created in the seventeenth century would have been even more elaborate, flourished with the baroque. The style appeared flowing yet spare, perhaps art nouveau, though she knew little about the art style of the time period.

"I was hoping you could explain this to me," Jacques said. "It appears perhaps Dumas put the joke on all of us."

She stepped forward, wary of her periphery, and also not about to forget that the building was on fire. Contained? How did one contain a fire to one floor? Perhaps that's where the goons were. Destroying BHDC's files.

The more time she wasted, the more incriminating files Lambert was able to destroy.

"It's not indicative of the baroque time period," she said. "I would expect gilding, some miniatures painted on the sides. Of course, time might have erased any detail work. May I?"

Lambert nodded eagerly and she picked it up.

It was light. The wood must be walnut, or perhaps mahogany; she couldn't be sure with the white paint. The cover was latched on two opposite sides. Interesting. It wasn't a lock and key, but rather a sliding latch mechanism, and it wasn't gold or silver, but bronze. Again, a surprise.

Wouldn't a gift from a queen, rumored to be worth an untold sum, at the very least, be offered in an elaborate setting?

There were words engraved around the rim of the box cover. Annja traced a finger along the raised carvings as she read, *"Tous Pour Un, Un Pour Tous?"*

Lambert met her wondering stare with a shrug of shoulder and splay of his hands. "Ironic, isn't it? That Dumas was able to dupe so many. I had always wondered if he had based *The Count of Monte Cristo* upon his own treasure findings. This proves it."

"If Dumas found the treasure, then why did he die in debt?" Annja asked.

"Extravagant spending, a childlike lack of understanding for the value of money and goods," Lambert said.

Details Annja knew anyone could know about the writer by reading a simple biography.

She opened the lid. There was nothing inside, save a soft red velvet lining. If it was from d'Artagnan's time it had aged

ery well. But the condition of the fabric led Annja to believe
was much newer.

"There was nothing inside?" she asked.

Lambert shook his head. "I would tell you if there had
een. Honest."

He probably would have. If only to flaunt his find, she knew.

"This could not be the treasure," she said. "It could not have
een placed in the tunnels during Queen Anne's time."

"Perceptive, but dull as a horse," Lambert said snidely.
There never was a treasure. It is a hoax designed by Alex-
ndre Dumas, for—I don't know!"

"It couldn't be." She replaced the cover and smiled at the
ying that Dumas had made famous: All For One, One For
ll. The musketeers' call to adventure, their claim to protect
e king and each other. "The map was in d'Artagnan's sword.
umas couldn't possibly have found the sword and planted
outside Chalon to be later dug up by—"

"Treasure hunters?"

He implied she'd stepped from her profession to the dark
de. She wasn't about to join ranks with this pirate.

"No, the sword and the map are real. Dumas must have
und the treasure during his research—perhaps he found the
py of the map in Fouquet's papers? Or even Mansart's?"

"Possible."

"And when he found the treasure, he then decided to leave
hind this box for future treasure hunters." She tilted it and
spected the bottom, which was lined with a disintegrating
ash of green velvet. "It looks a trinket box. Maybe some-
ing created to go along with the release of *The Three Mus-
teers*. 'All for one—'"

"None for all," Lambert spit and slapped the side of the box
it went flying out of her hands.

Annja wasn't quick enough. She lunged, but felt the woo
as it skimmed the tips of her fingers. It hit the marble floo
with a dull crash, but did not shatter as she expected; only th
lid cracked in two and clattered across the floor.

"What a waste of time!" Lambert railed. "And at so grea
an expense."

"What expense? You plunder. It costs you nothing mor
than time spent stalking your marks until they lead you to th
treasure!" Annja shouted.

"It cost me the entire third floor. Because of you. Yo
know too much."

"Most of it was freely given by you when you spilled th
beans to me the other day."

"I—! For a pretty young celebrity, you have an obstinat
manner about you."

"I've nothing of the sort. You wanted to spill, and you did

"I am doing this for Toby!"

Annja crossed her arms over her chest and tilted her hea
"Is this the part where the villain details his evil plan befor
the hero tries to take him out?"

"A villain?" Lambert scoffed. "In the eyes of a simpl
woman who has no more knowledge of the workings of th
genetic code than a monkey. Do you understand the value
mankind to successfully construct a human clone?"

"No, actually I don't. And I don't need to know that it
replace lost loved ones, or populate factories with mindle
drones. All I know is that your research is playing God and d
stroying human lives in the quest for a nonessential science

"Nonessential? It is our future. It is our means to immo
tality!"

"It is morally wrong."

"Morality is an invention of the personality," he hisse

grandly. "It is something we creatures require to uphold judgment against others. We crave that accusatory judgment, the ability to place ourselves above another, to lift our souls. I am of the light, I judge none and I serve all."

Annja coughed, and glanced aside.

"One man's morality is another man's sin," Lambert said. "Science is always the scapegoat! What you cannot understand, you seek to destroy. And yet, throughout the ages, science has never ceased to open our eyes. We feared the plague, and then science created a microscope so we could study germs and learn and understand that fear. We are but atoms and light, Annja Creed." He pounded his chest fiercely. "These are but borrowed bodies—the soul is the great equalizer."

"You've killed babies!"

"How dare you throw that accusation at me."

"I read the files."

"The subjects died naturally *after* successful births."

"Naturally? They died because of genetic defects you introduced through your incomplete and fallible cloning process. And what of the mothers who gave birth to those unfortunate babies you've documented in your files? Where are they?"

Lambert lifted his chin, silent in his crime.

"Dead?" she asked.

"Never."

"Were they aware of what their bodies were being used for? The woman I followed as she left here the other day— she's pregnant. She believes this a fertility clinic. She has no idea, has she?"

"I've had enough of your accusations. You've got the musketeer's sword. Keep it and be happy for your treasure."

Annja blew out a frustrated breath and toed the divided pieces of the box cover.

"It's interesting, one man's notion of treasure, isn't it?" she said. "I hold little value in sparkling gemstones or piles of smartly stacked hundred-dollar bills. I do value an intangible history and verifying its truth. And while I may never consider myself maternal material, I do hold great value in a child. Why do you label such a treasure garbage? Because that's what you do with your research."

Lambert made his move. Annja bent her knees slightly, prepared to defend, but cautious.

The man went for an épée on the wall, brandishing it in a sweeping display before him as he approached her. Emeralds fixed to the hilt captured the minute spotlight and flashed green fire.

Annja backed up until her shoulders hit the wall.

"I've got my eye on a new treasure," he announced.

The épée swept the air in a hiss.

"It is another sword. A magical one."

"You believe in magic?" she countered.

"I believe what I saw when I watched you in the file room on the security cameras. You wielded a fine sword, Annja Creed. And you produced it from thin air. Do you deny I've got a recording of you fighting off my man with a sword?"

"Who can deny videotape?" she snapped.

"Where is it?" He approached, the blade held down and to the outside at octave, not threatening, but with a flick of his exposed wrist, it could be. "Bring it out of wherever it is you keep it. I want to see it."

She remained silent. Alert. Ready.

"I know something about you," he said in a singsong tone. "Your Monsieur Roux wasn't quite so careful as he should have been. Did you know about his visit to BHDC? He was most secretive."

"I know Roux was here," she said.

Well, she did now. Roux had come here? What was the old man up to now? She didn't like what he implied, because Annja could guess at but a few options if it involved Roux and Lambert's knowledge of the sword.

"Monsieur Roux brought along a piece of chain mail which he claimed was once Joan of Arc's. Ah, you find that intriguing, yes, as I did. Threaded within the chain links were four hair strands. Viable DNA evidence. My geneticist was able to extract DNA and sequence the entire genome."

"You're going to clone Joan of Arc?" Annja was stunned.

"We'll certainly give it a shot."

"But if the mind and the personality cannot be re-created, what is the purpose to having a child that resembles someone no one can recognize?" she asked.

"It is the *idea* of having a child with Joan of Arc's DNA. Trust me, there are people who will pay a ridiculous amount to make such a claim."

"Doesn't sound like people who have the right to be parents."

"Now you are judging, Annja."

He tilted his wrist and brought up the blade beneath Annja's chin. The tip did not touch flesh, but at the moment she wasn't actually concerned about injury.

"Roux also brought along what he referred to as a modern sample. A strand of hair that one must label—" the blade wept to the side to lift the ends of Annja's hair "—chestnut."

Her heart falling in her chest, Annja struggled to keep her expression neutral.

"He wanted me to match the DNA to markers in the historical sample. Answer the question of maternal relation. My geneticist matched mitochondrial DNA against dozens of genetic markers." Lambert tilted a foul blue gaze upon her. "I have the results, Annja. I will give them to you in exchange for your magical sword."

"You're barking up the wrong tree, Lambert. Why would you—?"

"Because I've done my research on your Roux and Joan. I know, Annja, I know."

"You know nothing."

"I will have the sword." He swung the blade.

Annja reacted, calling up her sword and meeting the oncoming blade with a clang that sent a shudder through her wrist and up her forearm.

Lambert smiled between their crossed blades. "Touché."

26

"You're not going to kill me, Annja, I know that."

"How can you be so sure? You know I had to dispatch the goon in the tunnel."

"Yes, but I've done nothing to warrant such punishment."

"You've done plenty against mankind."

"Such a statement merely proves your ignorance."

"I wouldn't expect you to sway from your stance, as deluded as it may be. But it's not my place to decide your punishment, Lambert. A jury of your peers should do nicely."

"No jury will convict me. The genetic cloning laws are so vague right now. And no one really understands the whole working process. A jury could not properly rule against something a mere high school education would never allow them to understand."

He feinted to the right, and then managed a stab to Annja's upper left thigh. She dodged but felt the burn of the blade through her jeans to slice flesh. The man was fast, and knew how to handle a weapon.

Annja backed over the fallen door and into the hallway. Smoke lingered at the end where she had previously gone on to explore the third floor. The air smelled sulfurous.

"What evidence are you destroying?" she said as she lunged to parry a thrust intended for her shoulder. Her sword wasn't meant for delicate fencing moves. Slashing and hacking was most fitting. "The files I looked over the other day? A laboratory that contains embryos waiting for implant in an unsuspecting female's womb?"

"I'll never tell."

A twist of her wrist brought her sword blade diagonally before her thighs, blocking Lambert's attempt to draw blood.

Annja's shoulder hit the door and she jumped away from it. The contact stung. It was hot as a stove burner. Only a fool would attempt to open it and go through.

Evidence was going up in smoke. Her best bet? To incapacitate Lambert and call the fire station. The sooner the fire could be put out, the better the chances of saving the incriminating data and files.

But the man would not be put back. He continued to advance upon her, a crooked grin revealing a narrow row of bright teeth.

Their blades clattered. Annja found she really had to concentrate on the fencing skills Roux had taught her, to match her opponent's every move. No slashing or hacking this time. She would not simply run him through. This man needed to answer for his crimes.

"You're quite skilled, Mademoiselle Creed."

"I've studied sixteenth- and seventeenth-century masters."

"That explains your neglect of proper form. I was fencing champion of 1985, junior division."

"Good for you." He thought her form lacking? Had she

proper foil, that would change. It mattered little. "What steered you toward evil?"

"There you go again. Judging!" In proof of his championship status, he lunged gracefully, blade tip coming under Annja's chin. She hadn't anticipated that move. "How much for the sword? I must have it," he said.

A flick of her wrist—her sword's *quillon* sliding along his blade—swept his threat away. "Impossible."

"It is Joan of Arc's sword."

That hadn't been a question.

Annja swept low, but her opponent deftly leaped from harm's way. He made a gleeful dash down the hallway toward the reception area where she'd entered through the damaged door.

"Your brother wouldn't have wanted you to harm more children!" she called after him.

"You never knew Evil Gentleman Tobias!" he called out in something resembling a wicked sneer. Or perhaps a delusional pirate's cackle.

Arriving at the reception area, Annja took a moment to draw in a breath as Lambert paced between the desk and the front doorway, which was still ajar. They both needed a breather. Clear air wasn't on the menu. Smoke flooded the hallway in their wake. Annja could taste the smoke on her palate.

"I know things about you, Annja." Lambert tapped the air with his sword blade. "As well, your Monsieur Roux believes certain things about you. I did some research on the man."

"On Roux? He's an enigma. It's not like he's got a Web site or a presence on the Internet."

"But there is a notation about him in the history books. Fifteenth century."

With a forced chuckle she tasted the gritty murk of smoke. "He's an old man, but he's not immortal."

"I disagree, and you know I'm right." Lambert paced the reception floor, behind the glass-topped coffee table lined with magazines. He circled the air before him with the sword tip. "One must have an open mind to study science, Annja."

"Scientists are infamous skeptics."

"Then I am not the norm."

He could say that again.

"I've spent the better part of a day searching historical texts on Joan of Arc, and discovered a small notation on a soldier who traveled in her retinue. Rumors told he was also a wizard. I guess that wizard was your Roux."

"Roux's no wizard," Annja said.

"Perhaps not in the sense that we've come to associate with magical spells and wands. And yet, when there's a magical sword involved, one tends to err on the side of the possible. Roux was supposed to be Joan of Arc's protector. He obviously failed. The man witnessed Joan burn at the stake outside Rouen.

"Now, who do you think might have taken something of her person away with him? A man who felt guilt at not being able to save the one woman he had chosen to protect? A man who wanted to make things right? And what could he take? A soldier would eye a sword," Lambert said.

"I'm sure all her possessions were confiscated by the Inquisition. It would have been impossible for a mere soldier to lay claim to anything the martyr once owned," Annja said.

"Yes, a martyr. Like you, Annja? Do you battle evil for the forces of the good?" He swung up his blade, catching Annja's sword close to the hilt. It was a powerful hit, but Annja worked through the blow by extending her hand upward. "I confess I came up short when researching your history. The television Web site provides the standard bio and educational background in New Orleans, but as for the real history, such as parents and place of birth? You remain an enigma, Annja."

"A girl's gotta keep some mystery about her."

"Yes, you believe that all you want, Annja. The greater mystery lies in the sword, though. Explain how it works," Lambert challenged. "Do you speak to some higher power as Joan once claimed to speak to God?"

"Get over yourself, Lambert. You're barking up the wrong tree. There's no such thing as wizards, let alone a magical sword."

They crossed blades and drew up close. Devastating madness flickered in Lambert's blue eyes. Annja genuinely feared her opponent, not for his prowess with the blade, but for the demented ideals he sought to protect. And for the damning knowledge he'd put together about her and the sword.

"It is her sword," he said in a tone touching admonishment. "And I'm guessing it chose you. How else to explain it magically appearing and disappearing when you will it?"

"I don't believe in magic," Annja said.

"Nor do I. But I do believe in destiny."

Destiny. A word that had taken on new meaning in Annja's life since taking Joan of Arc's sword to hand. Now she believed in things that she would have never given a second thought to previously.

How dare she question another man's destiny?

"My brother's death set me on this pirate's life," Lambert continued. "It is my destiny to cure the sick. To give them new life. Just as you were destined to gain Joan of Arc's sword. To fight opposition with it. Did the wizard gift it to you?"

He was still guessing. But he was right on the money. How could he speak so confidently of something even she did not have all the answers for?

Lowering his blade, Lambert reached out with his free hand. "Just let me…touch it."

"Gladly." She drew back and made to deliver a direct hit to his forearm, hoping to disarm him, but sight of black smoke clouds billowing into the room stopped the action. "Your fire is no longer contained! Get out!" she shouted.

Lambert twisted and a gush of thick smoke enveloped his head. Smoke spewed down the hallway in rolling waves. The man gagged and choked. Annja bent low and lunged to grab him by the waist. He punched her head with his right hand, the sword hilt making the blow all the harder.

Struggling against the woozy pull that wanted to black out her consciousness, Annja wobbled. If she blacked out, he'd leave her behind to burn.

How must death by fire feel? To have stood before the nonbelievers and to have prayed to a God that would no longer listen. To be so young, and to be punished for following the only path that had been clear to her.

And to know her protector, Roux, had not been there for her. Had she felt helpless? Or had her faith made her fearless when it was most needed?

What do I have faith in? Annja wondered fleetingly. The sword? My ability to win against evil? Myself?

She gasped, but that was the wrong thing to do, for opening her mouth drew in more smoke.

Did the lungs fill with smoke and choke the victim unconscious before the flames burned through flesh? Or did a victim suffer the horror of feeling their flesh melt from bone fully conscious?

Thoughts of such an agonizing death cleared Annja's brain. This fire would not take her down.

She managed to swing around and fling Lambert toward

the door, still ajar from her entrance. He took the hint and slipped outside.

Head still pounding from the hit, Annja scrambled across the marble floor, coughing on the thick smoke. The rubber boots gave her traction. She made her escape right behind Lambert.

Neon curls from bars and distant restaurants edged the night. To her left, the Eiffel Tower twinkled, its peak jutting out in the distance. The rush of cars gliding by on the nearby *périphérique* sounded like ocean waves.

Fire crept behind her. Smoke filled Annja's nostrils. She rushed away from the building and into the center of the street where Lambert stood coughing, bent over at the waist. Breathing deeply, she filled her lungs with fresh air.

Could she ever purge the nightmares? To be consumed by fire…

"Is it that you cannot control it?" Lambert called. "If you let go of the hilt is it gone?"

Annja hadn't realized she'd released the sword to the otherwhere. It had become an intuitive part of her. When needed, it arrived, ready. When not, it slipped away.

No sword can protect you from the accusing flame.

Biting back a scream, she shook the nightmarish cries of her predecessor away.

"Tell me how it works, Annja. I must know!"

"Stop trying to figure out something even I don't completely understand."

He strode over to her, épée to hand, but not threatening. "Yet you can call it into existence whenever you wish."

"That is as it appears." She had no sense to keep her secrets right now. Smoke coiled in her lungs and dizzied her brain.

"You are quite accomplished. You control it well," he said.

"As you seek to control life?"

"It is not so simple as you define it, Annja."

"It appears that simple."

The shrill of police sirens alerted them both. Far off, but the alarm grew closer. She hadn't alerted the authorities. Had Roux? Or maybe Ascher had guessed her destination.

"Points for you, Annja Creed." Lambert offered a surrendering bow and then pointed his épée over her head. "Pity. All documentation of wrong-doings will be lost."

The fire had begun to rage on the roof. The ground floor, still dark and silent, spewed out smoke like a monster furnace.

"So you admit that what you've done is wrong?" She spun to face Lambert, who kept a keen eye down the street for the oncoming police cavalcade. "Why would you destroy your research?"

"I would be a fool not to keep backups and copies," he said.

"You could do a good thing if only you'd focus on what is right."

"Your *right* is my obstacle, Annja. I cannot work miracles if I am forced to ridiculous parameters by lawmakers who have no knowledge of genetic cloning."

He approached cautiously, head bowed and épée tracing the ground. A smear of soot brushed his cheek. "The evidence to your secret is going up in flames as we speak. Roux was keenly interested. I wonder should I reveal the findings to him?"

"Without proof, nothing can be believed of you, Lambert. You're a liar and a thief and a—"

"A pirate?"

"Yes. A biopirate."

"I like the sound of that."

She hadn't meant to fuel his demented fire.

"You think you have defeated me?" He chuckled. A snap of his wrist thrust his weapon to *en garde*.

Annja called up her sword and met the challenge. She aimed for his left shoulder, but Lambert's dodge placed his heart in harm's way. Annja felt the blade enter Jacques Lambert's body. A warm splatter of blood spotted the back of her hand. The heart tremored—she felt the throb ride her blade—and she quickly withdrew.

Blood spilled from Lambert's chest.

"No!" She had not intended to kill him.

Abandoning her sword, Annja caught him as he wobbled forward.

"It wasn't supposed to happen this way," she muttered frantically.

He would never have killed her. The man merely enjoyed the duel, in matching his skills against hers. He had said he'd not wanted her dead.

"You've killed me?" he gurgled. Blood dribbled from his mouth.

Annja helped him lay down on the tarmac. A cursory glance found the road empty, but the sirens, which had momentarily receded, were closing in. They must be tracking the fire without a destination address.

"Quick." He gripped her arm. "Go inside. Get my heart!"

"Your—what?"

"I've cloned all my organs." A cough of blood spattered her bare knee.

"The building is ablaze," she said. If she risked reentry, exit would not be possible.

The man had cloned his own organs? This was too much. "It's not that simple."

"Words of my…father," Lambert whispered. He coughed on his blood. "It is…never so simple. I need…Toby."

The man had created an empire in the memory of his lost twin brother. Had his vision not been corrupt, perhaps the medical community would have embraced BHDC's research in therapeutic cloning. There was so much about Jacques Lambert that was right.

Had she done the right thing?

Of course not. She hadn't wanted to kill him.

"Toby?"

Annja, embracing a sudden welling of sympathy, squeezed Lambert's hand and leaned over him. "Toby would have been proud of your research, and your desire to help children as your brother could not have been helped."

He breathed, nodded, and his head fell limp in her hands. Annja lowered his skull to the ground. The police sirens sounded but a block or two away.

"I'm sorry," she said.

A dead body. Blood on her clothes and hands. Not a situation Annja wanted to be caught in.

Standing, she took off for the alley across the street, and ran into the narrow darkness until she arrived at a Dumpster. Pressing her back to the hard steel container, she bent forward and gasped to clear her lungs.

At the end of the alley, sirens wailed.

Shaking her head, she struggled with what she had done. Many times before, she had killed to protect herself, to protect others, to protect the world from evil.

So why, this time, did guilt clutch her heart? Jacques Lambert was a delusional man, yet his research—the legal research—could have helped many.

It would happen someday, the therapeutic cloning. And it would be legal and right.

She nodded, summoning her wits about her. Now was no time to freak out. She had to believe that her sword would not strike at any who did not deserve it.

And if she thought of the other benefit, then things were almost right. The BHDC building was going up in flames. And with it, Lambert's death would keep the secret of her sword.

Annja turned and clung to the steel lip of the Dumpster. Some of the action at the end of the alley was visible.

Not far behind the police, a black Renault pulled up across the street from the burning building. A man jumped out from behind the driver's seat to look over the destruction. He shoved a hand through his tousled hair. He wore pajama bottoms and a housecoat over his bare chest.

Annja crouched and peered around the edge of the Dumpster to see inside the car. A woman, who looked to be screaming—make that moaning, desperately—reached out for her husband. He ducked his head inside the car, raising his hands in an I-don't-know-what-is-happening gesture.

Annja recognized the woman. The pregnant woman she had followed from BHDC the other day. Her moans were labor. Obviously, she had come to the one place the BHDC doctors had recommended.

The husband managed to snag a police officer, who, after frantic gesticulations, spoke into his walkie-talkie. Summoning an ambulance to take the laboring woman to the hospital?

If only she could go to her. How to find out the woman's name? To know if her baby would survive Jacques Lambert's experiments.

27

Ascher had been the one to alert the police.

Annja didn't hang around long. It was never wise to remain at the scene of a murder. Until the fire was extinguished, no one could know if there were salvageable documents. Something that might clue the police to the travesties that had occurred behind the steel doors of BHDC.

Surely, Jacques had employees who would carry the torch for him in his absence. At the very least, Annja could rest assured this particular lab had been destroyed.

How many more were attempting to clone human beings? It was a race to play God that could never be extinguished. But if the media reported on it properly, then more people could be educated about what genetic sciences could and couldn't do. No parent would seek to replace a dead child, knowing the personality could never be duplicated.

And perhaps, with education, the political arena could be taught that stem cells donated by couples going through infertility treatments were a viable means to valuable research that could save thousands.

So long as that research continued to be policed.

ANNJA STOPPED BY the hotel across from Notre-Dame and checked out. Her notebook and laptop were still there in the small closet where she had stashed them. Bart McGilly called while she stood looking from her hotel window over at the centuries-old beauty of the cathedral.

"I appreciate you looking into the cloning laws for me, Bart, but it's too late. Lambert…died in the fire."

"Unfortunate, but probably better in the long run. You coming back to American soil anytime soon?"

"Not for another week. I just got an assignment from my producer. I'm off to Ireland to chase faeries."

"I'd laugh, but for some reason I think you're serious," Bart said.

"I hope not. Belief in faeries? So not going there. Thanks, Bart. We'll lunch at Tito's when I get back to Brooklyn. My treat."

"Excellent. I miss you. Talk to you later, Annja."

She hung up. A twinge of regret poked her briefly. As much as she loved him, she knew she wasn't the woman for him.

"Don't go there, Annja," she told herself.

On the other hand. She had caught herself a fine Frenchman, without even trying. Everything about Ascher Vallois appealed to her, once she got past his initial deception and theft of the map. He had only done what any desperate man might do.

"Hope that last kidney is all right," she muttered. "Poor guy took a beating these past few days. Bet I could beat him in a race across the city."

And climbing, leaping and dodging, she thought, remembering their *parkour* run. Now, that was definitely something she would try again. Without the thugs on her tail next time.

BEFORE RETURNING to her car, Annja detoured to the Hôtel-Dieu, which was right across the street from Notre-Dame. It didn't take long to locate the woman who had given birth last evening. Annja stood in the doorway to the guest waiting room. From her position she could see the nursery viewing window. The woman she'd followed the other day to the café stood before the window with her husband. Both cooed and waved at one of the bundled infants behind the glass.

A healthy baby girl, she'd overheard them whisper. Their dreams had been answered after years of unsuccessful fertility treatments.

Annja could foresee no possible way of sleuthing her way into the nursery to check the baby's records—the nurses were like tigers on the prowl, very protective of their tiny charges.

Was it her responsibility to inform them the mother had been a guinea pig in an illegal cloning operation? Could she do that to a helpless infant? Force it to endure medical tests to prove it was a clone? How did one prove it was a clone? Wouldn't DNA tests appear as any other normal human?

If word got out, the media would have a heyday. The baby's parents would be kept from her. She would become an orphan surrounded by a strange circus of media, medical and scientific personnel.

A little girl lost, yet surrounded by a curious and inadvertently cruel world. And yet all she would crave was to be held by her parents.

Sniffing, Annja tilted her head away from the scene. She swiped the back of her hand across her cheek. She wasn' crying. Maybe.

It wouldn't change things to mourn over what was missing from her life. There were plenty of children and adults in this world without parents. The world was a cruel place. The baby behind that glass would have to learn to suck it up if she wanted to survive.

But survival would be much easier in a loving family.

As for alerting the medical staff of the baby's possible genetic beginnings…?

Annja felt not knowing this truth was best for everyone involved.

ROUX HELD d'Artagnan's rapier *en garde* as Annja entered the study. He was being playful, his left hand propped at his hip and a jaunty defiance crooking his grin.

Annja wasn't feeling the humor.

She called Joan's sword into her hand and swept it before her, slicing the air and speaking a warning to back off or risk injury.

"You in the mood for duel?" Roux challenged. He drew up the rapier before his face and looked at her, the blade drawing a line between his steely eyes. "You wouldn't risk damaging an artifact, would you?"

Stalking right up to him and sweeping a low slash that should have cut him off at the ankle—had he not jumped into the air—Annja gave him the silent answer. The old man was spry, she'd give him that.

"Why the angry energy today, Annja? Didn't the treasure hunt go well?"

"We found it. Maybe."

Dodging his lunge, she guessed he wouldn't poke her with the blade, but then again, one could never be too sure about Roux.

She would never completely trust him. And this new information about his skulking about at BHDC only served to remind her that Roux did have his own purposes.

"What's going on with you and Lambert?" she asked. "I know you've been to see him. He was very cagey about knowing something about me. Something that would change my world."

"When did he say that to you?" The duel forgotten, Roux let down his guard and almost lost an ear, had Annja not stopped her slash but an inch from his scalp. "Annja, dear, hold your venom. You really wish to do me harm? I'm not in collusion with the man, if that's what you believe."

"You hadn't even heard of BHDC until I told you days ago. What was it I said that had you running to Jacques Lambert? I can guess, but that would just be too awful."

"And what do you guess?" Completely oblivious to its value, he pressed the point of the rapier into the toe of his leather shoe, propping his palms casually over the hilt which still lacked the pommel. "That I'm curious about you, and the sword, and the whole she-has-inherited-Joan's quest thing?"

She didn't want to ask. She didn't want to know.

Yes, you do.

What good would knowing serve? There was nothing to know.

"Did you bring Lambert a DNA sample from Joan of Arc? Was that her chain mail?"

Lifting up a belligerent chin, his silence told Annja all she needed.

"And mine?" she whispered. She didn't want that answer. Not in a thousand years could she want that answer. Roux had obtained a sample of her DNA? From what?

"Lambert was to call me the moment he had results. I'll ring him up right now, if you wish me to."

"Too late." She thrust out her right arm, splaying her fingers to release the blade. It disappeared.

"It is a wondrous thing," Roux said, reverence making his words husky. "The sword and its attachment to you. Don't you wish to know? What if you are—?"

"Not listening." Annja spun and stalked toward the door. 'Can I trust you'll send the rapier on to the museum in Lupiac?"

"Yes, Annja, but—"

Still walking, she turned and fished out the pommel she had carried in the pocket of her jeans. Giving it a toss, she lobbed it right into Roux's palm.

"BHDC burned to the ground this morning. All research and DNA evidence went up in smoke with it," she said.

"No, that's—" Noticeably shaken, Roux dropped his gaze along the floor. His hand shook. The rapier blade curved violently, then he snapped the blade out to cut the air. He suddenly looked every bit the five hundred years he had lived. "Her mail—I suppose that was lost?"

Annja nodded.

"I was so close."

"Close doesn't count," she said.

"Don't you want to know?"

Annja swallowed back the first word that came to her tongue, and instead shook her head negatively. "Sorry you lost the chain mail, Roux. Thanks for…" For opening up a whole new mystery for me to ponder. "We'll meet again. I look forward to it. *Bonsoir.*"

He waved and stepped back to sit on the edge of his desk.

Annja did not look back. She fought the urge to turn and

race up to him and embrace him as a daughter would her father. The man simply wanted answers. She understood his pining. But she couldn't give him what he wanted.

And she wasn't ready for what he wanted to offer her.

ASCHER TUGGED a T-shirt over his head as Annja arrived at his hospital room. He was getting dressed to check out. She'd scanned his chart, hanging outside the door. They'd sewn up the bullet wound and prescribed him Vicodin for the pain.

"Annja!"

"You're looking rested, Vallois."

"And you're…"

He scanned her attire; she was still dressed in the clothes she'd worn all day yesterday, which had included their adventures in the bowels of the city. Blood stained her hip, and dirt and soot scuffed her jeans. She hadn't seen a comb in ages and she was tired.

"Ready for a real vacation," she provided.

"Sorry about that. Next time I invite you to Paris it will be strictly for leisure."

"Did you say leisure or pleasure?"

"Pleasure? You would accept the invitation?" he asked.

"You'll have to wait and see."

An enthusiastic wink preceded his crossing the room to pull her into a hug. It was a friendly we-survived-a-great adventure kind of hug, which relieved Annja. She was in no condition, physically, to volley any flirtations.

"Did you get the box?" he asked.

The man did have a one-track mind. Focused on riches as usual. "It went up in flames with the entire BHDC headquarters."

"What? After all our work?"

"We did spend a lot of time tracking the elusive thing. I did
get a chance to look it over, though. I'm guessing it was a sort
of trinket box, put out to advertise *The Three Musketeers*. It
had All For One, One For All carved around the box top."

"But that means…this was all a wild-goose chase?"

"I don't think so." She sat on the canvas folding chair next
to his hospital bed. It felt good to sit and not be tense. And to
not have to stand before Roux and face his disappointment.
"I think there really was a treasure, but someone claimed it
and left the box there in its place."

Ascher settled on the edge of the rumpled hospital bed, white
sport socks in his hands. He let out a heavy sigh. "Dumas?"

"No. He died a pauper."

"Like our Charles de Castelmore. It had to have been in
the mid- to late-nineteenth century if what you say about the
box is true."

"Yes, which rules out any of d'Artagnan's contemporar-
ies, including Fouquet and Mazarin." Annja zipped open her
backpack and pulled out a notebook where most of her notes
on the lost sword and this whole adventure were scribbled.
"But Auguste Maquet…"

"Who forced Dumas to sign a document guaranteeing to
pay him wages—"

"Which he was never paid because Dumas was in financial straits—"

"Died a rich man," Ascher concluded.

"Exactly."

She found the page where she'd copied the notation regarding Maquet's building a home in Dourdan and living rather
well, much to the surprise of his friends and family. No one
was sure how he managed it—for all were aware Dumas had
stiffed him the owed monies.

Pleased she'd solved the riddle—though it was only con
jecture—it fit well enough into her idea of history. Annj
waited for Ascher's reaction.

"You're wishing you never invited me to the dig, I bet." Sh
walked over to the window. Fading wooden roof slats pro
tected the bird market on the street across from the hospita

"Never." From behind, he put his arms around her wais
"I did lose a treasure that could have financed a new additio
to my fencing school."

"You'll find a way. You're an industrious man. Besides, th
treasure was long gone before we got there," she said.

"I also lost a kidney."

"You can survive with one. You'll be fencing in no time

"But I did get the girl."

She turned in his arms. "Sort of."

"You are going to leave me for another adventure?"

"I've already got a new assignment. I have to be in Irelar
by tomorrow afternoon."

"That gives you twenty-four hours. The Chunnel will sho
you to the British Isles in less than two hours. You can sta
the day and have lunch with me at the Eiffel Tower?"

"Isn't that a little touristy?"

"So you'll stay?"

"A girl should never refuse a free meal," she said.

Epilogue

Alexandre had a way about him. He could divert a man's attentions and get him to work. Work furiously. Work desperately. Putting words to paper.

And Auguste had enjoyed his years collaborating with the man. It was satisfying work, though it was far from fulfilling. He knew history, and read much, and had ideas. He was a born treasure hunter, if only on paper. But now he had little to claim as assets beyond a small apartment on the Left Bank.

His financial straits had forced him to draw up a document that would ensure Alexandre pay him one hundred thousand livres over the next six years to keep Auguste quiet about what works, exactly, they had collaborated on. Auguste then agreed to renounce all claims to future royalties.

He simply wanted the monies owed to him. Yes, he understood that Alexandre was no better off than him, but Dumas had squandered not only his own money, but also that which

should have been paid to Auguste for his work in the firs
place. That damn château Dumas had built in Saint-Germain
en-Laye being such folly. He was generous, yes, but recklessly
so. It was almost as if the man did not know the value of things

Alexandre agreeably signed the document. It had stunned
Auguste at the time. But he and Dumas had been true friend
over the years; perhaps his former partner had turned ove
a new leaf.

It had been over a year. Dumas had made no attempts to
contact Auguste. No money had made it into Auguste's hands
He should have expected as much. Blood from a stone an
all that. He'd been forced to start court proceedings. Duma
denounced him as a rogue and cheat. There was no way to wi
against one so famous and popular with all of France.

It was on a particular evening, as he whiled away a mis
erable defeat in a local tavern, that Auguste remembered th
map, copied carefully from Nicolas Fouquet's files while re
searching the musketeer stories. A map François Mansart ha
drawn up for Queen Anne. It would lead a very lucky mus
keteer beneath the labyrinths and catacombs on the Left Ban
to a royal treasure.

Auguste suspected Fouquet had intended to go after th
treasure himself, but he had been waylaid when arrested fo
embezzlement. And having ruled out d'Artagnan retrievin
the cache, Auguste had the smallest hope that the queen
treasure might still be intact.

It could really exist.

There was no possible way to navigate the keyless ma
but Auguste had an idea that it was somewhere close to th
Val-de-Grâce. Where else?

It would be an arduous venture, crawling about beneath th
city with no means to navigate the twisting passages on th

nap. But he was desperate. After breaking ties with Dumas, he quickly found that no publisher was interested in what Auguste Maquet had to write. Who was he?

He tapped the box Dumas had given him. Painted white and flourished with ridiculous commercial detail. A trinket designed to promote the book. All For One, One For All danced around the top. It was worthless, as Dumas's friendship had turned out to be.

"To a successful venture," Auguste said, and he raised his last bottle of Anjou wine to his lips.

Seventeen days later, Auguste Maquet retired to a quiet countryside estate near Dourdan. The motto engraved across the decorative stone ribbon over the doorway read *Selon les Mérites.*

"As I deserve."

James Axler
Outlanders®

SERPENT'S TOOTH

A combination of reptilian and human DNA, the Najah are the revitalized foot soldiers of the Earth's ancient alien masters, the Annunaki. Surviving the megacull of humanity, these half-cobra warriors vow to avenge their near extinction and usher in a new age on Earth. From its underground war base in northern India, this monstrous force launches its cleansing fire. Kane and his allies have one hope—a renegade female Najah, reptilian and ruthless, whose alliance is both a promise...and a threat.

Available February wherever books are sold.

ROOM 59

THERE'S A FINE LINE BETWEEN DOING YOUR JOB—AND DOING THE RIGHT THING

After a snatch-and-grab mission on a quiet London street turns sour, new Room 59 operative David Southerland is branded a cowboy. While his quick thinking gained valuable intelligence, breaching procedure is a fatal mistake that can end a career—or a life. With his future on the line, he's tasked with a high-speed chase across London to locate a sexy thief with stolen global-security secrets that have more than one interested—and very dangerous—player in the game....

Look for

THE finish line

by

cliff RYDER

GOLD EAGLE®

Available January wherever books are sold.

www.readgoldeagle.blogspot.com

GRM595